A
MARRIAGE
OF
INCONVENIENCE

Also by Daisy Vivian

The Wild Rose: Meg's Tale
Fair Game
The Forrester Inheritance
Rose White, Rose Red

A
MARRIAGE
OF
INCONVENIENCE

Daisy Vivian

Walker and Company
New York

First published in the United States of America in 1986 by the Walker
Publishing Company, Inc.

Published simultaneously in Canada by John Wiley & Sons
Canada, Limited, Rexdale, Ontario

Library of Congress Cataloging-in-Publication Data

Vivian, Daisy.
  A marriage of inconvenience.

  I. Title.
PS3572.I86M3   1986   813'.54   86-15787
ISBN 0-8027-0935-4

Printed in the United States of America

10 9 8 7 6 5 4 3 2 1

for my beloved Batya,
of course.

"Of all the Bedlams, marriage is the worst,
With endless cords, with endless keepers curst.
Frantic in love, you run and rave about;
Mad to get in, but hopeless to get out!"
John Wilmot,
Second Earl of Rochester

A
MARRIAGE
OF
INCONVENIENCE

=1=

THE EVENING PARTY had been the talk of the neighbourhood for a month, but as the carriage moved smoothly
through the summer dusk Clarissa St. Minver, called Clair
by half her acquaintance, wished for the thousandth time
that she need not attend. What was one to say to those
ostentatious well-wishers who would insist on extending
their condolences over the fact that one's long-arranged
"understanding" had evaporated into the air? And what *was*
one to say to one's long-intended as he stood in the receiving line beside his new fiancée and his odious mama who
had never approved of one in the first place? It was sure to
be a trying evening. A purgatorial experience of the worst
kind.

The silence was broken only by the sounds of the
jingling harness and the occasional clucking of the driver as
he encouraged the horses who moved as languidly as if
they, too, were reluctant to face the entertainment of the
evening. Sir Wilton St. Minver, still distinguished despite
his years, sat as ramrod-straight as he had done in the
guards. On either side of him, his daughters in their social
finery were a fitting complement: Clair in a sapphire-blue
gauze which would sharply accentuate the bright cerulean
of her eyes, and Dolly, being younger, in virginal white
muslin. They had been silent as the night for most of the
three-mile drive to Landon House, but, just as they approached the gateway, Dolly's long-pent sentiments burst
out as if she could restrain them no more.

"I vow, I shall never forgive him! It will be as much as I can do not to fly at his throat! I swear that if I speak to him this evening it will be for the last time, and if I meet him or his new sweetheart in the village, I expect I shall cross the street to avoid them!"

"I hope you will do no such thing," said Sir Wilton with a mildness which perfectly illustrated the amity between himself and his children. "It would be uncivil in the extreme and quite unworthy of you. In addition, I believed you liked Greville immensely? I recall that it was not so very long ago that he was your idol and it was 'Greville this' and 'Greville that' as if no such nonpareil ever before existed. And now he is to be cast into the outer darkness simply because he has not lived up to the expectation of marrying your sister? Dolly, you disappoint me."

His youngest sniffed disdainfully. "You know perfectly well, Papa, that I do it for Clarissa's sake. It is true that I always looked forward to having Greville as a brother by marriage, but, now that he is going to marry Miss Austruck for her fortune, I expect that I have long misjudged him. You know that there was a long understanding between him and Clair, and now he has betrayed it for mere gain."

Her sister seemed to take no umbrage at this frank discussion of what were generally her own affairs, but said (albeit with a wry little smile) "I do not think you should say *mere* gain, Doll. I believe Miss Austruck is very well fixed in the thousands. I expect that since Greville had none of his own, he had to seek it out. Certainly Landon Hall and the grand style of living must make great demands upon the purse. I don't expect that Mrs. Landon ever denied herself anything at any time."

"Clarissa," said her father, on the rising note which his daughters understood to be cautionary. He was, of course, quite right. It was scarcely the thing to criticize a woman merely because she had stood between oneself and personal happiness. But, to put an end to it, Clair must have the last word as usual.

2

"I hope, Doll, that you will not shame me by going all about this evening hinting at things for gossips to chew upon? I shall be quite overset if you do. Greville and I—Mr. Landon, I suppose I must call him now—were great and good friends, which I hope we shall always be, but we were not, as you well know, *betrothed*, and there is no reason at all to slight him on my account. No, nor his bride either." She tossed her pretty chestnut head. "I certainly do not intend to do so."

They had passed the lodge now and were on the drive itself, proceeding slowly because of the crush of carriages ahead, and Clarissa looked up at the imposing country house with the great admiration she had always had. It was a lovely old seventeenth-century place recasing the original Elizabethan manor, the improvements (somewhat dubiously) ascribed to Inigo Jones. However that might be, the result was a treasure, and she never entered it without a lift of spirit. Time would tell if the tradition continued into this evening. As children she, Greville Landon, and his sister Estrella, had been inseparable. Clair had run in and out of the hall as though it were her own home. Estrella was gone away, long since married to a Virginia planter, but the old sense of familiarity remained.

The front hall, when they reached it, was crowded. Folk had come from all over the county and were laughing, chatting, calling out obstreperous greetings to each other in the way of country dwellers of all classes. They milled about without restraint, elbowing each other and banging against the two guardian suits of Nuremberg armour in a fashion that threatened to make the metal warriors come alive to defend themselves. Through a doorway Clarissa could see the older ladies in the small salon, sedate in dark silks, comparing social minutae, while in the gun room the old bloods had gathered to guffaw artlessly among their contemporaries, clapping each other about the shoulders and talking of racing and hunting, hunting and racing. Sir Wilton hastened to join these gentlemen, but the young women continued on into the rear parlour, a chamber which had, from time immemorial, been set aside as a retiring room for ladies on occasions such as this. Clair had not looked forward to her appearance there, and she was not disappointed.

The conversation, going along at a fast clip of overlapping dialogue, came to a tumbling halt the moment the St. Minver daughters entered the room. In truth, it would have been an astonishing thing if it had not happened, for Clair's probable appearance or nonappearance had been the single most popular subject in the neighbourhood since the party had been announced. Ever since it had been known that Mrs. Landon would be welcoming her prospective daughter-in-law to Landon Hall before the London wedding and the continental tour of whatever spots that dreadful Napoleon had left open to English travellers, speculation as to Miss St. Minver's disposition had been rife. Well, my dear, everyone who counted in the county was likely to be there. Wild dogs at the crossroads could not have kept them away!

Pierette Hughes, of course, was the first to take advantage of Clair's arrival. Fairly dripping unspoken commiseration, she sidled insinuatingly across the floor, lemon-yellow draperies awaft, and embraced the newcomers with the familiarity of long acquaintance, Dolly first and less effusively, then Clarissa.

"My darling, you look wonderful!" she assured her victim, then pulled away a step to be sure that what she said was true. "That shade of blue is quite ravishing with your hair and eyes. I can't think *how* you have pulled yourself together when everyone knows what you must be feeling. I am sure we all applaud your courage!

"Don't we?" she asked, turning to seek the corroboration of the others, and they agreed with pretty smiles and hard, curious stares. Ravishing. Courageous.

Miss St. Minver had never been considered beautiful in the conventional English fashion: her high-cheekboned face was too unusual for that, her chin too pointed, her eyes too tilted in a suspiciously foreign way that perpetuated envious jibes of supposed irregularities in her ancestry. There was even now, as always, that impossible manner of hers, that placid acceptance of always being the center of attention. She smiled at Pierette and at the others, disliking these cats as much as she knew they disapproved of her, but she was not allowed to say so. She dissimulated instead, dropping her eyes in the accepted fashion, murmuring her thanks for their kindness. When, turning away for a moment, though, she caught her sister's wondering gaze, she winked roguishly, deprecating all this fal-lal.

"We all think it quite wonderful that you have come tonight," Pierette went on, drawing Clair a little to one side, but speaking in a bray designed to easily carry to the others. "It is so brave of you, and everyone is ranged on your side." The others nodded emphatically and pulled sympathetic faces.

"We have made a resolution to demonstrate our partiality, you see. Not that we will be rude to little Miss Austruck, but she is certain to be sure what she is up against."

It is not being done on my account, thought Clarissa. *Not one of you has ever cared a whit for me, nor I for you.* "That would be too unkind, Pierette," she protested dulcetly. "Think what the poor thing must be going through in a world full of utter strangers. It is not as if she has the background for it."

Miss Austruck was known to be the daughter of a manufacturer from one of the grimy towns in the north which had little, if any, society in which to learn the social graces. There was much to be said for growing up in a secure and restricted world, however confining it might eventually become.

"Why, we do not even know her," Clarissa went on. "She might even turn out to be just our sort."

"She isn't," said gruff Miss Beeton firmly. "I have it on good authority that she was very condescending to little

Miss Flint in the lending library." Every one of them was concerned with their standing in Miss Flint's eyes, for how else could they expect to have the newest novels at the earliest opportunity? To a strong degree, one's standing was determined by how one treated the librarian. No one saw anything in the least odd about this.

"And she is very stiff, they say," Lydia Leslie added, "very proud. She passed Mrs. Grimes in her carriage without so much as a nod." This impressed her hearers, though they all knew that Mrs. Grimes was sure to be here with the rest of the world this evening, despite any snub intended or otherwise. "Not our sort" they had all agreed to agree, but they were attending the evening party, nonetheless. For her soul's sake, Clair knew, she herself could not have avoided this evening's confrontations. The world would have publicly pitied her, and that was something she could not allow.

Besides this, she would not ever subject Greville Landon to such outré behaviour. They had, with Estrella, been daring partners against social hypocrisy at too many gatherings of this very kind, for her to betray their old friendship now. They had been confidantes for too many years, and the devilish thing was that she understood all too well why it was not herself who was the bride-to-be. The neighbours would side with Clarissa but for reasons of social solidarity rather than true sympathy. There was, in fact, a considerable spitefulness behind their smiles and kind words.

When she had finished with her toilette, Clair bit her lips and pinched her cheeks to heighten the colour. She and Dolly left the room with their little pointed chins held at a determined angle, knowing that when they were gone the women would say little, but communicate through the small signs of raised eyebrows, pursed lips, and covert glances. In point of fact, the ladies in the room made their last-minute arrangements quite hurriedly and followed the St. Minver sisters closely behind for fear of missing a single moment of the great and intriguing drama they expected to unfold before their eyes in the ballroom.

The way to the dancing was up the long staircase and through the picture gallery where Mrs. Landon and her son, holding court as certainly as any monarch of old, would welcome their guests and present Miss Austruck. There was, of course, a certain amount of waiting while the company filtered through the receiving line, but the pictures provided a certain amount of relief from the tedium. Family portraits were numerous, all sharing the same distinctive Landon nose and small eyes. There were one or two handsome landscapes and a few items from the collection of the late Henry, Cardinal of York, the brother of Bonnie Prince Charlie and known to Jacobites as King Henry IX, as well as a rather fine portrait of that very prince, painted in Rome by Laurent with a kind of satiric elegance, as though he were secretly deriding the claims of The Young Pretender. The young women had hardly time to catch their breath from the stairs, however, and had not even approached their hostess before they were quite besieged by beaux. The young women they knew might be envious, but the young men were all delighted attention.

Though Mrs. Landon stared at them coldly across the crowd, Dolly was pretty and fresh, while her sister was the acknowledged fascinator of the county. Countless young men had sighed for her, but, believing she was promised to Greville Landon, had rather kept off. Now they crowded around her like young schoolboys at a gingerbread booth at the fair. Clair, for her part, smiled and flirted with them, twisted them easily about her fingers, and cared not a rap for any. Dolly, though, enjoyed herself hugely, the game of romance being new. Firmly, the older girl drew her away from her admirers and propelled her toward the line.

"Hostess first, my pet; flirtations later. Mrs. Landon is in a snit already because we had the audacity to accept her invitation. We must not rile her further."

But Dolly's eyes were trained upon the handsome figure

of a man on the other side of the gallery who was inspecting the pictures with a cynical eye. "Lud, Clair, you know everyone—who on earth is that?"

The gentleman was undeniably handsome in a severe sort of way and his expression as he looked at the family portraits accentuated his air of remote disdain. Broad-shouldered and perfectly fitted, his hair curled about his ears in the fashionable Brutus cut, while his sideburns lent length to a jawline already too pronounced by far. Whilst others in the room were convivially relaxed, he alone had the air of holding himself aloof. *He looks*, thought Clair, *as though he has been on quinine for a year*. And, indeed, his slightly jaundiced complexion lent credence to her observation. She had no idea who he was.

They were about to move along when a shrill voice, vastly resembling the cry of a captive peacock, cut through the hubbub like a sharp knife.

"Dolly! Clair! Clarissa St. Minver!" The two girls winced, for they knew the voice all too well.

"Oh, Lud," Dolly murmured despairingly. "It is Lady Dedham. I think I shall just go on, Clair, since she seems to wish to speak to you."

"My dear ones! What a delight! Approachay-voo, approachay-voo at once!" she cried, in strident and badly-accented French.

There was no help for it, and they must face her all alone without even Papa as bulwark. Hatibell, Lady Dedham, was a sort of connexion from their late mother's side of the family, of whom they had little knowledge and less concourse. She lived a fortunate twenty miles away on the far side of the county and rarely deigned to travel, believing, perhaps rightly, that her own establishment most suited her comfort and her own company most suited her taste. Many people were happy that this was so, for her ladyship had the unfortunate knack of raising almost universal irritation in the way that some lucky few have the knack of loving. She was, however, of a tall and handsome figure like all her family and made an arresting appearance. People who did not know her sometimes made reference to the portrait busts of matrons of ancient Rome. They could not know how little Lady Dedham actually resembled the nature of those stoic individuals, for she was dedicated to self-indulgence in the extreme degree. Fortunately, her tastes were ordinary, or she might have been a very Medusa. With all her vast wealth she could certainly afford to be anything she chose to be. As it was, she surrounded herself with life's little luxuries, retained the same servants whom she had badgered into obsequiousness through years of effort, but paid them so well that they thought of her as an amiable eccentric rather than a demanding taskmistress.

She had always by her some personal companion to do her bidding. There had been a long string of them over the years, mostly young and dependent, whom she could treat in shockingly bad fashion without the expectation of rebellion, then pension off with a good dowry when she decided to choose another. A young woman of that sort stood beside her now and, as Sir Wilton's daughters approached, the old woman thrust her forward.

"This is m'niece, Phyliss Powley! One of that unfortunate brood at Chesterton, don't y'know." She spoke as loudly and as unconcernedly as if the young woman were stone deaf and had no notion she was being explained. "Pleasant enough gel, but sadly lacking in conversation. Pity *you* ain't young and needy, Clarissa. I've always liked your spirit, and I wouldn't mind having you about. You are deucedly amusing, I've always thought, and I require much diversion."

She nudged Miss Powley rudely. "Well, speak out, gel! Cat got your tongue? These young ladies of fashion will think you are a stuffed figger if you don't look out." She laughed raucously at her own sally. "A stuffed figger, hah!" Their near neighbours turned, but seeing who it was, turned quickly away again for fear of being drawn in.

The young woman extended her hand. "Good evening,

Miss St. Minver, Miss Dolly. I have heard so much of you from all quarters that I feel I have known you for an age." Her smile was the pleasantest thing about her, for it was warm and guileless, quite transforming her face, which was of the same Roman mould as that of her aunt, handsome but chill. With the smile there appeared at the corners of her mouth, two dimples which altered her entire aspect, she led one to believe that she was gentle, well-bred, and not at all intimidated by her relative. She tucked her hand firmly under Lady Dedham's elbow as if to draw her to one side and said, "I believe, Aunt, that the young ladies were only just on their way to pay their respects to our hostess. Perhaps we will have an opportunity of a good chat a little later in the evening."

Her forthright words took both of the St. Minver sisters rather by surprise, for who in the world had ever heard Lady Dedham addressed in such terms before? But the old creature herself seemed not to mind in the least. "Oh, yes? I daresay you are right, m'dear, though who in their senses would wish to be drawn to that person's attention I cannot imagine. Airs and graces from here to eternity! If I had not been plagued with curiosity to see this new creature of Greville's, I shouldn't put up with her." She grimaced. "Can you imagine what she had the effrontery to say to me when I went to make my addresses? 'So you came, Lady Dedham?' she says, for all the world as if I had broken through the hedge. 'Yes,' said I (I was that taken aback that I came perilously near to losing my manners), 'and if you ain't kind to me I shall stay forever!' Hah! 'I'll stay forever' is what I told her. That stopped her for the moment, I can tell you.

"Well, you two pretty things go make your bob to her and congratulate Greville prettily on his acquisition." Her eyes grew kinder. "And you, Clair, keep your chin up, there's a good gel. Men does what they please in this world mostly, but the consolation is that they must live with their consequences afterwards.

"Hah!" Her sharp, hacking cry cut through the flummery of the occasion and lifted Clarissa's spirit immeasurably. "Hah!" Dreadful as she could often be, nothing would be allowed to go quite wrong with the world so long as Lady Dedham kept her head above ground. "When you come back," the old woman promised, "I shall introduce you to young Rackham over there. My nevvy and a prime catch, if I do say so. Promised, though, to Phyliss, so don't raise your hopes. Hah! Don't raise your hopes, I say, of becoming Viscountess Rackham!"

This was all said in such a piercing and audible tone that heads turned once more and even Miss Powley was disconcerted. "I pray you, Aunt, do not say such a thing," she begged. "You know your scheme can never be."

"Not from a want of emotion on Rackham's part," said Lady Dedham stoutly. "You needn't imagine I am going to let you waste yourself on that psalm-singer you are so caught up with, eh? I've promised you a dowry, but I don't mean it to go to the likes of John Wearthy."

Miss Powley, trapped into a discussion of her private life in this very public setting, blushed furiously, which changed the marble cast of her complexion quite strongly, suffusing it with a rosy glow which was much becoming. "Rackham and I are merely friends, Aunt, no matter what construction you wish to place upon it. I can never marry him for I cannot think of him in that way. I know you would like to unite the two branches of your family, but, I assure you, it shall not be done through Alexander and me."

But Lady Dedham was not to be beaten off. "He cares for you, I know. I expect you will come to your senses one day soon."

Eager to escape this intimate discussion, the St. Minver sisters turned away, but just as they did so, Clarissa found herself being jostled from the other direction as the press grew stronger. She was propelled forward and took one or two little steps to regain her balance, which provided a

11

difficulty in still another direction, for she found herself thrown up against the broad masculine chest of the gentleman who had been examining the pictures, but was now bearing in each hand a cup of claret punch, not so carefully as he might have done, for one cup slopped over and stained the ruffles at his wrist an angry red.

"Oh," Clair apologised when she saw what had happened, "I am so sorry!"

"Not at all," the gentleman answered frigidly. "I appreciate how difficult it is to keep one's head in a crush such as this."

"Not my head, perhaps, so much as my footing," she replied.

Then Dolly wailed.

"Oh, Clair, it has gone on your gown. Look, your new gown!"

Clair looked down, surveying herself. There was a small, but vivid scarlet stain on the sapphire gauze. "Oh, drat. So it has. I see, sir, that we are in much the same plight."

From behind them Lady Dedham's caw said, "Rackham! Here, sir!" exactly as she might have done to a pet terrier or spaniel.

"If you will excuse me," said the gentleman, trying unsuccessfully to navigate past the sisters, but Clair's intention had been much the same and her movement, unfortunately, in much the same direction. They collided again to the annoyance of both. The claret slopped again and the gentleman's other wrist went scarlet. His long jaw tightened, but he allowed himself no recrimination. His look said everything.

And Clair's made eloquent reply. She drew back, as he did, and they edged past each other as warily as sworn enemies.

"Rackham, here! Ah, I apprehend you have met Miss St. Minver, another of my connexions. Have you been introduced? Miss Clarissa St. Minver, my nevvy, Viscount Rackham. Alexander, what on earth have you done to your wristbands?"

"Charmed," said the viscount, acknowledging the introduction, but clearly expressing the opposite of his word. "Miss Powley, Lady Dedham, I have brought you some claret punch."

"You seem to be wearing a bit of it," Miss Powley observed in a sisterly way. "What an unfortunate accident."

"Yes," he said, looking at Clair in a chilly way, "unfortunate. But what can one do in a mob such as this? I shall know better another time." He turned back to Clarissa with a measure of grace. "I truly regret my clumsiness, Miss St. Minver. The damage does not look to be extensive, but I shall be happy to make it right."

She actually found herself smiling at him. "Not at all. There is only a drop or two near the hem. I daresay it will come out. In the meantime, I doubt that anyone here will notice,"—she laughed a little ruefully—"for, I expect with all this press, no one will see my hem at all. I confess I am heartily glad I did not wear the sandals that were made to go with with this gauze."

"If you will allow me, then," he offered, "I will make what reparation I can by forging a path through to the receiving line. I have been fetching drinks for my aunt and her friends. I daresay I am getting rather good at cutting through."

Try as she would, Clarissa could not understand the very obvious change which had come over this gentleman. Who would have believed, after his previous chill, that he could be so thoughtful? She looked at him and then at his aunt, Lady Dedham, seeking some sort of link, but found none. Then, gazing at Miss Powley, she thought she understood his change of heart. It was the product of his unrequited attentions, of course. The rejected suitor wished to impress his beloved with his innate virtue. Well, she did not require another witness to her probable discomfiture.

"Thank you, sir, but I expect I shall make my way well enough."

And, indeed, it was like a Red-Sea parting as people saw who she was and where she was going. The long line of waiting guests simply evaporated before her, and Clarissa saw that there was no help for it; her time had come. She found that she was quite alone, for Dolly had already made her curtsey and Papa, it seemed, was still downstairs with his cronies. There was nothing to do but set her jaw, fix her smile, and move forward.

Greville seemed astonishingly the same, all smooth cheeks and fluffy hair that made him look like a misplaced angel. For a brief moment her heart leapt, remembering how it had been, but a deep breath took care of that. *Schoolgirl infatuation*, she reminded herself sharply and, with that tonic, adjusted her smile to a more genuine aspect and made her curtsey.

An odd thing was that Greville showed no awareness that anything untoward was going on. Certainly his pretty companion seemed unaware of her role in a local drama. That she was pretty, one had to admit, and obviously held her groom in adoration, for she smiled and blushed and all but trembled at his every word. Lettice Landon might have been seen to draw herself up as if for battle at Clarissa's approach, but Greville was all affability.

"Can this really be you?" he said in his old familiar way. Greeting her with outstretched arms, he drew her toward him in a brotherly embrace and kissed her on the cheek.

"So you have consented to come to us at last! I have told Miss Austruck everything about you."

"Everything?" asked Clarissa with a social smile. She could feel Mrs. Landon's eyes drilling into her back. "That must have been wearisome." She turned expectantly toward the bride. Greville presented her.

"Georgiana, this is Miss Clarissa St. Minver of whom I have often spoken. Clair, my bride. I do hope that the two of you will conceive a dote and become as dear to each other as each is to me."

He pressed Clarissa's hand affectionately. "Clair, you have always been my 'other sister' and I hope you will welcome Georgiana to the family."

The two young women merely stared at each other: Clarissa because she could not believe that Greville was being so obtuse; Georgiana because it was her nature to let the other person make the overture. Mrs. Landon's smile gleamed frostily.

"I expect that you are quite enchanted with my new daughter, aren't you, Clarissa?" she asked. "Two who are so fond of my boy cannot but be fond of each other."

Clair, schooled in this line of country since she had, as a child, first realised Mrs. Landon's instinctive dislike of her, summoned up her most engaging nature and leant forward to brush her lips against Georgiana's cheek.

"I think you cannot fail to be happy with Greville as a husband," she said. To her surprise, she realised as she spoke the words that she meant them. She had always loved Greville, but was not love partly a desire for the other's content? Her expectations of him had not been met, but no promises had ever really been made. Certainly she did not envy the girl having Mrs. Landon as a mother.

"Oh, Miss St. Minver, I hope I shall become as dear to you as Greville and Estrella are. I shall need a great many friends, I am sure."

"We all need friends," Clair said blandly. "The difficulty is in telling who they are."

"I daresay we shall be hearing of *your* betrothal soon?" asked Mrs. Landon with a false air of bonhomie. "Time passes so quickly, does it not? I remember how sweet you looked at Estrella's wedding; like a jonquil, though I, perhaps, would have chosen another colour. For the complexion, you know."

Since Mrs. Landon had been quite firm about the colours at the time, Clair let it pass, but she could hardly ignore what was further said.

"I do hope, dear, that you will not choose to become one of those dreadful Blue Stocking Ladies who abjure the comforts of matrimony to risk being ape leaders?"

The insult was direct since the term all but implied that

one was unmarriageable. Georgiana's eyes widened at the words, and even Greville, adoring of his mama as he was, had the grace to seem disconcerted.

"Ah, there you are, my dearest," said a masculine voice at Clarissa's shoulder. "I had only turned about and you were gone. Will you not introduce me to these charming people?" He took her hand firmly and placed it in the crook of his arm.

Though Clair was inwardly seething at the crass impertinence of the man, the look on Lettice Landon's face was delicious. Clair found herself torn between rage and gratitude.

"Mrs. Landon, Miss Austruck, Mr. Landon, may I present Viscount Rackham?"

"Viscount? . . ." asked Mrs. Landon faintly.

Alexander Rackham bowed over her hand lingeringly. "I hope you do not mind that I came along to meet all of dear Clarissa's friends," he said suavely.

"Rackham?" asked Greville. "I say, weren't you at school with the Ruans?"

Rackham allowed himself a genial smile. "Ruan major just above me, Ruan minor just beneath, actually."

"We must talk, old man. Are you in the neighbourhood now?"

Alexander shook his head. "I have been staying with my aunt, Lady Dedham, but I have a house in town. Berkeley Square. You must come when you are up for the season." He turned to his hostess. "And you, as well, madam. I daresay I can find you sponsors at Almack's.

Lettice Landon's smile was arranged upon tightly pressed lips, but her fluttering nostrils revealed the true depth of her feeling.

2

"How DARED YOU, sir? Do you know—can you even remotely imagine what you have done?"

The elegant music swirled about them, but Clair, stiff with suppressed fury, could not abandon herself to the rhythms.

"Do you reverse?" Alexander Rackham asked, then moved as if she had assented. Clair found her body following his lead faultlessly. They were well-matched partners, but her lips were still compressed in annoyance.

Mrs. Landon had done well by the occasion. The local quartet of musicians had been tripled for the occasion, happily augmented by players from Pargate and Rottenhaugh. They played well, considering; almost always together.

Rackham smiled coolly down into her face and backed her about the room in time to the music. "This new *valse* tempo is quite appealing, is it not? Has rather a sweep. Almost—you could say—sensuous, eh?"

Clair moved perfectly but made no reply.

"Pray, Miss St. Minver, do not scowl quite so heavily or they will think we are indulging in a spat."

Her tone was bitter. "We are mere acquaintances, Sir Alexander. I think we hardly know each other well enough for a spat."

"I doubt that. In fact, I am convinced otherwise, but what have I done to bring on the clouds and rain save rescue you from the mouth of the dragon? My word, I thought she would eat you alive and spit out the bones. I must say, I find your ingratitude alarming."

"You need be alarmed no longer if you will but return me to your aunt."

His slightly twisted smile grew perceptibly broader. "But I find this so diverting."

"And I find you, sir, both impertinent and forward. I will thank you to stop smirking at me as if you have just pulled off the greatest coup of the season!" She actually scowled at him. "Take me back, if you please!"

But Rackham made no motion to relinquish her. "If we cease now, they will talk their heads off, don't you think?"

"Let them, then," Clair said between clenched teeth and tried to remove her hand from his clasp. His fingers only tightened.

"Relax, if you please, Miss St. Minver. Listen to the music. *One*-two-three, *one*-two-three. There, that is better, eh? Now, then, try to look diverted. Gaze up at me in that adoring fashion little Miss Milk-and-Honey gazes up at Landon."

Try as she would, Clarissa could not help sneaking a quick look in the direction he indicated and, further, could not resist a smile. Georgiana *was* looking up at Greville rather like a mooncalf. Rackham caught it at once and beamed back at her with devilish abandon.

"That is better. So-o-o *and* around. You are quite convincing, now. I believe the crisis is past. Shall I take you back to Lady Dedham now and abandon you to your fate?"

Surprisingly, the thought of it put Clair into a state. She said nothing, but, Rackham, holding her in his embrace, perceived it at once.

"Ah, so I am *not* useless, after all?" The dance drew languorously to an end. "Very well, we shall go back, but I shall stick to you like a discreet burdock.

"Unless there is someone you fancy in that mob who besieged you when you came in? I could convey you in that direction, if you like?"

The situation was becoming quite alarming for Clarissa was certain the eyes of everyone were upon them. She both wanted to be rid of this smirking jackanapes and dreaded being left to face the company alone. "No, please . . . oh, dear . . ." For the first time Rackham dropped his quizzical expression and looked alarmed.

"Madam, are you going to weep?"

Her little pointed chin went out. "I shall certainly do no such thing, sir. Kindly take me to Lady Dedham."

"If you insist, though the price of respectability is demmed high."

Clarissa perceived with dismay that the social climate had quite changed by the time they left the floor. Disapproving matrons who, in the past had all but frozen her out as a threat to their daughters, now fawned with fluttering fans. Gentlemen crowded about to scribble their names on her card while they were able. Even Dolly, chatting with a young subaltern, gave her an astonished look from across the room. Only Mrs. Landon, abandoning her post at the door, glowered suspiciously. Clarissa knew that their hostess was not convinced, but was forced to accept what had been implied by Rackham's action: that odious Miss St. Minver had captured a prize far greater than any she might be supposed to have lost.

Only Lady Dedham was not cordial. "I am not amused, Clarissa," she said behind her fan, "and you may as well know it. You have made a spectacle of yourself and brought discredit upon the whole family."

The young woman tried for a demure expression, even attempted to seem contrite though only achieving an aspect which infuriated her relative further. Pulling the chit away a little so that his lordship should not overhear, Lady Dedham muttered at her fiercely, "You know perfectly well that I have a scheme for Rackham and my dear Phyliss. I shall be much obliged if you do not upset it by your caperings."

Since Clair well knew that the truth would come out

shortly that she and the viscount were *not* betrothed and were hardly more than strangers, she could protest with a clear conscience. "Nothing could be further from my mind, cousin. If you would only let me explain . . ."

Lady Dedham drew herself up to her full, imposing height. "I expect there is nothing *to* explain," she said grandly. "I apprehend that you now know my mind and we need say no more of it."

"Perhaps that would be best," replied the girl faintly. *Least said, soonest mended.* No word of hers was likely to penetrate her ladyship's shield of invulnerability of opinion. Rackham was edging toward them, but Lady Dedham was looking in another direction.

"Ah, there is your father. I hope your conduct has escaped *his* ears, at least." She raised her fan imperiously, and Sir Wilton obeyed the summons.

"Lady Dedham. It has been an age."

She snapped her feathers to with a flourish. "Yes, Wilton, an age, though I have twice heard that you were in my part of the county and did not call."

"Dull business, I fear, madam. Hardly a social journey."

She sneered. "Dull? I had heard it was for a marathon of cards."

Sir Wilton refused to be intimidated. "Perhaps it was," he said with the sort of finality which leaves no further room for discussion, but as it was accompanied by his usual gentle smile, Lady Dedham's only recourse was to sniff audibly in irritation. Viscount Rackham, though, appeared to take a great interest in the conversation. His gaze rested speculatively upon Clarissa's father, then he turned graciously to his aunt, drawing her fire.

"May I engage your ladyship for this dance?"

Lady Dedham coloured. "Why, I don't know. What is it to be? I don't step out to these new ones, you know."

"I believe it is a country dance, madam, at which I believe you were once celebrated."

Her colour went higher with pleasure. "Perhaps I was,

but that don't mean I am still. Old bones are brittle. Where is Phyliss? Why ain't you dancing with her?"

"Because, dear Aunt, she is not a *contredancer*, and you are. Pray, do not disappoint me, nor give the lie to what I have heard, eh? Let us show them all how it should be done."

Clarissa had never expected to see her mother's cousin transformed into a coquette, but it took place before her eyes, an unexpected delight. Some ghost of a girlish past fairly illuminated the old woman's face as she elegantly extended her hand.

"With pleasure, sir," she said and allowed Alexander to lead her out. There were a few astonished looks, for no one had seen her upon the floor within memory, but they were nothing to the expressions of admiration when the dance began.

The two lines formed, the musicians struck up with an alacrity they had not previously shown. Lady Dedham, inflamed by the opportunity, turned, promenaded, pranced, and paraded with the best of them. So much admiration did she excite in her execution that when a second contredanse was called to follow the first, she was overwhelmed with potential partners. Rackham surrendered her and returned to Sir Wilton and Clarissa with a smile.

"And they say she is an old lioness," he remarked. "It is not so, as you can see. The lady merely needed to remember who she was."

He looked about them. "But, I say, where has Miss Powley got to? I don't see her on the floor, nor have I seen her for half an hour." He spoke as if he had every right to command her presence, but Clair, recalling the young woman's protestations to Lady Dedham, doubted that his rights extended so far as his desires. Perhaps this was the way of the very rich, to expect that the world danced to their tune? To be sure, she herself had so danced earlier, but, grateful though she was for his finesse in extricating her from Mrs. Landon's clutches, she was not resigned to further intrusion of that kind.

But then, she reflected, it was Miss Powley his eyes were seeking, not her own. And a lucky thing, too, for she knew they could never get her. He was just the sort who most annoyed her: overassured, overbearing, and oversetting to a fine degree. She did not envy Miss Powley if the girl were forced to marry him against her inclination.

As the dance concluded, Lady Dedham, eyes bright and colour high, was escorted back to their little circle from one direction, while Miss Powley came from another. The difference being that Lady Dedham was essentially alone, her partner soon retreating, but Miss Powley was not. The old woman quickly asserted what she saw as her right of interrogation.

"Well, miss, and where have you been when I might have needed you? Careering about, I expect, wasting your time." She lifted her old-fashioned quizzing glass and stared at the man who accompanied her niece.

"And who, pray, is this?"

In truth, the gentleman seemed an odd duck to find in company such as this, (if, indeed, he was a gentleman at all by the standards of the Haut Ton), for he was in appearance hardly a merrymaker. He had a long, serious face with a grimly disdainful expression as he looked about him. His clothes, sober to the extreme of drabness, were serviceable but clumsily tailored. His boots were heavy, the heels worn lopsided, his linen coarse and badly laundered as if he cared not a whit for appearances, but only dressed to cover his sparse frame. Miss Powley beamed as she introduced him.

"Lady Dedham, Viscount Rackham, Sir Wilton, Miss St. Minver, may I present my friend and teacher, Mr. John Wearthy, the eminent social historian?"

"Teacher?" demanded Lady Dedham suspiciously. "What do you mean by teacher, miss?"

Rackham merely looked down at his boots.

Miss Powley was too effervescent to notice that her

22

companion had made less than a favourable impression. "Mr. Wearthy," she explained, "is the founder and first president of the Pargate Society for the Undertrodden."

"So this is where you have been spending your free afternoons?" asked Lady Dedham. "In a Society of Thingamabobs?"

Phyliss Powley patiently corrected her, but, if she had expected compassion, she was mistaken. "Never heard of it!" said Lady Dedham unequivocally, implying by her manner that what she was ignorant of could not exist. "What does it do?"

Mr. Wearthy, though, was not about to let an opportunity pass through incipient hostility.

"Our society, Lady Dedham, of which I am proud to be the president," he intoned as if he had practised long and diligently, "is dedicated to a great and needed purpose; to wit, the moral uplifting of those who, in these terrible times, have fallen along the way. The sinners, certainly, but as well the publicans and the Pharisees."

"How extraordinary." Lady Dedham looked at the man as if she must have misunderstood, but preferred no further enlightenment.

"And just what is it you do with—or should I say, *for*—these undertrodden, Mr. Wearthy?" the viscount asked with every appearance of sincerity. "Do you have a shelter, say, or a soup line, or perhaps a hospital or dispensary of some sort to which one might contribute?"

"Oh, we are always happy to accept donations, sir," Wearthy announced with alacrity. "You can be sure it will be put to work in a good cause."

"What sort of work, sir, if I may ask?"

"Well you may, well you may. Tracts, for example; hymnals and scripture cards; and, of course, there is the question of subsistence for the teachers."

"Oh, yes," said the viscount understandingly, "the teachers."

In the deep brown wells of Miss Powley's eyes something flashed as if she understood something of what the viscount was implying which the moral-teacher did not yet fathom. With an air of putting him firmly in his place (though her words were addressed to her aunt), she said, "I shall be one of those very teachers, you see."

"You?" asked Lady Dedham in a thundery rumble.

"Mr. Wearthy has done me the honour," Miss Powley went on, "of seeking my hand in marriage."

Her ladyship looked rudely down her long nose. "Preposterous!" she said. "You are going to marry Rackham!"

Miss Powley was kind, but very firm. "I think that is very unlikely, Aunt, for, you see, I have already told Mr. Wearthy yes."

— 3 —

THE EXPLOSION DETONATED by Miss Powley's announcement still reverberated the following day. Prosser, the
house maid, was just clearing away the luncheon things
when through the dining-room window she saw the heavy
but elegant closed chaise coming up the long drive from the
road. The St. Minver home being small, the staff was
equally abbreviated; three servants being the norm except
in times of particular festivity. Today was hardly such a
one. Leaving the last of the crumbs to be swept off the
snowy linen, but replacing the decanter of flower wine on
the sideboard, Prosser sought out Dolly in the small parlour.

"Miss Dolly, look, someone is coming. Someone substantial from the look of it." Dolly agreed but could not
help wondering what manner of person would travel in a
closed carriage in such balmy weather as this. She hurried
to the stairway and called up to Clarissa.

"You'd better wake Papa, Clair. Someone is coming."

Clarissa laid aside the mending she had taken up—really
one had no time to oneself these days—and looked out
toward the drive. She did not actually recognise the vehicle, but from the style, slightly old-fashioned though polished and burnished to a high degree, she had a sinking
feeling that she was acquainted with the occupant. With a
muted note of annoyance, she hurried along the passage to
her father's study. It was an understood thing that he was
never to be disturbed from luncheon until teatime, but

severe trials call for severe measures, and she suspected that the remainder of the afternoon would be trying indeed.

She tapped on the study door, but there was no answer. Again, more loudly, rapping on it, actually. Rattled the knob, calling out her father's name. At last opened it to be confronted with the sight of Sir Wilton upon the settee, feet up and resting on an arm of it, a silken handkerchief laid lightly across his face, the fabric fluttering gently with each breath. She repeated his name softly, then said it again accompanied by a slight joggle of the shoulder.

"Papa. Papa! Wake up. Someone is coming."

The reaction was immediate, though perhaps not quite coherent. "What? Eh? What? Who is coming?"

"I don't know who it is, Papa, but I fear it may be her Ladyship."

Sitting up, Sir Wilton shuddered. "Am I to be haunted by your mother's kinfolk for the rest of my life? What does she want, d'you suppose? Not to hash over last night's affair, I hope? It is no business of mine, after all." He rose reluctantly and absently stroked the rubbed spot on the settee's leather arm where his heels habitually rested. "A bit shabby."

"You could remove your boots when you lie down for your nap," Clarissa reminded him, but he answered her with one of his disarming smiles.

"In that event, I should not be so quick on the ready to greet unexpected guests, should I?" He ran his fingers through his thinning hair. "I suppose we must admit that we are home?"

Clarissa urged him gently toward the stair.

Lady Dedham, when Prosser admitted her, seemed to be attired in a kind of fashionable half-mourning. She was wearing a round gown of deep violet bombasine finished at the bottom with a broad flounce of purple crape, a spencer composed of dark purple cloth cut without a seam and ornamented with the same crape. Her bonnet was a large-brimmed (one might almost say huge) affair of still another purple shade (which did not quite harmonise with the others), the brim ornamented with large, hollow plaits of violet. She was nothing if not majestic, though the costume seemed unnecessarily heavy for a summer afternoon, but her manner was agitated in the extreme. Without preamble, she began her lament the moment she entered the hall.

"Ah, Sir Wilton, Clarissa, what a wretched creature you see before you. To think . . . to *think* of the ingratitude, the cynical thoughtlessness of the girl. Sneaking away behind my back to consort with such a person, to consort wi . . . with . . ." A large silken square (violet) went up to stifle the impending sobs.

Tender-hearted as he was, Sir Wilton could not bear the unhappiness of anyone. His deepest enemy would have had his sympathy. "My dear lady," he said, "My *dear* lady!" He looked about helplessly at his daughter. Clarissa indicated with a look that the visitor should be escorted into the parlour. And so she was, leaning on Sir Wilton's arm and Dolly's frail shoulder.

"A bit of hartshorn will do the trick, I daresay," remarked a dry voice from the doorway. Clarissa looked round to see that Viscount Rackham was standing there, cool and elegant in smooth white breeches and claw-hammer tails, carefully drawing off his gloves and dropping them into the handsome, high-crowned hat which Prosser was holding. Clarissa was relieved to find that her previous reaction to him had not been aberrant, but that he annoyed her quite as much today as he had done last evening. Her response had not been a mere social error.

"What ho, Miss St. Minver, are you ready for the second act?"

"I do not know what you mean, sir," she said coldly, "but I expect it is something quite cold-hearted."

"Oh, quite. But do you not think it is all rather like a play? Last night the situation set, today the second act? Who knows what the denouement will be. I warn you, she has been to her lawyer already this morning."

Clarissa was prevented by the manners instilled in her at Miss Pecksniff's school from saying what she was thinking about his odious remarks. She could only accompany him into the comfortable little parlour, where Lady Dedham was asking plaintively, "Is there a bit of hartshorn about, my dears, or some other restorative?"

Neither Clarissa nor Dolly, healthy girls both, had ever felt the need for ammonium carbonate and so could not readily supply the need, but tea was cried, and a glass of cordial water in the meantime.

Lady Dedham swooned back against the settee, but discovered that her bonnet would not allow complete surrender, so sat forward again and pressed her open hand across her face, peering with half-opened lids through the fingers. "I am undone," she moaned. "Oh, Wilton, I am undone. What shall I do? I am undone."

Embarrassed, her host crouched beside her, helplessly patting her other hand. Not easy, for the heavy rings impeded his action considerably. "Will you not tell us, dear lady, what has come about that has so unnerved you? Nothing short of tragedy can be worth this anguish, surely."

"The money," she said with sorrow, "the money cannot be saved."

"The money? What money, madam?" He looked to Rackham for explanation.

Lord Rackham groomed his moustache with the back of a long finger. "I daresay my aunt is unduly agitated," he suggested. "The fact is, you see, she feels she made a bad bargain and wants out of it."

Lady Dedham moaned into her handkerchief. "You make me sound like either a fool or a mercenary."

A look of unexpected kindliness came into Alexander's eyes. "I know, Aunt, that you are generally neither, but in this case, I am bound to own . . ."

Lady Dedham managed to look both outraged and put upon.

"Let me explain. You have met my aunt's niece, Miss Powley," Rackham continued to Sir Wilton.

"Indeed, a lovely creature."

"Yes, she is, and as charming as she is beautiful. Well, my aunt, you see, settled a certain sum of money upon Miss Powley and now she wishes she had not. The settlement was arranged contingent upon the completion of an agreed term of companionship with my aunt, the sum to be paid over to Miss Powley as her own property, a sort of dowry, if you like. Not merely a salary—it is more substantial than that—and besides Miss Powley was given her expenses as well, but it *was* a legal arrangement. Her ladyship has visited her solicitor this morning and been told that, since the term has expired naturally, save for a few days which Miss Powley had every intention of serving out . . ."

"Not in *my* house!" Lady Dedham interjected. "I want her out of my sight!"

Sir Wilton waited for Lord Rackham to go on, but, when he did not, was forced to ask for elucidation. "But if the contract is legally fulfilled?"

The viscount nodded. "Exactly. Just what the lawyer told her, but the use to which she believes the money will be put sticks in her craw."

Sir Wilton understood. "Ah, the parson or whatever he is?"

Rackham made a satiric little quarter bow. "Founder and President of the Pargate Society for the Undertrodden, actually. The P.S.U. Quite a virtuous little man, wasn't he? Extremely *moral* at any rate."

"Oh, quite," agreed Sir Wilton, "but," he looked nervously at her ladyship "how can it concern any of us here?"

Lady Dedham moaned pitiously and clutched at her host's hand so fiercely that her rings cut into his fingers.

"I expect she will explain it to you once she has control of herself again," said Rackham.

Did her ladyship cry "Cruel!" in a strangled tone?

The tea tray came, and with it a basin and napkin with which Lady Dedham could refresh her swollen eyes. "I know I am making a spectacle," she allowed at last, "but who would have believed the ingratitude?" She cast a longing look upon her nephew. "And to think I wished her to marry *you*, my boy."

His lordship accepted this with wry good humour. "I admit, Aunt, that it is a blow to have a psalm-singer preferred over oneself, but I expect I shall somehow survive it, eh? Miss Powley is a rare creature, though, and it is sad to see her cast away on such a person."

Clarissa found herself for once in agreement with him. She could not imagine what a young woman of Miss Powley's undoubted advantages (if one looked indulgently upon Lady Dedham) could see in such a person as Mr. Wearthy. Perhaps there was a side of him not readily apparent to the majority of onlookers. Perhaps he was actively kind to a disabled mother, or followed secret charities or . . . or . . . She could think of nothing else at the moment, but such things might surely exist. Many people have unfortunate exteriors, she reflected, and forbidding manners. Still, Mr. Wearthy had not been a person to enlist popular support, had he? Suddenly the closeness of the crowded little parlour began to oppress her. It might react upon Lady Dedham, heavily swathed as she was, even more.

"Would you care for a turn in the garden, Lady Dedham?" she asked. The woman had sipped her cordial and drunk her tea and played out her scene; now she seemed to be in a mode of transition. It seemed obvious that she had come here for more than light refreshment, and yet she seemed in no hurry to get on with her business, only sat there, massaging her right temple reflectively. Finally, at Clair's words, she did rouse herself.

"Yes," she said delightedly, as if this were a new and novel idea. "Let us take a breath of air. Your mama always prided herself upon her garden. I hope you have kept it up?

Yes, let us look at it. I may have one or two suggestions by which you may profit."

Dolly, who had all this time been silent, though listening and watching like the cat in the corner, rose as if to accompany them, but her ladyship waved her away. "I am sure you have many little things to do, child. Clarissa will manage me nicely, I am sure." At which Dolly looked quite relieved for she found the old lioness, if not fearsome, unsettling in the extreme.

"I do have an errand or two to run. I shall be going to the lending library. Clair, shall I match your fabric at Miss Plumb's? I know you wanted fresh ribbands."

Clarissa hurried to her room to fetch a swatch of the fabric, leaving her ladyship in Dolly's care, but, discovering the material was not quite where she thought she had left it, was somewhat delayed in her return. As she came out of her chamber again she saw something quite unusual. Papa, at the opposite end of the passage, was ushering Lord Rackham into the study, his private retreat and *sanctum sanctorum* where even she, an hour before, had hesitated to enter uninvited.

How very curious. She would not have thought the two men would have much in common. Her quiet, gentle father was quite the antithesis of Rackham.

=4=

As THE DOOR of the book room closed behind them, Sir Wilton waved his guest to a seat, shy for the first time about the shabbiness of the room, the badly rubbed spot on the arm of the settee.

Alexander looked at the profusion of books, the sun-faded rug, the writing table, which was obviously made for work, not for show. Nothing new, nothing glossy or obtrusive, only the gentle changes inaugurated by time. It was a friendly room, which suited the man whose retreat it obviously was, but Rackham was afraid he was bringing discord into this pleasant Eden. He became aware that Sir Wilton was regarding him curiously.

"Now, Lord Rackham, what is it that you feel you threaten my hospitality by mentioning?"

Put so boldly, he had no option but to reply with equal forthrightness. "Sir Wilton, last evening . . ."

"Yes, m'boy, last evening?"

"Well, sir, it was mentioned that you had recently been in Lady Dedham's part of the country without calling upon her?"

Sir Wilton shrugged apologetically. "Lord Rackham, with all due respect to your aunt . . ."

"May I ask, sir, if you were in the neighbourhood of Foxform?" Sir Wilton's look grew wary.

"And if I was, sir?"

Rackham was aware that he was treading dangerously,

but he went on. "It appears that there is a fair amount of gaming there of late." Sir Wilton grew very still. He seemed nervous rather than offended, but he responded coolly enough. "There might have been some play whilst I was there, yes."

"Rather deep play, I believe. The word is all over."

Sir Wilton closed his eyes briefly and grimaced. Rackham felt overwhelmingly sympathetic. "It is true then, sir?"

St. Minver's body sagged as if the energy had quite left him. "Yes, my boy, I am afraid that it is true. Unless I can raise a good deal of money by the end of the month, I am a ruined man. Sir Francis is a deuced lucky player."

Alexander Rackham noted with approval that Sir Wilton did not try to evade nor shed the blame for his actions, but Rackham knew too much of Sir Francis to let it lie thus. "Yes, demmed lucky. Consistently. I wonder that he can still find enough players to make up a table."

Sir Wilton raised his head and looked at the viscount attentively. "Are you implying, sir, what you seem to be? Do you have proof of unfair play?"

"How nicely you put it. No, I have no concrete proof whatsoever," the younger man said with regret, "but I expect if one paid close attention over a period of time, one might find very surprising things."

"Even if you do, it will come too late to help me, I fear."

"What amount *would* put you in the clear, sir?"

Sir Wilton paced about the room. "I apprehend that you do not mean to offend, my lord, but you will grant that this is a touchy subject for me."

"Forgive me, Sir Wilton, if I am clumsy."

"No, no, not at all. I recognise that your impetuousness comes from a heart, not a head, though I fear I cannot avail myself of your generosity."

"A mere loan, sir, not charity."

"One which I should be hard pressed to repay."

"It is yours, sir, if you choose to avail yourself of it. I can give you a draft on my bank up to the amount you specify, which you can use at any time."

Sir Wilton looked at him curiously. "May I ask what prompts you to this, my lord? We are nearly strangers."

Rackham stood up as well. "Let us say, sir, that I know you for an honest man and I suspect that the man you played against is not. I should hate to see you forced to go to moneylenders when it is unnecessary."

"A personal vendetta then, is it? What has Sir Francis done to you?"

"Something like that. The gentleman in question (and I use that term only as a class distinction, you understand) was once my schoolfellow. I knew him to be untrustworthy then, and I cannot persuade myself that time has altered his nature."

"People do change," Sir Wilton said charitably.

Rackham sadly shook his head. The remark was in complete character for this truly gentle man, but it was, unfortunately, rarely true.

In the garden, Clarissa was having a difficult time of it as well, but for altogether different reasons. It was all she could do to keep from laughing out loud at the proposition Lady Dedham had just laid before her.

"You honour me greatly, madam, but I don't think . . ."

"That is the trouble exactly. You do *not* think. You have made up your mind before considering what I have said."

"But there is no reason, madam, for me to . . ."

"Piff-paff!" snapped her ladyship. "I see through you like glass, my gel. You think you are too precious to waste on the likes of me, you think that you are too well-fixed, and you think, I daresay, that if I mismanaged your life as I mismanaged that of poor Phyliss, you will be adrift indeed, eh? Is it not so?"

Clarissa was completely disconcerted, for all those things had just been racing through her mind. However, the old woman was her guest and, however remote, a connexion of her mother's, not to be dismissed rudely.

"Now see this," Lady Dedham went on, "perhaps the time has come to take a strong look at your life. Do you know where you are going, what you want to do with yourself?" She pressed the perspiration away from her temples and paused to catch her breath.

"Shall we return to the house?" Clair asked.

"What, go inside? Not a bit of it. Like any fool I am overdressed for a warm day." She continued their perambulation, walking carefully along the shell-covered walk.

"I know, I know, for some time now you have been the belle of the county, and it is a heady experience." She gave Clarissa a sidelong look. "Oh, I am not so old but that I can remember what it was. But *I* planned my life shrewdly. I do not mean to say that I chose my three husbands with an eye to their mortality, but each had a fortune. The second was glad to merge my money with his, and the third thought he had come to the rainbow's end!" She uttered that peculiar peacock laugh. "But I outlived 'em all!"

"Are you suggesting, madam, that I do the same? Have you a rich widower in mind for me?"

"Mind your tongue, girl. If I knew a rich widower, bless me if I would not set a cap for him myself." This extraordinary idea was announced so confidently that the girl had no doubt it was true. "I know that you thought you would be the next Mrs. Landon—we all thought you would—but those gods up there," she cocked her head, "decreed otherwise. It is no matter. Your time will come.

"What I have in mind is that you will come to me as Phyliss did, with a smart sum of money at the end of it. Two years and a bit of a nest egg, eh? What do you say?"

Which you will try to keep if I do not please you in every detail, thought the girl. "No, my papa has my dowry set aside, I believe. I am fully . . ."

"You are fully cognizant of the honour I do you . . . and

35

all the rest of it, I know. Pish, gel! Teach your grandmother to suck eggs. It is that I am a cantankerous old woman, I expect. Well, I make no pretence. I am not easy, but I should have thought that we were kindred spirits and that a gel of spunk could match me, word for word!"

The overdressed old harridan was so disarmingly frank that Clair could not help but give way to her desire for laughter. Impulsively she put her arm about the woman's shoulder and hugged her.

"Madame, I do assure you that should I fall upon evil times, you will be the first person I turn to."

5

"So you have won out over our aunt, but the fact remains, dear girl, that you have mightily disappointed me." Lord Rackham's tone was not exactly petulant, but there was certainly an element of injury. He was sitting in the wing chair, his feet upon a scarlet ottoman. Miss Powley merely laughed at his reproachful look.

"I fear I know you too well for marriage, Rackham," she said.

"Ah, Rackham is it now? Until very lately it was Alexander, as it has been for fifteen years."

"You make my very point. We have known each other since the schoolroom; how could I take you with any seriousness?"

"But are my faults so glaring as all that?"

She shrugged, a pretty movement that perfectly illustrated her graceful nature. "Glaring? Indeed, no. Only the ordinary drawbacks of the male sex, but I have seen yours at much too close quarters and with no veil of infatuation to lighten them."

He adjusted the lay of his collar, flicked away a fleck of dust from his sleeve. "I daresay you will tell me what they are."

"If you like. Perhaps it may improve you, though I doubt it." As if she were ticking off Leporello's list she began to enumerate. "You are merely vain, capricious, self-willed and with a healthy regard for your own advantage and an utter disregard for anyone else's opinion. You are kind enough in your own way—more to animals than people. . . ."

"I say, Phyl, do you remember that fox cub?"

"Little Aesop that you rescued from a snare? Of course I do. It is exactly the sort of thing I mean. You treated that poor, maimed creature with all the tenderness in the world, but I doubt if you *ever* put anyone before yourself in your estimation. Certainly you never put me there, no matter how you profess admiration."

"Well, but, Coz, that is exactly why we should suit so admirably. Each would know exactly what they were getting. You need security and a good marriage; I need a handsome, compatible woman for a wife. God knows, I would not ask much beyond the usual conjugal duties to ensure the line. We would go our own ways for the most part."

"A marriage of convenience, in short?" she asked regarding him affectionately.

"Well, yes. I suppose you could call it that. We get on well together, don't we? Except for minimal requirements, I would guarantee to stay out of your way, and you would be free to stay out of mine. I don't even dine at home all that much. You'd be free to make your own life."

"I would keep your house while you resorted to a certain set of chambers in Finsbury Pavement?"

"How the devil do you know about that?"

"A number of people have been happy to educate me. I rather wish they had not. Certainly no *wife* would care to know such things, Alex. The fact is, I know too much about you."

"That affair with Elena is about done, you know. It was never serious."

She raised a finger. "You see? You illustrate exactly what I mean. *You* are bored with the arrangement; *you* will make a change; *you* will, I daresay, pay the girl handsomely and move on to another conquest. To myself, if I were not careful, I suspect."

"Why are you trying to make me so uncomfortable, my pet? It goes against the grain. I think you need waste no sympathy on Elena. Like most Cyprians she has very little heart, only a gaping pocketbook. She will not suffer, I do assure you, either financially or emotionally. She is pretty and spirited and deucedly good in . . ." He hesitated on the brink of an indelicate disclosure, but quickly eased the statement into other paths, ". . . in the sort of society which I inhabit. But there is always another admirer for her and another pretty maid for me."

"And where will it end? You deny seriousness, but it is never serious with you, as the whole world knows."

"And it is because I am not serious enough that you will not marry me?"

She had been standing with an arm lying gracefully along the mantle, but now, with an affectionate look in her eye, she crossed the room and perched upon the ottoman before him. "I will not marry you, Cousin, because I do not love you."

"I should have thought that would be all to the good."

"Not in the sort of marriage I want for myself," she said seriously. "I know that Mr. Wearthy made a poor impression amongst all your friends with their fine clothes and that it was a mistake to bring him into that grand house. . . ."

Rackham chuckled. "I daresay he thought it all frightfully decadent."

"Don't laugh at him, Alex. He is a decent man."

"Oh, I will allow that, but I cannot for the life of me think what you see in him. He is not our kind."

Surprisingly, she agreed. "No, he is not. Pray, do not think me rude, but Alex . . ."

"We have been friends too long for me to think you rude. Rude was when I pulled your plaits; we are rather beyond that sort of thing. Say what you will, it will not make me bleed."

Despite herself, Phyliss was a little nettled. "Oh, then, I

am not concerned with the opinion of 'our kind' because I believe I have found someone better."

He passed a hand over his chin. "Not rude, but demmed close. You imply that I am inferior to this psalm-singer? Good Lord, woman, you ride the edge!"

She said nothing to this, only regarded him gravely.

"I cannot believe," he exploded irritably, "that you have converted into a Bible-thumper. You'll say you have become a Wykehamite next!"

"I have not said that. I am becoming the wife of a man I admire."

Rackham relented. "Well, old girl, I can only say 'more power to you.' You've overthrown me, and you've bested Aunt, and if you've done that, you can do anything, I expect."

The person in question entered the room just as he made that statement, but she affected not to have heard it. Instead she looked coldly at Phyliss Powley.

"That will be all, miss. You may go to your chamber. I expect you will wish to pack your belongings for your journey."

"Thank you, your ladyship," said the erstwhile companion demurely, but as she left the room she cast one of her sweetest looks upon Lord Rackham. "Good-bye, Alexander. Perhaps you will come visiting in Pargate one day."

Her cousin, who had risen from the chair at his aunt's entrance, now bent over Phyliss's hand. "Perhaps I shall," he agreed. "Shall I send my carriage round for you in the morning to transport you to your new home?"

"That will be unnecessary, Rackham," said their aunt. "I am not such an ogre that I will not allow Miss Powley the use of my chaise, no matter what has passed between us."

Phyliss curtsied. "Thank you, your ladyship."

As the girl went out of the parlour and ascended the stairs it would be unlikely if she did not hear Lady Dedham say forcefully, "I do not know *how* you could sit there chatting with that person when you know how she has abused my trust."

He raised an eyebrow amiably. "Well, now, Aunt, is that really the case, or could it be construed that a part of the error is your own?"

Her reply was thunder. "How dare you, sir!"

He put his arms affectionately about her shoulders and drew her against his chest. It was an odd thing to see that stately matron lay her head gratefully upon his shoulder. "Oh, Alexander," she said again, "how do you dare?"

"I dare, madam, because, despite your horrific temperament, I hold an endless regard for you, and you know it. Let Cousin Phyliss go. Send her off with your blessing or you will always be sorry. It will mar the joy you have had together. Do not think of what lies ahead for her."

She raised her head. "But to think of my money going to such ends."

"Is the money really yours?"

She pulled away, half-angry again. "What on earth do you mean?"

"Now, now, do not overset yourself. I mean no disrespect."

"What then?" she demanded, only half-pacified.

"You signed the dowry over to Phyliss in return for her acting as your companion. You retained no clause allowing you to choose her husband, or even that she must take one of a certainty. Would you cheat the girl of her rightful due?"

"Why, no, but I . . ."

"The money is as surely gone as if it never existed. It can only hurt you if you attempt to hold on to it in this way."

Lady Deadham heaved a sign and visibly relaxed. "I suppose you are right, Alex. I *do* hate it that you *always* seem to be so, but I agree. I have been an old termagant."

He kissed her on the brow. "A Devil's daughter, indeed."

"Enough. I shall speak to her before she leaves and

concede that she shall have no more difficulty from me in the matter. She is a good girl, after all, and I shall have a rare time replacing her."

This seemed to strike a spark in Rackham's eyes. "Have you thought of whom you will ask?"

"Not really. I have considered one or two."

"I would try Sir Wilton's girl, I think," said Alexander with an elaborately casual air.

"Would you? Dolly, of course you mean."

"No, I was thinking of Clarissa."

"Too late. I have already made the bid and been laughed at for my pains."

"Have you?" he asked, rather in surprise. "How enterprising you are, but, if I can make a suggestion, you might just ask again. The circumstances may have altered, if you understand what I mean."

Lady Dedham knit her brow. "Altered? Because of young Landon, do you mean?"

"Just try," counselled Lord Rackham. "It can do no harm, and you might be surprised."

But, even as he spoke, another thought occurred to him. By Gad, what if . . . ? Brilliant! It was a brilliant idea!

6

MISS PLUMB'S SMALL shop on the High Street was both a collection and dispersal point for feminine news of every sort. The men gathered at the Hand of Glory tavern or the coffee house, but the women liked to be surrounded by the odds and bits of luxury which Miss Plumb provided. Today it was particularly well filled, for this was Burriton market day, and many of the country people, the small farmers and tenants, were about. They thronged Caunsehead Street, which led from the market, and the ladies stopped to chat with Miss Plumb (as much a fixture as her mother had been before her) to order five yards of the black sarsnet (two-and-tuppence the yard) against an expected mourning, or a bit of yellow ribbon for the eldest girl, even a silk rose to enliven last year's summer straw, and, yes, new ribbons for it as well.

The St. Minver sisters were popular here, for they, Clair in particular, led local fashion, and what Miss Plumb sold to them, she might hope, by mentioning it, to sell to someone else. But the girls had not had a happy morning. Papa had gravely spoken to them of business reverses and said that the gardener must be cut back to one day a week, cook admonished to concentrate on nourishing but economical meals, and the upstairs maid let go entirely. She had found another position, in any case, and it was the announcement of her defection that had alerted Sir Wilton to the economies able to be practiced in the household. Prosser, naturally, would be retained. The household could hardly run without her, but with the added upstairs duties, she would not be able to function as lady's maid. The girls would have to do for themselves in that area. He managed without a valet easily enough, he reminded them. They would have to learn to do the same.

It seemed only logical, then, that the young ladies go shopping, that occupation, as everyone knows, being the sovereign antidote for economical depression of the spirits. They could tolerate the loss of the gardener, would not greatly miss the upstairs maid, and neither had any great taste for elaborate cookery; only Prosser's departure would have been a major blow. They missed her even now, for they were used to bring her shopping, and it was difficult to remember to carry the little shopping basket oneself.

They needn't linger, after all, for they already knew the great tale of the day, having attended the ball at Landon House themselves, but it might be amusing to hear it reported and contrast the undoubted exaggerations with the realities they had seen. However, it was a little uncomfortable to find *themselves* still a topic of speculation—or Clarissa, at any rate, for, though Dolly had now more or less officially made her debut into country society, she had danced with too many partners to be linked with any particular one of them. They had the sense, though, that their fellow shoppers were glancing at them from under their eyelids and whispering behind their fingers in much the same way the 'friends' in the attiring room had done at Landon House.

The St. Minvers need hardly pay attention, in any case, for the tattle objectively concerned them very little, if at all. What was done was done, and if Greville was to marry his heiress then that was how the world fell out. Certainly, since Papa had suffered reverses, he could hardly be generous in the matter of Clair's dowry and, so, Greville would have had to look elsewhere in any case, as well as . . . ah, but it was too fatiguing to follow the line of conjecture when one must decide between two shades of cream silk paduasoy. So deep were they in discussion with Miss Plumb that they scarcely noticed that the shop had grown ominously silent until they heard the unexpected voice of Greville's mother.

"Why Clarissa, what a joy to see you!" she said with grossly false amiability. "And Dolly, what a spark you struck the other evening. I am sure there are a dozen broken hearts in your wake." The unusual affability was quite shocking since for years past (indeed, since it had appeared that Clair might join her family) she had been reserved in the extreme toward the sisters.

"And here is dear Georgiana with me. Georgie, dear, do you remember Miss Clarissa and Miss Dolly St. Minver?"

More than one small smile went about the shop at this question, for everyone there knew in what relation Miss Austruck and Miss Clair stood to each other. What they had not expected and, perhaps, what the very participants had not expected either, was that today, the crisis being past, the two young women felt a definite regard for one another: Georgiana for the verve and forthrightness of Clair, and Clair for the heiress's undoubted simplicity. What a pity it was that Mrs. Landon's daughter-in-law should have no one to befriend her, quiet little grey mouse that she seemed to be. Remember? Of course they remembered each other.

Mrs. Landon could not wait upon this budding friendship, however, for she had greater news to report. "I know you will be excited by this, Clarissa. I have had a letter from Estrella with wonderful news! She is going to have a child! I cannot tell you how much I look forward to a voyage to America when Georgiana and Greville are settled."

It seemed quite a triumph. Not only had her beloved son acquired an heiress, but her daughter was allowing her to acquire a grandchild. Her triumph over despised Clarissa must surely be complete. But then the true blow fell. So subtly was it lowered, so exquisitely dispatched, that

Clarissa did not, at first, understand what had come down. It was said in a tone which pretended to be confidential, but was calculated to carry throughout the shop.

"So sorry to hear about your father's reverses, my dear. They do say that Sir Francis is known for playing close to the bone. I own I always thought your father a more temperate sort of man than to be sucked into so steep a game as that must have been." Mrs. Landon was past mistress of effect. She seemed pleased with the result. The dawning of understanding on Dolly's face was slow in coming, but Clair absorbed the kernel of malice immediately. So this was what had precipitated Papa's tale of 'business losses' and push for economy. Her heart went out to him, for she knew how hard it must be for him to bear. His home and daughters were everything to him.

Clair knew there must be some riposte with which to retaliate, but for once her quick tongue failed her. "Why, I . . ." she began, wishing uncomfortably to retain both decency and the day. "Why, yes, Papa is luckily such a good player that one night's bad run is nothing. I expect he will take it back the next time they play."

"Yes, I am sure," purred Mrs. Landon. "But such a pity that one's future depends upon a trick of the cards, eh?" She smiled dazzlingly, quite ignoring the fact that her late husband, Greville's father, had been such a dub at the tables that he was welcomed as a pigeon wherever he went.

"Do you mean to say," asked Georgiana wide-eyed, "that your father actually gambled away everything he owned?"

Clair could almost *feel* the attention of listening ears. This was hardly a topic for public discussion. She tried to carry it off with a light laugh. "Well, not everything, but our standard of living will certainly be eclipsed temporarily."

"Oh, you poor thing."

"Unless, of course, there is a marriage in the offing," said Mrs. Landon with an air of administering the *coup de grace*. "And how *is* Viscount Rackham?"

"I am very well, madam," said a voice from the doorway. "How very kind of you to ask."

"Ah, Miss St. Minver, I have been looking for you. I had it in my mind that our appointment was for the lending library." He doffed his hat gracefully, bowed to the other women and to Clair's sister. "Miss Dolly, how glad I am to see you." Dolly blushed furiously, but Clarissa smiled warmly. The man was becoming a regular St. George. Well, she could enter into his charade.

"I beg your pardon, my lord, you are, of course, perfectly right. We have been dawdling over nothing more than a few ribbands. Shall we go then, Doll?" Dolly seemed a little bewildered by it all, but she agreed with alacrity. To be left behind at the probing mercy of Greville's mother was more than she cared for.

"Miss Austruck," said Clarissa graciously, "I trust you will give my very best to Greville. Perhaps you and he will come to tea one afternoon before you return to London?" She made it quite clear that Mrs. Landon was not included in the invitation.

"What a fortuitous meeting," the viscount said as they came out into the sunshine. "Almost as if we had rehearsed."

Clarissa still found his self-assurance extremely irritating, but she had reason to be grateful. "You have twice rescued me. I should not like you to think I have no appreciation, sir, but, really, we can find our way to the lending library alone."

He made a little, mocking bow. "But then *I* should feel deprived. I ask you, Miss Dolly," he appealed to the younger girl, "is that a just reward for my performance?"

Amused, Dolly agreed that it was not. "What harm can it do? Whatever anyone believes has already been settled, surely?"

Clair reluctantly agreed, but she had the certain feeling that a web was being woven from which it might not be so easy to escape. "Very well, sir, to the library, but no further."

"What on earth were you doing in Miss Plumb's shop, of all places, Lord Rackham?" asked Dolly animatedly. "It hardly seems to be one of your haunts."

"No," he agreed, "but I had been delegated to return a certain purchase which my aunt made, but found unsuitable; a bit of thread and some net not worth twelvepence."

"What a strange lady she seems to be," marvelled Dolly. "I own I find her fascinating and frightening at the same instant."

Rackham chuckled. "If you mean to suggest that she is mad, then the answer is uncertain. I believe she takes the custodial responsibilities of wealth quite seriously, even to the value of a shilling. Luckily, as I was passing through the village on my way to visit your father, I was able to do her errand."

"Which you have not done, I believe," Clair pointed out.

"By Jove, in the excitement of meeting Mrs. Landon I quite forgot it. My carriage is just across the way. May I offer you transportation?"

"We really do need to visit the library," Clair explained. "You need not wait."

"Thank you, moddom," he said as wryly as if he had been a servant whom she had summarily dismissed. Clarissa coloured, but Dolly seemed to have missed it all.

"You are visiting Papa?" she asked in wonder. "What on earth for? Have you been gambling with him, too?"

"Not at all, miss," the viscount said affably. "In fact, I hope to offer him a solution to his problem."

"But why should our father's welfare matter to you?" asked the girl. "With all respect, I believe you are hardly acquainted."

"Ah, but what I know of him, I like," said Rackham as if that closed the subject.

=7=

WHEN RACKHAM HAD disclosed his plan to his mother the previous evening the viscountess was much surprised. "Married, my dear? But I had believed that Miss Powley had accepted the proposal of another man. Surely you will not be instrumental in disrupting the relationship?"

"No, Mama, it is not Phyliss I mean to offer for."

His mother turned quite pale and she all but stared him out of countenance. "Alexander, it is not . . . I mean to say . . ."

Lord Rackham looked at her in surprise. "What is it that I do not mean to say, Mama?"

Lady Rackham was a woman of about forty-five, though she looked very much younger and, in fact, her many flirtations over the years had kept her young in heart and attitude as well. Though her behaviour had never been scandalous in any way, the attention of others had been vastly beneficial. Now, however, she laid her hand across her breast as if to still un unduly palpitating heart. "The . . . the one you plan to marry . . ."

"I do not believe you have ever met her, Mama, although it is probable that you have heard of her."

His mother took a trembling breath and almost consciously willed herself to relax. Slowly the colour seeped back into her cheeks. "Alex, my boy, tell me that it is not . . ."

"Not whom, Mama? I swear I do not understand your agitation."

"Not . . . not . . . Finsbury Pavement?" she asked.

Lord Rackham looked at her in astonishment for one long moment, then he responded with a shout of laughter.

"Elena? Good gad, Mother, what do you take me for? Elena ran off last Tuesday, I believe it was, with Basil Clapham, and I shall miss her, but the farewell note which arrived in yesterday's post says that she expects to be very happy. She also hopes that I will not be so cold-hearted as to refuse my blessing."

"And this does not affect you? She is quite right in thinking you are cold-hearted."

Rackham was visibly taken down. "I really don't see why. Dammee, Mama, the gel left *me*, not I her." His air of being put upon suffered, though, when he added, "Besides which, I have saved myself the smart little *parti* which I was prepared to settle on her when we took our separate ways, as I had every reason to believe would be fairly soon."

"And you do not mind that she has preferred another man?"

"Why, bless, you, it has saved a great deal of trouble all around. Why on earth should I mind? Basil will take fine care of her, I do assure you, since his inheritance is twice the size of mine and he has no taste for cards."

"I am sure it must be a comfort," said the viscountess, a little acidly, "to know that when I go, yours will outweigh his? Perhaps you can buy your little Cyprian back from him. My word, what you men put women through!"

Rackham, guessing that she was in danger of beginning a tirade on the inequality of the sexes, kept his mouth closed so as not to antagonise her. Lord knows, she was right, but what could he do about it, after all, save give each woman her just due? Ladies were ladies and Cyprians were Cyprians, and he doubted whether either would seriously care to exchange for the other.

"Who is it, then?" she asked after a period of expectant silence.

Rackham had opened his gazette and was deep in a news

article concerning the proposed abolishment of the netting tax, a dangerous notion in his opinion, "Umm? Who is it?"

"Alexander, *please* give me your attention." He put the gazette down reluctantly.

"What is it, madam?"

"Who . . . is . . . the . . . girl?" she asked, carefully framing her words as if he were slightly slow in comprehension. His gaze slid back to the paper.

"I see that they are playing *The Noble Jilt* at the Argyll Room in Upper Regent Street. Strangely poor acoustics there. Postage stamp of a theatre, and you can't hear a thing."

"Perhaps it is you, my son. You do not seem able to hear *me*, and I am only across the table."

Rackham put on his look of misunderstood injury, which he knew from past experience would always turn her affection toward him, and said patiently, "The gel, Mama, is Miss St. Minver."

"What? Not one of Sir Wilton's daughters?"

"The eldest, m'dear, Miss Clarissa."

"But *she* is all but promised to Greville Landon! You cannot go so far as to disrupt an already recognised understanding!"

"You have already said that, Mama, when you believed it to be Phyliss," he objected. "Am I to have no choice at all?"

She saw that he was laughing at her.

"In any case," he went on, "I think you had better explain the circumstances to Greville and to the pretty little heiress he has got himself engaged to. I do assure you that whomsoever Miss St. Minver marries it will not be Landon. And, I gather, Mrs. Landon is very glad of it."

His mother's usually placid periwinkle eyes all but snapped. "I should think so. I have never met the girl, but she has a reputation for a sharp tongue and very little discretion."

"I hope you will try to love her, Mama. For my sake," he said blandly.

"If you are serious about this, I will surely try to do so,

despite my doubts." After a moment she added, "But it is more important that *you* hold her in regard, is it not?"

This seemed not to have entered Rackham's mind at all. "As a matter of fact, I like her immensely. She is a fine, spirited girl with a keen sense of humour, but, honestly, ma'am, I see no reason why it should be a matter of any great moment? It will be a marriage of . . . what was it Phyliss called it? . . . ah, yes, a marriage of convenience, I think she had it."

"You discussed Miss St. Minver with Phyliss Powley?" asked his mother faintly.

"Of course I did not, Mama, though I could have, for they know each other slightly. No, no, this is a business arrangement, pure and simply, beneficial to us both. Mutually advantageous."

"And what does Sir Wilton say to this?"

"Why, nothing. I have not yet spoken to either of them on the subject. Did you think I would do so before discussing it with you?"

8

"I say, Rackham! What a surprise!"

The man who approached them was quite simply startling in his handsomeness, though both Clarissa and Dolly were far too well bred to openly show their admiration.

"What on earth are you doing in a hole like Burriton? And surrounded by such beauty, too." He doffed his hat and bowed as gallantly as current custom would allow. Rackham, however, did not seem particularly well disposed toward him.

"Miss St. Minver, Miss Dolly—Sir Francis Carlton."

Carlton was not tall. Rackham towered above him, but he had the lithe body of an athlete, though in miniature. His hair, which fell carelessly across a wide brow and curled about his ears, was the colour of burnished bronze, and his face might well have made his fortune in another age, for it was the very countenance of Titian's *Adonis*, a painting Clair had often seen at Landon House as a child before the family reverses had required its sale. It was a chiselled profile which would not have been out of place on an ancient coin, but a sensual smile, which curved knowingly about Carlton's lips, lent a decidedly pagan touch.

Clarissa took Dolly's hand defensively. The man's magnetism was quite astonishing. His blue eyes seemed almost to burn with intensity.

"Where have you been, old man?" he asked Rackham. "We have missed you. The table seems hardly the same."

Then he turned back to Clarissa. "Miss St. Minver? Not Sir Wilton's daughter, by chance?"

And Clair knew him for who he was. Had she not heard his name mere minutes ago from Mrs. Landon's lips? He was the man who had ruined Papa.

Clarissa looked at him coolly. "Yes," she said. "I believe I have heard of you as well, sir."

Sir Francis chuckled, and his eyes seemed to twinkle. How could he have such charm and be a villain? "And you have heard nothing good of me, I'll wager. I cannot imagine what folk find so reprehensible in my behaviour, but there it is. If only I more enjoyed my sins, I would not mind the many which common repute adds to my list." He clapped Rackham on the shoulder in a friendly fashion. "I expect our friend Lord Rackham, here, will give me a good character, eh? Will you vindicate me in the lady's eyes, Alex?"

Rackham merely looked sour. "What are you doing in these parts?" he asked. "Have you exhausted the amusements of your estate?"

"A matter of business, old fellow. The minor acquisition of some property hereabouts." Clarissa and Rackham exchanged looks. "Then I am off to London again, my short respite over." He turned back to Clarissa. "Do you know London, Miss St. Minver? Upon my soul, I believe you were made for it!"

"I have been there, but I do not know it well."

"Then I hope we shall have the pleasure of seeing you there again, and soon. Beauty is wasted in the country with no appreciative eye to see it. I expect you would be a sensation at Almack's."

"I do not know if I would care to be a 'sensation,' Sir Francis. My world may be small, but I think it worthwhile."

He refused the setdown. "It would be a crime against humanity, Miss St. Minver, if you allowed yourself to be buried in the country forever. It is good as a retreat, but there is another whole world out there which you have yet to experience. You are no true country mouse, miss; nor, I suspect, is Miss Dolly. Come into the light where you will be appreciated."

"I am sure that Miss St. Minver can take charge of her own life, Carlton," said Rackham brusquely. "If you will excuse us, I believe the young ladies have errands to accomplish."

Sir Francis cocked a roguish eyebrow. "And you are accomplishing something of your own, I suspect. Well, let it be. I am not a man to spoil sport of such a sympathetic kind." He bowed again. "I hope to see you and Miss Dolly another time, Miss St. Minver. Perhaps your father will allow me to call?"

"I am certain you know my father well enough to judge your welcome, Sir Francis. You will excuse us?"

They moved on toward the lending library, but Dolly seemed to go with reluctance and looked back over her shoulder longingly. "What a fascinating man," she said in an undertone to her sister. "Isn't he handsome?"

"Oh, come along," Clair said impatiently. "Handsome is as handsome does." Rackham looked at her out of the corner of his eye.

But at the door of the library she, too, looked back at the handsome wastrel just as he was bending low over the hand of Georgiana Austruck, while Mrs. Landon stood by beaming with pride. Clarissa could not imagine why, witnessing this, she felt obscurely annoyed.

Later that day she found even further cause to be annoyed.

Rackham had driven them home in his carriage as he had suggested (not the staid old-fashioned closed carriage of Lady Dedham, but his own chaise behind a high-stepping pair of greys), had gone into the study with Papa and remained for the better part of an hour. He emerged, chastened but charming, joined them for tea and drove off again. His attitude and manners had been, on the whole, so exemplary that Clarissa found them suspicious. Her previous observations of him did not lend themselves to this view of Alexander Rackham. All that she had seen suggested that he was too brash, too self-concerned to be all convincing whilst donning this aspect. But, since he was Papa's guest, not her own, she felt she could say nothing of it.

However, Papa said something puzzling at the supper table which increased the mystery. "Clarissa, I have something to discuss with you. Will you join me in my study when we have done eating?"

She looked down at her plate, feeling the stares of both her sister and of Prosser, who was serving the meal. She even felt Dolly kick her foot lightly under the table, but she refused to respond.

"Something rather interesting has occurred," said Sir Wilton after he had motioned her to a seat on the leather settee and he himself was at his chair at the desk. "I expect that you knew all about this, but I must say that I was perfectly unprepared. It was a real bolt from the blue."

She looked at him worriedly, a little frown forming. "What is it, Papa? Is it the money?"

He ignored her query and went straight to the heart of the matter as he saw it. "The fact is, my dear, that Lord Rackham has offered for you."

Clarissa was stunned. The notion of marrying Rackham was so preposterous that it seemed to fall into the category of improbables that included the sun nevermore rising, the collapse of the Bank of England or the idea that she might go as companion to Lady Dedham. Her father watched her shrewdly, noting the variety of emotions which seemed to flit across her face.

"Is it an equal surprise to you as well?" he asked.

"I had no inkling of it." In a few quick sentences the girl outlined her introduction to Lord Rackham and the two encounters with Mrs. Landon.

Sir Wilton was contrite. "My child, why did you not tell me things had come to such a pass?"

"Because you might have chosen not to attend the ball in a mistaken notion of saving my pride," answered Clarissa honestly. "I *had* to go, Papa."

He agreed. "I can see that. In any case you wanted to see the new bride, eh?" he asked with an amused expression. "I think most women would, despite the cost. I only blame myself that I was not with you when I was needed."

"It was a trifle delicate, but Lord Rackham *did* impress Mrs. Landon."

Sir Wilton began to fill and tamp his pipe. "From your tone, I conjecture that you do not care for the man?"

She began to answer hurriedly, then stopped and re-phrased her answer. "To speak honestly, I do not know him at all well and yet I own I should not care to spend much time in his company. I find him impulsive, often boorish, and certainly irresponsible."

"Then I may refuse his suit with a clear conscience? Or would you prefer to do so yourself? He returns tomorrow for an answer."

Clarissa was alarmed. "As to whether I will marry him?"

"As to whether he may press his suit," her father assured her. "I think he would not force himself upon you."

"Papa, do *you* like him?" she asked curiously. He took time to light his pipe and settle back in his chair.

"I confess I rather do, though I know no more of him than you do. In some ways he reminds me of myself at his age. What is it you said of him? Impulsive, irresponsible, and boorish? Add brash and bullying and I daresay you would have found me very much like him."

Clarissa flatly disbelieved her progenitor. "You, sir? Never! Why, he . . ."

"Young men are much the same, Clair; at any rate they differ very little. Certainly they are a different species from young women, and the understanding between the sexes at your age is limited at best. Will you hear him out?"

"Father, may I ask you something in confidence?"

If he was taken aback by this change from affection to familial formality, he did not show it, but assented with a nod. Clarissa, though, looked somewhat daunted.

"Has your consideration of Lord Rackham's suit been at all affected by a view to my security?"

For the first time he seemed perturbed. "What do you mean?"

She looked more uncomfortable. "Your business losses, Father. Mrs. Landon very kindly let me know how they came about when I saw her today." She told him of the meeting at Miss Plumb's and of the meeting with Sir Francis as well.

Her father sighed. "There is no doubt, my pet, that I shall be financially straitened for some goodly time to come, but do you truly believe that I would stoop to auctioning off my children?"

"Oh, Papa, no . . . but you *might* be overly concerned about my future and Dolly's.

"Lord Rackham is, after all, a rich man," she added.

"Despite being a boor?" He held up a hand to stave off an explosive response. "May I ask you only to discuss the matter with Rackham? Such marriages are not altogether rare, you know."

"I would rather marry for love than money."

"I daresay you would. So would we all in some degree or other. It is the unrelentingly romantic British soul, I expect. No Frenchman would admit to such a thing, and a German or a Swiss would not even admit that it existed."

"Very well, Papa. Do not worry your head. I will listen to his addresses for your sake, though I am bound to say I think the whole affair to be suspect."

At the door she turned back to him. "Are you certain he was not joking?"

Clarissa was so subdued when she came down the stairs that Prosser was concerned. "Is everything all right, then,

Miss Clarissa?" The girl only nodded absently. From the garden the melodious jug-jug of a nightingale drifted on the air.

"There it is again," said Prosser. "I ain't heard a nightingale in our garden for years now." She smiled reminiscently. "The last I heard was the night Mr. Greville went away to London. Don't you remember it, miss?"

Yes, Clarissa remembered how the thrush had sung that night. And oftentimes before, for it had been . . .

"Miss Clarissa, where on earth are you going?"

She tried to keep her voice and manner languid. "Just into the garden for a little."

"Without a shawl? You'll catch your death."

"I shan't be long," Clarissa promised.

The night was quite still, weighted with the scent of woodbine, and she heard the nightingale warble again, the nightingale which had not been heard in this garden since Greville Landon had gone up to London and the great world. Lifting her skirts against the dew, Clarissa moved along the familiar paths, which were as legible to her in the starlight as in the full light of the moon, directly towards the small pavilion in the center of the garden.

The summerhouse had been built in the reign of George II on mock-Palladian lines, deliciously mimicking in diminuitive elegance the grandeur of larger edifices. Though it had been conceived for the dalliance of lovers, it had served first as a playhouse for the St. Minver sisters and later as a personal domain in which to entertain their friends such as Greville and Estrella, and the rest of their circle. In the time of early adolescent rebellion, of infatuation, and ephemeral romance, it had even served once or twice for innocent evening assignations. It was then that Greville had developed his virtuosic repertory of bird calls. If Prosser remembered the nightingale well, so did Clarissa.

She did not enter the pavilion, but stood well outside. "I heard your call. Why have you come here?" she asked the shadow lurking within.

"Come into the shadows," Greville cautioned. "Someone may see you from the house."

"I would rather they saw me standing alone in the starlight," she said sensibly, "than drawn into heaven-knows-what compromise."

"Good Lord, Clair, don't you trust me?"

"You must go away at once." But curiosity was rampant. "Why are you here?"

His voice betrayed both longing and a certain satisfaction at her question. "I was afraid I would never speak to you alone again."

She accepted that easily enough. She had felt much the same way when she had seen him with his fiancée, but she spoke censoriously. "You should not be doing so now. What do you want?"

There issued a deep sigh from the summerhouse. "Won't you come in here where I can speak to you properly?"

Lud, how she wanted to, but she remained rooted to the path.

"I wanted to explain," he said softly. "I wanted to make it right between us."

She felt her heart wrench. "There is nothing to explain, Greville. You are betrothed."

"I always dreamed it would be you, Clair, but Mama . . ."

It would always have been "Mama." She recognised the genuine anguish in his voice. "I loved you, Clair. Do you understand that?"

"Yes," she said sadly. "I know that. But I have no fortune. Is Georgiana very rich?"

"Yes," the answer came dully, without rancour or bitterness, "very rich. Her fortune will bring Landon Hall back to what it should be." He tried to clear the huskiness from his voice but it crept in unwanted, "Oh, Clair, if you only knew how . . ."

Clarissa stood there shivering a little despite the warmth which still rose from the earth. There was no moonlight, but everything seemed sharp and clearly etched. She suspected it would remain so in her mind. "I do know, Greville." She understood all too well how things had fallen out, but she understood as well what she must do. She saw clearly. Too clearly.

She began to back away from the summerhouse. "Goodbye, Greville."

"No, Clair, wait!" he whispered hoarsely. "For one last time . . ."

"I have to go in now." She walked away, then suddenly wheeled and came back. "And Greville?"

"Yes?" he answered hopefully.

"No more nightingales."

"No," he said with resignation. "No more nightingales."

As she ascended the steps to the house, she reflected that she had never seen him in the summerhouse at all, only heard his voice through the woodbine.

"My word, miss," said Prosser as she came back into the house, "you did not stay out there very long."

"No," Clair said, "it was too cool without a shawl."

== 9 ==

PHYLISS POWLEY, PORTMANTEAU in hand, moved briskly through the streets of the holiday town. Pargate was at its best in summer when visitors from all over England thronged to its pretty shell beaches. But there was another Pargate as well, she had discovered. Phyliss had left the coaching house a quarter of an hour before. Ordinarily she would have taken a hack, but the distance to the hall, the bright sunshine, and the thrilling scent of the sea persuaded her to walk.

"Can I take yer bag, miss? Lemme carry it for yer. I don't ask much, just gissa penny, miss."

She looked down at the ragged waif who tugged at her skirt. Pale and undernourished, he looked as if he could hardly manage her heavily stuffed portmanteau, but, as well, she suspected that within that narrow chest might burn a fierce spark of independence. He had not simply begged for money, after all; he had asked to earn it.

"Do you know where to find the Pargate Society for the Undertrodden?" she asked. He gave her a sour look which sat poorly on his innocent face.

"Are you one of them, then, miss? P'raps you'd better take yer bag, then. I don't have a taste ter come home by weeping cross."

Phyliss could only stare at him blankly. "By weeping cross? What in the world do you mean?"

"Ain't you one of them 'repenters,' miss? If not, I begs

yer pardon. I only thought, since you was wanting ter go there, y'see, that you was mixed up with 'em."

"I expect I am 'mixed up with 'em,' as you say, but I believe you have a wrong idea. I know Mr. Wearthy very well. He is a good, kind man."

"Near as I can see, he's nought but a jerry-mumble, miss. I'm sorry if he's yer friend, but I knows about him. I seen him handin' out his tracts, ain't I? Might better be handing out food, is what I says."

Phyliss looked down at him indulgently as he toiled along with her luggage. "I believe that Mr. Wearthy considers the sentiments found in his tracts to be food of sorts," she said. "Food for the soul."

"Well, you can't eat tracts, miss, and that's a fact."

"Are you hungry now?" she asked. She looked about. They were crossing a shabby square on the far side of which was a pie stand. "What do you say to a hot meat pie?"

His eyes were longing, but he set his shoulders stoutly. "When you pays me, miss, I can buy me own meat pie." He switched the portmanteau from one hand to the other. "I'm thinking I should charge you extra for the weight. I never seen such a load. Whatcher got in it? Bricks?"

She had to chuckle appreciatively. She knew how heavy it was, for she had carried it a distance herself. "No bricks, but I have a few books that I felt I might need."

He looked at her incredulously. "Books? Whatever for?"

At the pie stand the beady-eyed vendor eyed her avariciously.

"A pie for the boy."

He grudgingly handed the waif a pie. "And for you, miss?"

"Only for the boy. He is hungry."

His reply was scornful. "Boys is allus hungry. Especially this boy." He sniffed disdainfully, "Look at him." The waif was, in fact, an amusing sight, his eyes half-closed in ecstacy, the flavourful drippings oozing out of the corners of his mouth.

"You know him, do you?" Phyliss asked.

"Course I knows him. One of the fixtures of the square, ain't he? A thief, too. Stole pies from me mor'n once, didn't he?"

"Well, you're being paid for this one," Phyliss reminded him sharply. "Is it good?" she asked the boy. He nodded, mouth too crammed to answer. "We'll have another, if you please." The pie man rolled his eyes.

"Bottomless pit, he has in there, miss." A thought occurred to him which lighted up his eyes. "I say, you wouldn't care to make amends for him, would yer, and pay me for all them pies he nicked?"

Phyliss looked the man straight in the eye. "I may be from the country, sir, but I am not so great a fool as that.

"Are you finished?" she asked the boy. "Then we had best be on our way."

By the time they had reached Harrowfield Road and the headquarters of the society, the lad was fairly staggering, but Phyliss had not the heart to shame him by relieving him of his burden. "How much extra do you think I owe you?"

" 'Cor, at least a pound!" Then he flashed a scalawag grin. "But you bought me them pies, didn't yer, and stood up to Mr. Peacenark. I figgers we is about traded even."

"Mr. Peacenark is the pie man, I take it?"

He tapped the brim of his broken hat. "You takes it correct, miss. I expect you'll see a bit of him if you stays about. He's one of your society, ain't he? He's your worthy Mr. Wearthy's left-hand man, I b'lieve."

"Right-hand man?"

But the boy looked at her darkly. "I knows what I says, miss. You keep an eye on them two."

She assented. "I shall certainly bear your advice in mind. Who should I ask for if I want to find you again?"

"Jeddy Pike, at your service. Shall I just carry this inside for you?"

Phyliss knocked sharply at the door but received no answer. When she had knocked again, she laid her ear to the door, but there was no sound from within. "Try the knob," Jeddy suggested, and when she did, it opened easily into the dank and unprepossessing interior.

As many times as she had visited the society, she had never seen the place like this before, bleak and echoing. It had an almost untenanted look, hardly alleviated by the rows of hard benches, or the rough deal table littered with papers of uplifting sentiment. Everything seemed dusty, the floor looked unscrubbed in a long while. Godliness had so overtaken the place, it seemed, that there was no room for its companion.

Jeddy wrinkled his nose. "Needs a bit of air, don't it?"

A little disconcerted, she called out Mr. Wearthy's name, but there was no answer. "What will yer do now, miss?" Jeddy asked.

Phyliss sank onto one of the benches. "I must wait for him, I expect. He must come back sooner or later.

"Perhaps you know where he lives?"

"Lives here, miss," the boy said with a curious look. "I thought he was yer friend and you'd been here before?"

Phyliss blushed. "I've been here before, but the subject of his living arrangements never arose." She had no idea why she was explaining this to a mere child. "He would walk with me to my coach, you understand. Perhaps we would have tea, but I *never* enquired as to his living arrangements, Jeddy."

He cocked an eyebrow. "Is like that, is it? You're sweet on him?"

She did not retreat from the question. "Perhaps I am." Looking about, an idea came to her. "Would you like to earn a few pennies more, Jeddy?"

Suspiciously, "Doing what?"

"Why, look at this place. An inch of mud on the floor, dust everywhere. But I expect we could clean it up soon enough, between us. Even you said it needed airing out."

He wrinkled his nose in a comic fashion. "Aye, it needs that. But should we take the liberty, do you think? Some people resents having it pointed out that they are dirty."

"Never mind that. Why don't you see if you can round up a broom and a bucket?" Whatever might be said of Phyliss Powley by Lady Dedham or any other detractor, it was not that she was unwilling to set a hand to work. Though she was not one of those who follows the world about with a whisk brush to capture stray flecks of lint, she had an aversion to untidiness and certainly to bad smells. With an air of determination, she unbuttoned her gloves and began to remove them.

The door opened behind her, and John Wearthy entered the hall. "Miss Powley, what are you doing here? I was not expecting you for another two days.

"And who is that boy?" he asked, pointing to Jeddy, emerging from the back rooms with the requested bucket and broom. "Boy, who gave you permission to go poking about in my private premises?"

Phyliss laid a calming hand upon his arm. "I did it, Mr. Wearthy. I felt the place could do with a bit of housewifely attention."

His look was resentful. "It never seemed to bother you before."

Phyliss tried to laugh away the tension. "I've never seen it in the sunlight before. Really, it does require some attention, don't you think?"

She was struck again at the way his dour handsomeness appealed to her. From the first time she had wandered into a meeting of the society—not wandered, exactly, since she had come with her married sister, Constance—she had felt a deep attraction for this working class "gentleman" with such an idealistic view of the world that he could organise a society such as this to combat its evil.

"Where shall I put this, miss?"

"Mr. Wearthy?" Phyliss asked, referring the question to her betrothed.

He looked about him. "I suppose I have let it go a bit. Do you want a job, boy? You can begin it tomorrow if you like."

"Do you not have a meeting this evening?" protested Phyliss.

"I daresay they will accept the dirty floor for one more evening. In the meantime, we must find you somewhere to live for a day or two." Intercepting her demurs. "Only until things have been made ready, you know." Phyliss guessed that he was speaking of the legal matters concerning the financial settlement.

"Do you know of such a place?" she asked.

He nodded. "One of the women in the society lets rooms not far from here. I expect she will be glad of the extra money. Her name is Mrs. Peacenark. A quiet, biddable soul, I have always found."

"I will take you round, miss," Jeddy volunteered. "I knows where it is."

"I believe I met her husband a little earlier," Phyliss said to Wearthy. "He is a pie man?"

"Nothing wrong with that. The society is built on the common ground of working-class lives, you see."

What a noble man he was, to be sure.

— 10 —

At about the same time Phyliss Powley was greeting her betrothed, her cousin, Lord Rackham, returned to the St. Minver household. The family servant, Prosser, beaming brightly, met him at the door and ushered him into the parlour as she had been instructed.

"Sir Wilton will be with you directly, sir. In the meanwhile I shall just bring you some tea, shall I?" Then, seeing his look, "Or a nice glass of flower wine?"

Sir Wilton came into the room just in time to countermand the suggestion. "Whiskey, I think, Prosser. Lord Rackham looks a bit too robust to fully appreciate flower wine."

"Very well, sir, I am sure you know best, though I did offer tea."

"Yes, Sir Wilton, I will vouch for that," agreed Lord Rackham, "the tea was first offered." Which both placated Prosser and amused his host.

As befitted the occasion, the opening moves were slow. Some little time was spent on the weather. (A particularly sunny year; good for the hay, but chancy for the corn.) Politics followed, both local and national. (The Commons, you know, have defeated the ivory tax, but I daresay the Whigs will reintroduce it in the next session.) And there was the constant threat of the Noncomformists to the Church of England. All was discussed in that languid way of men who know that the important topic has yet to be broached, but neither quite knowing which of them is expected to introduce it into conversation.

It was, as it fell out, the visitor who brought the matter in by asking after the health of Sir Wilton's daughters, for all the world as if he had not spent a substantial time in their company the preceding day. It was feeble, but it provided the necessary setting.

"Speaking of the gels," said Sir Wilton, clearing his throat and looking as if he wished to be anywhere on earth but where he was, "I mentioned to Clarissa a bit about, you know, your very generous proposal."

"Generous? Not at all, sir. I flatter myself that it shows only a feeling for what is proper in these matters."

"However that may be, sir, I regret to say that I spoke to her straight out about it, you know, and . . ."

"Good afternoon, gentlemen." Clarissa, herself, appeared in the doorway bearing a covered tray. "Prosser and cook were so busy in the kitchen that I volunteered to bring the tea to you myself."

"Tea, my dear?" asked her father. "I distinctly . . ."

But Rackham had already leapt to his feet. "How very nice of you, Miss St. Minver. Tea is exactly what I had a taste for, though your father's whiskey is really top-notch."

"Shall I pour, Lord Rackham?"

Sir Wilton had rarely seen his daughter in such a docile guise.

"Very kind of you. Milk alone, if you please, no sugar. And may I say how well you look today? Are those the ribbands you purchased from Miss Plumb?"

"How very good of you to notice such a trifle, sir. I am certain Miss Plumb will be as gratified as I am by your consideration."

Sir Wilton, quite bemused by this chain of events, slipped quietly from the room without a word, confident that he would not be missed for some time. He had it in his mind that his eldest daughter was quite capable of dealing with the proposal in her own way. His departure, of course, lent an air of tacit approval to the idea of Rackham presenting his brief in whatever fashion he might choose.

And Lord Rackham chose, quite soon, to come directly to the heart. He sipped the tea, but seemed disinclined to run a second time through the side issues of weather, crops, and politics. "May I assume, Miss St. Minver, that your father has relayed my request to address you?"

Any more infatuated man might have been taken aback by the calm look of calculation which he received in return, for it would have boded ill for any swain seeking romantic confirmation. Rackham, of course, sought exactly the reverse. Not to put too fine a point upon it, his inducements were similar to those with which he had plied Miss Powley (with Finsbury Pavement not at all entering in), and quite soon the conversation fell into the paths of point and counterpoint in a way of which any board of directors might have been proud, except that it entertained certain clauses and considerations at which any director who was a gentleman might well blush.

"My own carriage and pair—limited conjugal duties—a waiver of dowry because Papa still has Dolly to think of— freedom of movement—own friends so long as no breath of scandal is attached." These were not all on Clarissa's side alone; the discussion moved backward and forward between them with a multitude of small but pertinent details.

"My word, Miss St. Minver, you have given this some deep consideration," at one point said Rackham.

"Does it put you off, sir? Should I have blushed and stammered?"

"By no means! Your candour is refreshing." And they went on. Neither was overly demanding on the whole, certainly not so, considering the nature of the proposal; nor were many instances left uncovered at least by implication.

The tea was sipped, grew cold, and fresh hot water summoned, however, before Clarissa issued her final demand. It was prettily enough said in the manner to which they had accustomed each other, but it could easily have brought down a less sturdy house of cards.

70

"It is my certain wish, Lord Rackham, that we be wed before the fifth day of August. I hope that will not be an inconvenience?"

Prosser heard it from the dining room and relayed the notion to the cook, whose eyes grew quite round. They knew well enough what the condition was all about. In the parlour Rackham's eyebrows went quizzical. "Not undue haste, of course, but rather early, surely?"

Clarissa said nothing and for once dropped her eyes. Then he understood.

"Ah, the Landon nuptials are on about the twentieth of that month, as I recall?" He acquiesced gracefully.

"Certainly, Miss St. Minver, the date can be of no real significance, since it is a French marriage after all."

Her family was not so much astonished as completely baffled. Lady Dedham sent a note of congratulation which hovered somewhere between delight and outrage. She had managed to link two disparate branches of her family, although not the ones, nor in the manner, she had planned. Only Prosser, remembering the singing of the nightingale in the garden, understood what might have prompted the change of heart on the part of her young mistress.

Everyone in the county, on the other hand, understood the reason for the quite unseemly haste of the nuptials. A certain amount of sly smiling took place behind hands and unfurled fans, a certain amount of bawdy humour arose from speculation as to which of the brides would first produce an heir.

And, somehow, in the flurry of arrangement, Miss Austruck and her fiancé never came to tea at the St. Minver house. No one was really surprised. What did rather astonish everyone was the manner in which Alexander's mother welcomed her into the fold.

Lady Rackham, in consideration of her talk with her son concerning the sacrament of marriage, was inured to the sort of woman he must have chosen, for who but a calculating creature of no quality would have agreed so capriciously to such an arrangement merely on the basis of an aborted love affair? For her ladyship it was no great thing to lay aside the responsibilities she held as reigning matron of the family, but to lose those rights to a chit of whom half the county was talking about was quite another matter. The only consolation was that it would so put Lettice Landon's nose out of joint, and she and Mrs. Landon had, from time to time over the years, struck sparks from one another. She did not wish to promote an open quarrel, but she had no objection to Lettice's discomfiture.

She was of two minds, then, as she waited in the small salon of Powerbury for the girl to make her entrance. Clarissa had arrived, so much she knew, for the house had buzzed with it, but she had waited calmly behind the shut door of her own boudoir, not even allowing her son to enter when the pair arrived. She had dressed carefully in burgundy-red taffeta, the colour because she thought it suitable, the taffeta because she liked the majestic sound of its rustle-rustle. Her hair was put up in a braided coronet, and she wore the famous Rackham rubies. If she was to go out, it would be that she went in style. She had been waiting now for a quarter of an hour, and her fingers had begun to drum impatiently upon the arm of her chair. But when the door opened and she saw the pretty creature standing there hesitantly, she was surprised at her own affability.

She was surprised, too, at the question she asked a quarter of an hour later and at the tenderness with which she heard herself saying the words. And at the uncompromising answer.

"Tell me, my dear, how you regard my son. Do you love him at all?"

There was no equivocation. "No, madam, not at all."

And Lady Rackham was quite as satisfied with that reply as with any she might have had. It showed the girl to be straightforward and, quite possibly, of a compassionate heart.

What more, besides her obvious beauty, could one ask?

— 11 —

"THE TRUTH IS," wailed Clarissa, "that I know I have made a terrible mistake!"

Dolly, who had come into the elegant and stylish boudoir with every intention of dragging her sister off to view old Mrs. Searle's model farm in the Green Park, found her weeping instead of dressing for their outing.

"But, Clair, you have only been married a month. Surely you should give it a little time before settling into such despair? I expect it is only that you and Lord Rackham have yet to become accustomed to each other."

"What a fool I am," mourned Clarissa bitterly. "Doll, you have a fool for a sister."

"He hasn't actually been dreadful to you, has he?"

Clarissa blinked away her tears. "Who has been dreadful to me?"

"Lord Rackham, of course. Has he beaten you, or starved you, or forced his company on you when you would rather have been alone?"

Clarissa tossed her head scornfully. "Rackham? I scarcely see him. He is either at his club, or careering about town with his friends, or off in the country attending one of those illegal boxing matches. I only hope he will allow me a little time before he returns to setting up one of his Cyprians."

"You have heard of his former habits, then, I take it?"

"Heard? I can scarcely avoid them. Every gossipmonger

in London has gleefully retailed them to me as if they were the greatest entertainment in the world.

"Not that I am distressed by *that*," she added, her face clouding again.

"I would think, though, that he would have a little sympathy for your situation," Dolly continued, and in a moment devoutly wished she had not spoken, for she provoked such a baleful ferocity of countenance that she all but backed out of the room. Only her devotion to her sister stayed her. Certainly she had seen Clarissa suffering the vapours in the past, but never to the depths she seemed now to be plumbing.

The odd thing was that in these few short weeks since the wedding, her sister seemed to have changed all out of face from a bright, pleasant companion to this virtual stranger who now sat before her with tear-streaked face. The alteration was, actually, easily dated. Clarissa St. Minver had beome Lady Rackham upon the very date she had specified, the fifth day of August, the ceremony being performed in the little church at Burriton where the St. Minvers had held a pew for generations. For the first fortnight all had seemed to go well, a fact to which Dolly could aptly testify since she and Sir Wilton had been brought up to town by their new relation and installed in rooms not far from Berkeley Square. All the Haut Ton, it seemed, had been eager to entertain the newlyweds, and they were invited everywhere, perhaps because they were curious to see the sort of maiden who had finally captured the elusive Alex Rackham. They stayed to be diverted by his bride. Clarissa had promenaded, smiled, and danced her way through routs, levees, balls, and ridottos, seeming to delight in every moment. But then her humour changed.

On the twentieth day of August, Greville Landon took Georgiana Austruck in holy matrimony. Where the wedding of Lord and Lady Rackham had been quiet and unassuming, that of Mr. Landon and his bride bid fair to be the raree-show of the season. Mrs. Landon had not been seen in town for many years, and she had persuaded old Austruck, rich as Maecenas, to be lavish to the point of ostentation. Some few were impressed, most were amused. The newly popular Lord and Lady Rackham had been invited, although very late, too late to accept without raising eyebrows. A courier had arrived in the latter half of the second week they were married, but they had chosen not to attend.

"You don't want to go, I take it, Clair?" asked Rackham lazily. "I'll go along if you choose, but I should think it will be dreadfully dull. I mean—a country squire and a manufacturer's daughter? It's all been done before." He noticed, but did not comment on, the troubled manner with which Clarissa left the room.

The chapel, St. Cedric's-in-the-Square, had been pretty well filled—Georgiana's father had seen to that. Not that the town rocked with the news; the Haut Ton hardly knew the ceremony had taken place, but those who had been present and knew the ins and outs of the tale had been careful to see that the finer points were relayed to Lady Rackham. It was the least they could do, surely, for the new viscountess who looked likely to take the town by the ears.

Dolly had watched it all, of course, and, remembering the night she had looked from her window to see Clair standing in the center of the garden like someone gone daft, she had wondered how it would take her sister when the news truly sank in that Greville had married another woman. Now she knew.

Clarissa lolled her head over against her sister's shoulder like a child seeking comfort. "Oh, Doll, I am so unhappy."

But Dolly, with a wisdom beyond her years, would have none of it. "Only because you allow yourself to be. You have promised me an outing in the Green Park today, and I shan't let you off." She prodded her sister. "Come on, Clair, get dressed."

"I don't want to go out. I shall just stay here."

Her sister all but snapped her fingers in Clair's face. "You'll do no such thing. You promised to go to the Green Park, and I shan't let you off. Why, they even have cows there. And you can buy fresh milk just drawn!"

Clarissa rolled her eyes. "I could have had fresh milk, just drawn, at any time I chose back in Burriton. Why must I go to the Green Park?"

"Because, you silly, we might see the King. He is very fond of the place, I am told."

"The King is mad! They keep him locked up!"

"They let him out on good days," said Dolly firmly. "Get dressed."

It was quite true that Mrs. Searle's management of the little farm was conducted under royal patronage, and she, herself, was one of the attractions of it: an immensely dignified old woman wearing the wide panniers and tall hats of an earlier day. During the time of the American Wars the King had entrusted her with the task of supervising the tiny establishment, which consisted of a stable where the few cows were kept, a rustic cottage, and rambling roses tumbling everywhere. The royal patronage had made Mrs. Searle *a la mode*, the rooms of the cottage even having been decorated by the Princess Marie, fifth of the monarch's fifteen children. It certainly did her no harm that she was the aunt of the Prince Regent's current favourite, Beau Brummel.

"Perhaps we shall meet the Beau there, if not one of the royals," Dolly prophesied. "Or they say the ladies-in-waiting visit there after their duties with the Queen."

"You should not know a lady-in-waiting if you saw one, and neither should I." But, nevertheless, Clarissa dressed carefully, for one never knew who might be met.

She was just deciding between the lace shawl and the embroidered cashmere when there was a flurry of activity in the passage. The two sisters exchanged amused looks, but, as it continued, Clarissa quickly draped the cashmere about her shoulders and opened the door. And stepped back in surprise.

In the hallway was Prosser, who had accompanied Dolly and Sir Wilton up from the country, but here was a Prosser Clarissa had never seen before: red-faced and perspiring, almost stiff with anger. Her attire was disheveled, her Sunday straw, of which she was so proud, knocked to one side and broken at the brim. Two footmen were vainly attempting to restrain her flailing arms.

"What on earth is going on? Prosser, come to me this instant!"

"All I was trying to do, Miss Clair . . . Lady Rackham, I should say. I was coming up the back stairs, meek as a lamb, trying to find you and Miss Dolly when these ruffians . . ."

"Ruffians, me lady?" asked one of them in a suave and superior tone. "This person was coming up as if she had every right to go where she pleased! For all we knew she might be a housebreaker."

"I told you who I was!" Prosser protested. "And what's more I asked permission. I wouldn't go wandering through a strange house alone. What'd you take me for?"

The footman all but sneered. "Permission from whom, may I ask?"

"Why, from cook!" Prosser said in the self-righteous tone of those who have followed protocol exactly.

Clarissa would have interposed, but the footman gave no measure. "Cook? I don't know how it is in the country, missus, but in London cook runs the kitchen and nowheres else."

"How dare you to speak like that?" Clarissa said. "Apologise to Mrs. Prosser at once!"

The footman was visibly astonished. He looked at his companion, back to Clarissa, then, even, to Prosser. The command seemed to have shaken his world.

"What? Apologise for doing my duty?"

"There are ways and other ways of doing one's duty," said Clarissa coldly. "Do as I say at once."

"But, madam, what have I done?" The man's manner was truly insufferable. Clarissa suspected that this was to be a test of her authority and that, right or wrong, if she backed down now she would have no further command over the servants in this house. Before she could speak again, Prosser returned to the fray.

"I'll tell you what you have done! Look at me. Pulled about, my hat broken, my person manhandled! I always heard that *London* servants were the best in the world, polished and refined and superior to this sort of thing. Why, you're no better than a footpad!"

"What on earth is going on?" asked an annoyed voice from further long the passage. His lordship, the Viscount Rackham, splendid in a Turkish jacket, stood in the doorway of his dressing room, the smoke from his pipe curling about his head.

The footman leapt in. "This woman, sir—"

Rackham gestured indolently. "Mind your words, Mason. This . . . woman, as you call her, is Mrs. Prosser, and, as a trusted and valued retainer of Lady Rackham's, she is welcome in this household at any time.

"And she will be treated as any other upper servant, is that clear?"

Mason seemed to have difficulty finding his words. "Oh, but, yer lordship . . ."

"Is that clear, Mason?" Rackham repeated.

The manservant dropped his eyes. "Yes, sir."

"Very well, you may go." The man retreated hurriedly. Rackham nodded pleasantly. "I fancy that does it, my dear," and he made as if to return to his pipe and papers.

But, for Clarissa, the meeting was not over. "Prosser," she said, "please wait in the boudoir with Miss Dolly."

She strode after her husband and raised her hand just as he was about to close the door. "Rackham! A word with you, if you please." The closing door caught her fingers lightly. "Oh!"

"My dear! What have I done! I do beg your pardon!" He took her hand in his. "Are you injured?"

But Clarissa snatched it away. "Really, sir! How dare you treat me so shabbily just now?"

"Shabbily? But, my dear wife, I agreed with you completely. Mason was behaving very badly and needed my reprimand. I hope Mrs. Prosser is not too disturbed?"

"There was no need for you to interfere."

Rackham's eyebrows rose. "Interfere? In my own house?" His voice had a slight edge. "Am I no longer master here?"

"Of course you are master, I should be the last to deny it. But if I am to manage your household, I must stand before the servants, not trail along at your heel, sir. I fear you have only prolonged a process that would easily have been resolved."

He nodded, more understanding. "I begin to see."

"I hope you do, Rackham. Either the servants are in charge of the household or I am. You may have your choice."

The wretch actually smiled at her. "And if I come down on the side of the staff, then I might as well never have married at all, eh? Quite right, my dear. I ask your pardon."

His easy capitulation quite took the wind from Clarissa's sails.

"You . . . you agree!"

Rackham spread his hands. "Of a certainty. You are the mistress of the house. I relinquish responsibility very gladly. Such things are a bore to me. The household, in future, is entirely in your hands."

Seething inside, Clarissa spoke calmly. "Thank you, my lord. Will you be in to nuncheon?"

The slightest hint of amusement flickered about her

husband's lips. "No, I fear not. I shall be meeting Grave-send at the club, you know."

Clarissa swept from the room and along the hall with regal hauteur. "Doll, Prosser!" The boudoir door opened. "Come along at once. Dolly, be so kind as to bring my reticule? Prosser, your hat is a disgrace! We must find you another before all else."

The three moved majestically down the front stair. Mason, face calm and unperturbed, stood at the door. "Shall I fetch the carriage, madam?"

Clarissa gave him a melting smile and laid her hand upon his arm. "Thank you, no, Mason. It is such a lovely day, we have decided to walk."

"Walk, madam? Then, should I . . .?"

"Accompany us? No, I think not. We are going only a little way, but how thoughtful of you to ask."

Mason, bewildered, could only open the door like an automaton. "Very good, my lady." He had no intention of crossing her again.

The pretty little millinery shop had lifted all their spirits. Prosser, at first, declared for an almost exact replica of the headgear she had lost, but the sisters would have none of it.

"Too country, by half, Prossy," Clarissa declared. "Why do you think Mason felt so free to bully you? It was not because he is cruel, but because you have no presence."

"Presence, Miss Clair? I don't think I know what you mean?"

"Nor do I," added Dolly. "What is it you have in mind?"

Clarissa looked to the milliner for support. "A person may be up from the country and unused to London ways, but no one must ever see you cowed."

The milliner nodded understandingly. "I believe I have just the thing, madam." She went behind a curtain into her workroom and presently returned with a creation which quite took Prosser's breath away. Like her old hat, this was of straw, but a shining plaited straw of glistening black, high-crowned and elegantly severe. Not a fruit, nor bird nor flower adorned it. Except for a ribbon rosette to catch the hatband, it made no concessions whatsoever to frivolity. Prosser sighed in ecstatic content. The milliner placed it carefully upon the maidservant's iron-grey coiffure, settling it and adjusting it, before holding up a hand mirror so that it could be viewed from all around.

"Oh, miss . . ." Prosser breathed. "Oh, I look . . . I look just like a housekeeper!" It was the height of her ambition.

Perhaps I should buy one for myself, thought Clarissa wryly, *if that is what my new employment is to be.*

— 12 —

THERE IS PERHAPS no prettier thing in the world, to para-phrase an American philosopher, than the sight of the privileged classes enjoying their pleasures. Certainly it was true on this lovely morning in London. Strollers were everywhere, children with their hoops and nannies tumbled over one another on the well-kept walks of the park, pretty women, dressed in fashion, prettily fed the water-fowl which inhabited the reservoir. From the balconies, bow windows, and terraces of Arlington Street, the curious, unwilling to venture into the crowd unless it were enlivened by a personality of consequence, trained their eyes upon the park-folk.

But to Clarissa, Dolly, and Prosser, everyone there looked consequential. Still new to London, they were entranced by the mien and manner of the city-dwellers, their easy nonchalance, and, in particular, their fashion. The sisters kept a running commentary upon the dresses they passed. Here, a round gown of jaconet muslin to which an underslip of rose sarsnet lent a glow; there a dramatic (perhaps too dramatic for the hour) riding dress of emerald velvet; and beyond the little statue of Amor there was to be met a stately old galleon with the airs and streamers of a decade past.

The little farm was amusing in its pretension of rusticity, but the three country women were not as enchanted with goats and chickens as their neighbouring strollers were, though they were sometimes amused by the remarks they heard. "Why do chickens not fly away? Is cow's milk truly good for the complexion? Is anything so rank as the smell of a billy? Mercy, my dear, the creature should be bathed in *eau de cologne!*"

Mrs. Searle was affable to all, displaying a courtly old-fashioned charm, swaying gracefully in her skirt *à paniers*. She was aged, to be sure, but she seemed tireless, her energy amazing. At the moment her greatest consideration was engaged in preparing a syllabub for a stout lady of high complexion and a manner of rather overblown affability, fulsomely displayed as Mrs. Searle drew the milk warm from the cow's udder upon a portion of wine, sugar, and spice. It was evident that the recipient of this brew was a person of some consequence, though none of the three recognised her. The gentleman at her elbow was small of stature, but extremely handsome, and he smiled when he spotted them.

"Look, Clair," whispered Dolly urgently, "is that not . . . ?"

The gentleman called out their names with evident pleasure. "Why, bless me, if it is not my country neighbours! Miss St. Minver, I see that Lady Rackham has been successful in luring you away from bucolic pleasures to adorn our arid town society." To Clarissa he bowed deeply. "Lady Rackham, what an asset to our world you have already become."

"Good day, Sir Francis." Clarissa acknowledged him only with reluctance, the Carlton depredations upon her father's fortune being what they were. The stout woman returned her empty mug to Mrs. Searle and turned to them, still sporting a moustache of milk upon her upper lip.

"Your Royal Highness," said Sir Francis, "may I present to you the Viscountess Rackham and her sister, Miss Dolly St. Minver?"

The young women curtsied. Whatever they had expected from this morning's excursion, it was not to be presented to the unconventional and slightly declassée Princess of Wales. They had heard much of her long before coming up to London, but even more since, for her escapades were the grist of common tattle—her constant altercations with the Regent, whispers of an illegitimate son by an unknown father—as well as the very real and unfeigned joy with which the common populace accepted her as a thorn in her unpopular spouse's fleshy side. Because of the Prince's not-so-secret morganatic connection to another lady, it was said that Fitzherbert was his wife, Conyngham was his mistress, but Caroline was only his millstone. Whatever the truth of that might be, the royal pair had been estranged almost from the moment they met. All they shared in common was the daughter over whom they had fought for years.

"What pretty gurls you are," she said familiarly in a heavy Germanic accent. "Sir Francis, vere haf you been hiding dem?"

"They have just come up from the West Country, ma'am, to grace the last of the London summer."

"Ach, vat I vould not giff to take dere places in de country.

"Dat is vye I come here to visit Mrs. Searle," she explained to the sisters. "It at least giffs me de illusion of freshness, hah?" She laughed good-humouredly. "But ven I see such unspoiled faces like yours, it makes me almost satisfied."

"Your Royal Highness is very gracious." Despite the compliment, Clarissa was a little disappointed not to be taken for one of the *ton*. "We expect to accustom ourselves to town fashions quickly."

"Ach, not too quickly, pray. Your freshness vill be your greatest asset, *ja*, Carlton? De society here is quide cuckoo for novelty. No, no, *leibchen*, cherish your freshness while you can."

"And how is your esteemed father, Lady Rackham?" said Sir Francis, aptly shifting the conversation. "Has your ladyship yet forgiven me for besting him at cards?"

Even Clarissa had learned by now that it was considered

ill-bred to harbour resentment in such matters, or at least to show it. "Papa seems quite recovered from your depredations, sir," was said with an air of lightness she did not truly feel.

Dolly had, all this time, been standing quietly beside her sister, but staring almost transfixedly at Sir Francis. Clarissa longed to nudge her enough to break her trance, but Carlton took the matter into his own hands.

"Her Royal Highness and I were about to walk along the reservoir. Would you care to join us?" he suggested.

Dolly might almost have expired. "Oh, yes, please let us do so, Clair!" she breathed, but then had the presence of mind to drop her eyes before her anxiety could be too clearly read.

"If you would not feel we intrude, ma'am?" asked Clarissa.

"Ach, heavens no! Sir Francis and I are old, old friends and have each heard all de odder has to say. It vill be pleasant to have a pair of new voices, *ja*?"

"Very pleasant, indeed, ma'am," answered Carlton. He took Dolly's hand and tucked it beneath his arm, leading the way along the path. Clarissa followed, feeling very odd to be walking with the Crown Princess of England, and Prosser sedately came along behind.

"And vot do you t'ink of beautiful London, now dat you are here?"

Clarissa answered, suitably noncommittal. She was already finding that to be so closely paired with her Royal Highness was a mixed blessing. The woman seemed to be of the school that believed if a hint of scent was good, a heavy application could only be an improvement. The fact that it was a pungent patchouli only confirmed young Lady Rackham's inclination to an opposing view.

And yet the woman was pleasant enough. She had a sharp little nose like a parrot's beak and quick little eyes that seemed to look everywhere at once, missing nothing.

"Ah, dere is Lady Coyle and her . . . vot is de English?

. . . her *cicisbeo*." It mattered not that *cicisbeo* was not English at all, and that it had, in fact, become a commonly vulgar term had no bearing, though it seemed that Sir Francis believed so.

"I understand that the term used now is *cavalier servente*, Your Royal Highness," he said over his shoulder from ahead of them. "The other has taken on a different colouration."

"Ach, it is all the same. A pretty boy for a fading voman.

"You understand," she said to Clarissa as if they had quickly advanced to the stage of confidantes, "I shall not hesitate to do the same ven my time comes. One must still be amused, *ja*?" And she laughed so raucously that Clarissa looked about them nervously, wondering what the other strollers must think.

Suddenly Sir Francis came to a halt, waiting for the others to catch up with him. Glancing significantly ahead of them, he said, "Perhaps it would be better, ma'am, if we struck in another direction?"

The Crown Princess followed the direction of his look and snorted. *"Nein*, Carlton, vy should I accommodate myself to dot man's pleasure? Or do you t'ink I am afraid of him?"

"Certainly not, ma'am, I only wished to avoid . . ."

Disparagingly, she waved a hand at him. "Dot is nodding. I will not say bad t'ings if he don't say dem."

Clarissa saw that a group of people were coming directly toward them across the sward. Even from a distance it was easy enough to identify the Prince Regent's corpulent outline. He had been so often caricatured in critical cartoons that his bloated figure was more than familiar to the whole of Europe. Where once he might have been, in Sheridan's words, "an epitome of elegance," he was now rather more pitiful in his vanity. The heavy stays he wore could accomplish only so much.

The group was evidently coming from St. James's palace, and, both courses being constant, there was no way in the world that the royal couple should not meet. Apprehensively, Clarissa tried to catch her sister's eye, but the girl was all unaware, understanding nothing.

"The Prince Regent? Is it really? Which one is he? How exciting!"

"*Ja*, exciting," the Crown Princess muttered sourly. "Vait until you have seen him flopping about like a great sea animal!" She spoke in answer to Dolly, but her words were addressed to Clarissa, who found no possible avenue of escape. "You do nod know vot I put up with dis man. On our vedding night he was so drunk he slept vid his head in de grate. *Ja*, de grate of de fireplace. De First Gentleman, hah!"

The Prince Regent and his companions were much closer by now, and it was evident that recognition of Princess Caroline had sown consternation among them, for the Prince had stopped stock-still in the middle of the path and seemed reluctant to go any further until the danger of confrontation was passed. Then, perhaps, his courage returned, or perhaps his own better judgement, or that of his advisors, prevailed. In any case, he again came warily in their direction.

The Prince Regent had once been quite handsome in an overblown Hanoverian way, but now, past fifty, his vanity sometimes led him into snares. He dressed in a way more suited to a much younger man, and, indeed, the hyacinth blue of the coat he wore could never have been very flattering to a person of such high colour. It reflected against his skin in such a way as to give him a distinctly lavender hue. The skin itself had no tone and hung in unattractive dewlaps over the intricate folds of his immensely high cravat. He had for years led the fashion by carrying a gold-knobbed stick, but now, it was evident that it was used not for show but for support. His mode of locomotion was, in fact, not so much a walk as a manner of tottering along the path, half-supported by his companions. In no way was his appearance a credit to the institution of monarchy; nor, in the opinion of many, was anything else about him creditable. And they were not reluctant to speak out. Imprison them as he would, his enemies barked around his heels unceasingly once their freedom was restored.

But he could not imprison the Princess Caroline.

They stared fiercely at each other, the husband almost trembling with aversion, the wife seeking the vulnerable point as always. But they drew abreast, had almost passed, the moment almost saved, when the Crown Princess gave way to one of those unfortunate impulses which had alienated so many.

"Look at him," she jibed. "Dot man is one big fat pig! Vot a country dis vil be wid a porker for a king!"

The rage of the Prince Regent was a beautiful thing to behold, educated as he had been to public restraint. His plump cheeks ballooned, his beautifully lashed eyes spurted tears of anger which bid fair to run his mascara. Having not quite gone past, he did not turn around at this, though his words carried as well as if he had.

"I do assure you, madam, that if I am King of this realm or no, *you*, despite devil or god, will never be my Queen!"

On a personal level it was a distressing enough thing to have said, still, it could have been construed as one of those empty threats bandied by disaffected husbands and wives—but on a political level it was horrendous. For the Prince Regent of England to have said such a thing to his lawful wife in the presence of witnesses, was disastrous! Charges and countercharges in the courts of law had been flung with less provocation.

For Clarissa it was equally frightening to hear these great and powerful people wrapt in the bonds of such enmity. And she, too, had entered herself into a marriage such as this at bottom was, a marriage without love, a fiction of temporal convenience. Would she and Rackham, she wondered, come at last to the same sorry state?

=== 13 ===

PHYLISS, JEDDY, AND Mr. Peacenark could not help smiling
proudly as they looked about the meeting hall, though they
did so with exhausted sighs. This was the fourth Thursday
they had devoted to its rehabilitation, and it looked, perhaps, as clean as it ever could considering the vicissitudes of
its chequered past. From Peacenark she had learned that it
had been at various times a greengrocer's, a gin palace, a
slaughterhouse for small animals and fowl, and most recently a house or den for opium smokers. From time to
time, Phyliss believed, she could still catch a faint whiff of
the "dreamer's drug." Whatever had gone on here, the walls
and floors, in particular, showed the evidence of long and
hard traverse over the years. Though she ached in every
bone from the effort, she knew the boards would never be
truly clean. Her two helpers had been of enormous assistance, but only so much could be done.

The relationship between the urchin and the pie man, as
it fell out, was not so acrimonious as it had first appeared.
Since she had been living in Mrs. Peacenark's front lodging
room, she had discovered that there was a kind of mutual
camaraderie at this level of society, which was unknown at
the levels of respectability to which she had previously
been exposed. She sometimes felt that Mr. Wearthy did not
always understand the folk among whom he toiled. However unworthily, she felt, too, that he considered himself
their better by several degrees. Perhaps it came from his
uncompromisingly moral Scottish beginnings. It was cer-

tainly true that at the Tuesday- and Thursday-night meetings he harangued them in a way she felt they did not often comprehend. But what, then, brought them together with such regularity? It had to be more than the promise of refreshments of cheap tea and plain bread.

But there was little time for philosophic examination today, for this afternoon she had to visit Aunt Dedham's solicitor. She had tried to persuade Wearthy to accompany her, but he said, "I have a long-standing aversion to the legal profession." Phyliss demurred. "The terms of the dowry are quite clear-cut, are they not?" he asked.

"I do not know."

"Well, then you will tell me when you return."

If this behaviour seemed odd in one who was to administer the future of the money, it did not seem unduly so in the nature of the man Phyliss had begun to know since she had lived in Pargate. She did not exactly know the definition of a visionary, but she suspected that Wearthy might well be one. He inspired her with his moral strictures, but she sometimes wondered if his grasp of reality was concrete.

When, "Do you know anything of Mr. Wearthy's background?" was asked by the solicitor in the afternoon, she was forced to admit she knew little.

"Only what I have present knowledge of," she admitted.

"He has said nothing to you of his past ventures?"

She began to think she had been very foolish. "No."

The Pargate Society was not the first, he explained, and went on to detail three others of like pretension.

"Then, is he a scoundrel in your view?" she asked.

The lawyer looked down his long nose at that. "Something I do not pretend to know, Miss Powley. I follow instruction from my clients."

"In this case, Lady Dedham?"

"Of a certainty."

"And it was upon her behalf that this investigation was made?"

"It could scarcely hold any personal interest for me." He rattled the papers on his desk. "Your aunt is very fond of you, Miss Powley." She tried not to look disbelieving. "All she has done has been for your own good." It was increasingly difficult. "Not the money, you know. She is quite willing to fulfill her part of your bargain."

This took Phyliss quite by surprise. "She is?" Then she understood. "But there are conditions?"

"Only one," he said rather smugly, happy that he had disconcerted her. "She will not have the money made over to Mr. Wearthy."

"What does that imply? I fear I do not understand."

"Just that. The money is to be made over to you on condition that it remains in your hands."

"To administer? John Wearthy is to have no say in it?"

"Only through you."

Phyliss knit her brows. "I fear I do not understand the advantage to my aunt."

He leant back in his chair, smiling tolerantly. "There is none. The money is yours to do with as you see fit. As it comes to you, you may give it where you like," here he paused impressively, " . . . but the choice is yours.

"Consider, Miss Powley. It is a great deal of money," and he told her the exact sum.

"Yes," she admitted, "it is. It is a great deal of money."

When, before that evening's meeting, she attempted to explain all this to Wearthy, he, too, smiled tolerantly.

"I think that lawyer has bamboozled you, miss. When we are married, your property becomes mine."

"To administer, sir," she agreed, "when I place it in your trust."

"Trust? No, to do with as I like, Miss Powley, without consideration." John Wearthy's sparely handsome face had taken on a severity and impatience which his betrothed had never before seen. "It becomes my property, in point of fact, in much the same way you will have done."

"I, Mr. Wearthy?" She tried to make her answer light. "You make me sound like the veriest slave."

"Chattel, Miss Powley." He seemed intent on staring her down, as if by doing so he could command her spirit by the sheer force of personal magnetism. "The structure of matrimony is founded upon just that, my dear." The words of endearment came stiffly, as if they were forever alien. "The woman, being weaker, puts all her worries in her husband's care. The law agrees with this. The law knows what is best." He almost smiled. Certainly, his features assumed a more amiable cast.

But the seed of doubt had been sown. Phyliss, educated by Lady Dedham and unused to such male confrontation, stammered out her contradiction. "I fear, Mr. Wearthy, that you are mistaken."

"Mistaken?" His sallow complexion grew darker. "Of a certainty, *I* am not mistaken."

"Then I think *you* should consult with my aunt's solicitor, sir. The conditions of my receiving the money are quite other than you imagine. It will fall out that when we are married I will entrust the use of it to you, but, in fact, the final say will always be mine, I fear."

"That is quite preposterous! To come to you and beg for every sixpence? It is contrary to the law."

"Discuss it with the solicitor, Mr. Wearthy, and let us not quarrel."

"Well, though I fear you are wrong, I will do so. There is no great hurry, surely? We shall be married for a goodly time, shall we not?" He asked it with what Phyliss heard as forced lightness. And she believed she heard something else as well, did she not? The jingling of coin and the terror of losing it.

"Mr. Wearthy," she asked, "do you love me?"

"I respect you deeply, Miss Powley."

"No, no. That is not what I asked, sir."

His old impatience and surly arrogance at being catechised came to the fore. "We are engaged in a greater ideal than personal affection, Miss Powley, surely." He regarded her as severely as any ancient patriarch. "I had thought that your devotion to this cause . . ."

"I believe, sir," Phyliss said sadly, "that my dedication is no longer the question here. I was willing to share your ideals, but . . ."

His expression was very nearly bleak. "*But,* Miss Powley? I pray you, do not speak in haste or anger."

Phyliss's hands had for some time been nervously clasped at her breast, but now she dropped them. "I do not speak in anger, Mr. Wearthy, only in surprise."

"And in suspicion, I think. Well, I will not try to persuade you. As I would not beg for a sixpence, so will I not beg for more."

But as the hall was beginning to fill, they could not discuss it further.

John Wearthy's talk that evening (it was never called a sermon, as he was never called a divine) turned upon the subject of ingratitude and failed ideals. Phyliss understood that, for the most part, the thrust of it was intended for herself. She could not argue with this. It had come to her over these weeks that Mr. Wearthy's way and her own were perhaps quite different. Mere moral uplift could not, in the long run, count for much with Phyliss Powley. She had seen too many of the deserving poor struggling to make a life for themselves.

But if this was not the answer to aid them, what was?

= 14 =

THE MONTHS PASS quickly when one has been taken up, or so Clarissa found. All of the great world seemed to be enchanted by the new Vicountess Rackham and her pretty sister, Miss St. Minver. Without fail, they were invited everywhere, and the invitations fluttered in like a rain of confetti, invitations to card parties, opera evenings, the races, routs, musical soirees, dancing parties, and even to the circus which was exhibited in the amphitheatre of Astley's riding school. Dolly was inundated with beaux, but then so was Lady Clarissa.

As a quasi-business contract, the Rackham arrangement was going along famously, and on a day in late September the young marrieds were beginning their day together as they often did, lazily allowing the world to seep into their consciousness.

"And what is it we have tonight, your ladyship?" asked Rackham in a familiar way as he buttered still another muffin. "These really are delicious, you know. Cook is to be congratulated."

"I believe she learned it from Prosser," Clarissa suggested. "Do look how you are dripping the butter." She herself took only a bit of the fish and a touch of the savoury, since she had had quite a large early tea in her bedroom already. She knew, though, that her husband disliked breakfasting alone, and she accepted the ritual willingly as a part of her marital compact.

"As to this evening, I believe Miss Angelus is playing

Juliet, and we are spoke for both a rout at Lady Borrow-dale's and a lecture on Greek pottery at the Dellanoy Gallery."

"Miss Angelus is surely getting on a bit for Juliet?"

"It is, I believe, her farewell performance in the role."

"Well, I have seen it a half-dozen times." He rang the service bell.

"More tea water, Randolph; this is cooling rapidly. I believe the spirit lamp has gone out." He sighed expressively. "And that is all the evening has to offer?"

"I daresay there are a dozen alternatives cluttering my desk in the morning room, but I had believed these were the ones we had settled upon."

His lordship pulled a bored face. "It always happens, you know, and this autumn sooner than others. I am up to town for a bit after the hunting, and it quickly begins to seem the same and runs together."

Clarissa looked up from the folded paper which Randolph had presented to her. "What runs together, Rackham?"

"Everything. The parties, the balls; the exhibitions and the playhouses all show the same people, all repeating the same gossip over and over. Thank heaven the shooting begins next fortnight."

His wife carefully put the paper under the edge of her plate. "I surmise, sir, that you are trying to tell me something, but, pray, do not speak in allusive hints, for you know I am merely a country woman and do not understand such things."

He hooted at this. "The rising star of the social world does not understand her husband? Possibly too true. We scarcely see each other enough for such a climate to grow up, eh? But, seriously, Clair, you know exactly. It is all so tiresome!"

"Not to me," she answered. "I have never had such an exciting time, and I *adore* hearing all the gossip. It makes me understand the world so much better." She paused, a faint smile lingering at the corners of her mouth. "Have you heard about Madame Sylvestri that was?"

His ears could not but prick up, for the lady had once been the inhabitant of certain chambers in Finsbury Pavement. "What, Elena? What are they saying about the poor creature now?"

Clarissa ran her fingers through a ringlet, then patted it to lie more closely against her creamy shoulder. "Of course I don't know the ins and outs of it, but they are saying that before she spoke her lines with Lord Clapham she made a confession of all her past lovers. Do you not think that, in this day, such a thing is needless trouble?"

Rackham could not help grinning. "But what a remarkable memory!"

There were times, Clarissa reflected, that he was quite fun to be with. Tiresome often and demanding of others, but on his bright days he was sometimes most pleasant to be about. Not that she would dare admit such a thing. Particularly to him, for he would either scoff or run a mile. The first few weeks of marriage had been quite horrendous, but once the settling in had been done, all became quite placid. She had her own circle of friends, and he had his. Sometimes they overlapped, but not often. London was a great and various place with room for social roaming to the heart's content. More often than not, his were sporting coves, as they were called, and hers more of the mode. She had learnt to play cards with a dash, taken dancing lessons, listened to racy conversation with an innocence which lured the speaker to tell her more and more, but generally evaded the flirtations and proposed liaisons others tried to force upon her.

Something in her nature made it imperative to hold to the rules she and Rackham had laid down. Their marriage was to be free on both sides, but no scandal was ever to be attached. So far there had never been temptation strong enough to make her reconsider, but she sometimes wondered what would happen if the temptation ever came.

Uneasily she fingered the folded paper beneath the edge of her place.

Rackham threw down his gazette. "I wonder if you would feel in the mood for a little play at Almack's?"

Her eyes widened in surprise. Although she knew his fondness for the club, he had never made anything like a point of her attending with him. "I suppose we could cut Lady Borrowdale," she temporised, "though it would be a pity, for they say the Dreadful Duke is to be there, and I have yet to be presented."

Rackham threw her a mildly exasperated look. "Sometimes I wonder if you are fit to be left alone, though I expect he is not so dangerous as the world makes him out to be. Every family has its black sheep, and I imagine the King's brood can be no different. It is only that sabre cut which has given him his aura of wickedness.

"But there is no need to alienate Liza Borrowdale, if we do not require to remain too long."

His bride looked at him calculatingly. "Why are you so set on Almack's?"

His lordship merely shrugged. "No reason. A whim only."

"I expect that I am not to believe that for a moment. Is someone to be there from whom you fancy the protection of a wife?"

"Such as whom?" he laughed, but she fancied she had struck home.

Clarissa's mouth took on a humourous, pursed-up expression, as if she were savouring a special titbit. "Such as Elena, Lady Clapham, for instance?"

Her husband looked at first dumbfounded, then broke into a roar of appreciative laughter. "You minx, you knew all along about Elena?"

Clarissa shook her head. "No, but so many people have made a point of informing me that I could not pretend to ignorance for very long."

But then his look grew a little wary. "The fact is, you

see, the Landons have returned from their honeymoon journey. They are almost sure to make Almack's an early port of call."

Her fingertips again touched the paper, but she looked at him levelly. "And you think that your sovereignty should be established, is that it? Or do you believe they will be there of a certainty and that I should be exposed to temptation?" She carefully put down the pretty Meissen cup and saucer.

He raised an astonished eyebrow. "Do I detect a slight edge to your voice, my dear?"

"The business to which you allude is long over, Rackham."

That irrepressible grin again. "But the world has no notion of that, does it?"

So he was vulnerable to the talk of the ton, after all, was he? The notion truly surprised her, for her husband had never demonstrated any particular ardour. His weekly visits to her chamber were perfunctory at best, although conducted with grace and great good taste. Nothing had ever indicated that it was more than duty.

But she could see that talk about Greville and herself would not be pleasing to any husband. "Certainly, I will be happy to visit Almack's with you," she said.

"Not so great a crush here as at Lady Borrowdale's," announced Lord Tendril, superciliously staring at the denizens of Almack's through his quizzer, "but, upon my word, it seems to be all of the same people!" His companion, Sir Francis Carlton, had avoided Lady Borrowdale since their brief liaison the previous year, but knew exactly what was meant.

"My dear chap, it is generally accepted that a rout is meant to be a crush. It is the best way in the world of paying off overdue social debts in one fell swoop. Not elegant, certainly, but deucedly effective." His handsome face took on a veneer of faint contempt. "One does not expect much quality there, of course."

There was certainly a good deal of the quality here, for the subscription list of Almack's was carefully monitored by the Committee of Ladies, doyens of high rank, though the rule was that the gentlemen nominate and choose the ladies, and *vice versa*, so that no lady could exclude a lady, nor a gentleman a gentleman. Since the balloting was secret, a surprising number of prominent people were blackballed. One had to be very careful, for the tickets were not transferable, and if anyone turned out to be unsuitable, there was no opportunity of changing them, but one must see them forever. The Crown Princess of Wales, for example, would never be countenanced.

For a subscription of a smart twenty-five guineas, one had a ball and a supper once a week for twelve weeks. The ballroom was famous for its chaste splendour: gilt columns and pilasters, classic medallions, candles in cut-glass lustres. The room itself was nearly a hundred feet long by, perhaps, forty in width and had on one occasion been the setting for a ball at which seventeen hundred people were present. It was then that the conditions for entrance were tightened. Now the only mode of admission was by voucher or personal introduction.

In the gaming rooms the play was deep and constant, sometimes continuing for days at a time around the clock. Faro, which had started in the '80s, was an adaptation of the old Stuart game of basset, hazard was the most popular, while whist, curiously enough for such aristocratic surroundings, had begun in the servants' hall under the undignified name of swobbers. Sir Francis was well known in the card rooms, but tonight he had other things on his mind.

"And where, do you suppose, is the lovely Lady Rackham tonight?"

It was casually asked, but Tendril intercepted the undertone of interest. "Aha! Is the fair Clarissa to be the new conquest? I would think that you would think more than once before considering a dalliance with Rackham's wife."

The long standing coolness between Carlton and Alexander Rackham was well known, and the jibe meant to prick, but Sir Francis merely dipped a pinch of snuff in a lazy fashion. "All the more reason, old fellow," he advised. "Adds a bit of spice to the chase, don't you know?"

Lord Tendril did, indeed, know, for Sir Francis had cut as wide a swath through the distaff side of fashionable society as any man in recent history. His conquests were legion, and his reputation among the ladies both horrifying and spiced with the flavour of intrigue. There was a sort of game in existence in which participants wagered against each other as to how long the devilishly handsome Carlton would take to subdue a frisky mare, for it was always married ladies he chose. Maidens, he always averred, were too easy to make it worth his while. They would begin to languish from the moment he set his eye in their direction, and, from Sir Francis, such behaviour elicited only dry amusement. But, even though he knew it could not be, Tendril passed on the talk he had heard.

"They are saying, you know, that it is the younger sister you truly want, eh?"

Carlton did not deign to look at his companion but there was a hint of already savoured triumph in his voice as he answered, "Strategy, old chap. Lose the battle, but win the campaign, you know."

"Well, you shall soon enough have your chance," Tendril observed. "There they are now, Rackham and his lady, coming in the door."

But Carlton, who had seen them himself a fraction before the other, stepped out in quite another direction. The dandy lifted his quizzing glass to his eye and saw that his friend had paused beside quite another lady, one whom he himself had never before seen. Then he noticed the young man standing just beyond her and understood at once both who she was and the tactics of Sir Francis. Not only had the Rackhams arrived at Almack's, but Mr. Greville Landon had brought his heiress-bride to parade before society as well.

It was, of a certainty, vastly amusing to see the playing out of this little set piece. Rackham and his lady making the round, Carlton extending his enormous charm upon young Mrs. Landon, Greville Landon with eyes for none but Clarissa Rackham. Even at his most adroit, Lord Tendril could not remember arranging himself as the catalyst in such a quintet, but Sir Francis seemed to have moved almost instinctively to find the advantage in the situation without conscious thought. And now he was dancing away with Mrs. Landon, to whose husband Rackham had no alternative but to surrender his wife.

And, ah, yes, now Rackham was heading toward the gaming room, and Carlton was returning young Mrs. Landon to her husband, which left him with—of course— the original object of his attack, the fair Clarissa. What a master the man was. Rackham would never have directly relinquished his new wife to his old rival, but this way . . . brilliant strategem that. Worthy of a military mind. Pity Sir Francis wasn't out there against old Boney. Speculatively, he watched Carlton leading a still reluctant Lady Rackham about the floor. So he had not won her over quite yet, eh? It might prove to be a continuously interesting campaign. One worth watching. But, on the other hand, what was it that kept Francis Carlton and Alexander Rackham like hostile pups in each other's presence? That, too, might be interesting and worth looking into.

For Carlton, however, it was not as easy as it appeared. His handsome face creased into an amiable grin as he chided his partner. "My dear Lady Rackham, if you continue to dance so stiffly in my arms, the whole room will be talking."

"I am sure I do not know what you mean, sir."

"Consider for a moment. If one does not care—if a dance is only a dance—then one is quite assured and totally relaxed, giving oneself up to the music, don't you agree? Such restraint as yours would argue something quite different to anyone watching closely. It might even suggest an attraction which one is desperately trying to cover."

Hop hop step step glide. "Oh, pish! It could equally connote a deep aversion, sir, which one was, for the sake of politeness, trying not to reveal."

Sway with the music, step step glide. "Am I such an ogre, then?" He flung his hair back from his forehead almost coquettishly, a hallmark of vanity unusual in a man. Partly charmed by him, she relented enough to look up from under half-closed eyes.

"I am not sure. You have the look of the complete nonpareil, but you may recall that I have certain counts against you already."

"Your dear Papa? But I thought he had righted his ship and was sailing with an even keel by now? Surely Rackham has not been so niggardly as not to restore him?"

Clarissa opened her eyes in astonishment. "Rackham? Certainly not. Did you believe my marriage lines included a provision for the paying off of my father's gambling losses?"

Sir Francis raised his brows heavenward as if to feign innocence. "It would not be the first time such a thing has happened. But, I daresay, the mere fact of having an extravagantly wealthy son-in-law has recredited his solvency in some quarters. There are always those disposed to believe the best of a man when he is down. I daresay it is a flaw of human nature."

They rounded the bend of the enlongated oval of dancers and turned back the other way. "And you do not?" she asked.

"Would you prefer me if I were that sort of man? No, no, there are areas in which I give no quarter because I would refuse it for myself and play my hand accordingly. It has stood me in good stead so far."

"That I have heard," Clarissa agreed. Their conversation was interrupted as the dancers formed a long arch of lifted hands and the couple momentarily parted to separate, then traverse it together. "Does it not trouble your mind that you have built your fortunes on the ruin of others?"

He shook his head in mock sadness. "Do I have a small, still voice of conscience, do you mean? Not a whit. I daresay it was worked out of me at an early age. I had a rather north-country nanny. Flinty as the hills she sprang from, as I recall. Cold baths, unbuttered porridge and all that. Devilish uncomfortable at the time, but deucedly good for honing one's endurance."

"I do not believe you for an instant," said Clarissa indignantly as the couples formed a chain. "Who would subject a child to such a regimen?"

"*Au contraire*," he answered, but added cheerfully, "However, I must say, it prepared me for school."

"You were at school with Rackham, were you not?"

A shadow seemed to cross his face. "Too true," he admitted, but when she would have pursued the line of questioning, she found the subject had obliquely changed, or, more truly, simply skated away, for somehow she discovered that they were discussing other dancers on the floor.

"And Mrs. Landon," Carlton asked, "do you know her well at all?"

She wondered a little at his interest. "Scarcely. I grew up with Greville and his sister, of course."

"That would be the fair Estrella? I have not seen her in years. Does she well?"

"Tolerably well, I believe. She is to be a mother."

"A mother, fancy that. And you were saying about Mrs. Landon?"

"I know nothing of Georgiana."

"Is that her name? Poor thing. It must be heavy to be dragged about with a reference to the most unpopular monarch in history. Our history, at any rate. What did you think of the Prince of Whales when you met him that day in the Green Park?"

Clarissa was faintly shocked. "The Prince of . . . Really, you mustn't say such things, or people will hear you."

"Oh, I stole it from Charles Lamb." And with the dance music as an accompaniment he began to declaim with a perfectly straight face.

> "Not a fatter fish than he
> Flounders round the polar sea.
> See his blubbers—at his gills
> What a world of drink he swills.
> Name or title, what has he?
> Is he Regent of the sea?
> By his bulk and by his size,
> By his oily qualities,
> This—or else my eyesight fails—
> This should be the Prince of Whales!"

"But that is shocking! I hope this Lamb person was well drubbed for his pains!"

"Ah, it was anonymous, I do assure you. No man would be such a fool as to put his own name beneath it."

"No true man would have written it," she argued stoutly. He looked across her shoulder.

"And speaking of which . . ." he said. The dance turned them about, and she saw that the subject of their conversation had entered the room. The music limped to a close as the Prince Regent stood at the door for a few moments, chatting with acquaintances and basking in adulation, though perhaps it grew tiresome to hear always the same fulsome compliments, for his eyes began to roam restlessly over the waiting crowd as he listened. It was done with a kind of benign indifference . . . until his gaze fell upon Sir Francis and his partner. The normally expressive eyes narrowed, and the too-tender mouth pursed into a moué of annoyance. As the roomful of spectators watched him, he crossed directly to the pair, ignored Carlton, and spoke directly to Clarissa.

"My dear Lady Rackham, how delightful to meet you at last. Why has no one yet presented you? I have quite looked forward to the occasion ever since you came up to town. Will you be good enough to honour me with this dance?"

The room was agog, for the Prince Regent *never* approached anyone in this way, but informed his aides to present them to him. Even Clarissa recognised that it was quite unprecedented and hardly knew what to say. The whole of society was watching them attentively; the Regent had obviously intended a direct snub to her dancing partner, and was waiting, composed but obviously requiring an affirmative answer. She sought Sir Francis's eyes and thought she saw him give an economical yet very definite nod of his head.

Sinking into as deep a curtsey as her trembling limbs would support, Clarissa answered, "With pleasure, Your Royal Highness."

Prinney made a small gesture, and the orchestra struck up a popular *valse à deux temps* of which the Prince was known to be particularly fond. For such a large man of well known infirmity, he was surprisingly light on his feet, although Clarissa found the omnipresent creaking of his stays distracting. She supposed that he was required to initiate any conversation, and so they danced in silence for a few measures until, beaming down into her face as if he were paying her the great compliment of intimacy, he said familiarly, "I am nearly old enough to be your father, my dear, and so I feel I can take the liberty of chiding you. You really should amend your company or it will ruin you. That chap is rather a bad ha'penny, you know. Could spoil your chances in a week. What your husband is about, I don't understand."

Clarissa found herself flushing with chagrin. Despite the

fact that this overweight dandy in his absurdly tight trousers and heeled dancing pumps was her temporal monarch, she felt that he had no right to speak to her in such a way at only their second encounter. Particularly when she had not even been properly presented.

"You take my meaning, I suppose?" he asked, still beaming as if he were paying a compliment.

"Yes, Your Royal Highness," she managed to murmur through a tightly clenched smile.

"And take it well, too, I hope? As I say, it is only for your own good that I mention it."

"I am sure it is, sir. My husband, however, has nothing to do with it. I believe he did not even know with whom I was dancing."

He moved his faintly sweaty palm to a fresh spot on her back. "Ah, you see? While the cat's away! Perhaps we had better locate him, then, eh?" And, with no hesitation he walked her off the floor. "A bit of refreshment first, I think, to throw those watching ninnies off the scent?"

He spoke quietly into the ear of a gentleman-in-waiting who hurried off toward the gaming room. "And have you attended the new Lawrence exhibition yet? No? I shall escort you myself. A marvelous face taker. The only one to have captured my own real essence. Perhaps you could sit for him? I am sure the nation would be grateful to have preserved that pretty complexion of yours. So fresh, you country lasses.

"So, Rackham, here you are!"

— 15 —

It is not to be supposed that even the shabbier streets of Pargate were anything to compare to the dreadful slums and stews of Manchester and London, but there were, in truth, many who knew what it was to often go hungry to bed. Some of these were, of course, "the deserving poor," and others were of that kind to whom the cosy comfort of a tot of gin in tea made up for all the trials of a long and weary day. The guests of Mrs. Peacenark's lodging house fell loosely into a general area encompassing both degrees. Some of them lived by selling trinkets, souvenirs, or refreshment to the holidaymakers who came to the seaside, some even rented boats, but when a day was grey and business was slow or when the season was over, stomachs were often empty since they were people who lived from day to day rather than providently putting something aside. Even Mrs. Peacenark was in nature of the same sort, so that the board at which her lodgers sat down was one day groaning with succulence and a week later might be nearly barren.

"It was the way I were raised," she admitted to Phyliss. "Easy come, easy go. In my pa's house it were either feast or famine, as they say. Old habits die hard, miss. You know that is true."

It seemed to Miss Powley that the truth of it had never been so aptly illustrated than among the folk she found through the Society. Since she had been there, she had watched them come to the meeting hall, listen to Mr.

Wearthy speak, even sometimes leave a penny or two in the plate, but their lives outside seemed unaltered, their habits unchanged. She began to wonder, living among them as she did and listening to their conversation at table, if they did not view Mr. Wearthy's rotundly expressed oratory as a mere variety of entertainment, one cheap enough to afford. To make things worse, she sometimes found creeping into her mind a small—oh, infinitesimal—seed of doubt concerning the avowed purpose of the Society itself. She was beginning to find herself at home among these people, to like and even admire their fortitude—and to wonder if their morality was greatly different from anyone else's.

A worrying thing was that Mr. Wearthy, himself, had mysteriously dropped from sight. Since she had come to know him better, Phyliss had found her betrothed to be a man of moods, sometimes almost genial, but often withdrawn. This had seemed particularly to be the case since her own visit to Aunt Dedham's solicitor and her conversation about it with Mr. Wearthy. Sometimes, it seemed to her, she perceived a darkness of spirit in him which had not been apparent to her when she had first given her word to marry him.

The Society chambers had been closed and dark for three days now, the Tuesday meeting unled save by Phyliss alone. She had visited in the daytime of course, to continue her battle against dirt and dust, but with no sign of the Society's president.

"P'raps if we was to look into his rooms, miss?" Jeddy suggested, but Phyliss resisted such a notion. "But, miss, supposing something has happened to him? Supposing he's lying up there ill with a fever, or injured?

"Or," and he shivered deliciously, "dead, even."

Such a possibility had never presented itself to her, and the notion shook Phyliss profoundly. Despite her assumption of housecleaning chores, she had never been in Mr. Wearthy's private rooms above the meeting hall. It had never even occurred to her, since, having grown up in a large family, she knew the value of privacy. Now, worriedly, she was forced to consider such a move.

"Do you really think so?" She considered further. "Perhaps you had better fetch Mr. Peacenark as well. If it happens that something *is* wrong . . ."

He understood. "Yes, miss," he agreed and set out at once.

Left alone, Phyliss began to consider when she had last seen the Society's president. There had been a meeting on Sunday afternoon, then he had attended that inspiring chapel service with her on Sunday evening, which had featured Reverend Mr. Thomas and his silver trumpet—stirring to the imagination and thrilling to the soul. Then on Monday morning he had sent a message to remind her of some small task he had particularly wanted accomplished. And then no more. The brief note carried by Jeddy was the last she knew of him.

Peacenark arrived with a slightly scornful expression upon his face. Being a married man, he was used to the vagaries of the female emotions, and he was quite sure the trip was made for nothing, but if it would allay Miss Powley's fears it was worth it. Funny, how fond he and the missus had grown of her in such a short time.

The three climbed the narrow stairs and knocked at the door on the right hand of the landing. There was no answer.

"Try the other door?" Jeddy suggested practically.

Again no reply. Meaning merely to rattle it a little, Phyliss tried to shake the door itself, but, to her discomfiture it came open under her hand. She blinked in surprise. The room was empty.

No, really empty. Not a stick of furniture, not a scrap of curtain, not even a stray moral tract lying on the floor. Empty.

Quickly, they threw open the door to the other chamber. It was not quite so desolate. The bed frame was there, though stripped of mattress, the exposed cords looking unquestionably stark, and a chest was there in the corner. Jeddy opened it quickly.

"Empty, miss."

The two rooms were swept, the glass at their windows as clear as if a housewife had cleaned them only yesterday, but they were empty. Not a single trace of Mr. John Wearthy remained.

The solicitor for Lady Dedham leaned back in his chair and regarded Phyliss blankly. "So you say he is gone, Miss Powley? Gone? Simply vanished like a puff of smoke, without saying a word to anyone?"

"Not to anyone I am aware of," she answered. "Not to me at any rate." She returned his look levelly, her own filled with curiosity. "Did he call upon you as he said he would?"

The lawyer leant forward again, placing his elbows on his desktop, his chin on his hands. "Yes," he said at length and somewhat reluctantly, "Mr. John Wearthy—or, at least, someone who called himself by that name—did present himself here at my chambers. We had quite an interesting chat, actually."

"Please do not be mysterious, sir. If your conversation had bearing upon the gentleman's disappearance, please come directly to the point." Her voice was so like that of Lady Dedham that he realised his usual self-gratifying circumlocutions had best be set aside.

"Do you remember, Miss Powley, that when we last spoke, I mentioned certain aspects of his past?"

"Yes. I also remember that you seemed reluctant to enlarge upon them."

He nodded. She was *very* like her aunt, wasn't she? "Because *you* seemed rather reluctant to hear them, miss, and because my investigations had been made at the instigation of my client, Lady Dedham. I had every reason to believe that she herself would disclose them to you."

Only if it was to her advantage, Phyliss thought. During the time she had spent with Aunt Dedham she had learnt very well how that ancient mind worked. So far, it had not pleased her aunt to share these revelations. "And has she now authorised you to break the news to me?"

"No," he said, "but I see no reason to withhold the ensuing conversation with the gentleman.

"He came here, you know, very reluctantly, and for good reason. That is why he had hoped all could be settled through you, you see. When I presented him with the facts my investigators had marshalled, he took it, I must say, very well, very coolly. I explained the provisions of the dowry in much the same way, according to him, that you explained them to him. In short, saying that the money was yours, to be administered by you and that what you did with it was your own affair."

He wrinkled his brow slightly and assumed a judgemental air. "Could it be, do you think, that he felt you would not act in a properly feminine way in this matter?" It was said in such a way that Phyliss found it immensely annoying.

But had that been the case? Had Mr. Wearthy suspected that she was so strong-willed that she could not be easily managed? Perhaps he had thought there were other, easier, perhaps lonelier women out there who would give more freely of their portion. "He had other names than that by which I knew him, you say?" she asked.

"Several," said the lawyer, watching her carefully and with intense interest. Which way would she jump next, this disconcerting young woman?

Phyliss Powley did not at once gratify his curiosity, but merely sat in the chair reserved for clients and stared into nowhere, deeply engaged in consideration of her situation. Her face was so vacant of any expression that she seemed unmotivated by even the slightest awareness. This continued for a substantial time, the solicitor waiting patiently. At length she appeared to once more reanimate herself and turned to him with a certain sense of resolution.

"Very well," she said, "this is what I want you to do."

=16=

"Yes, Clarissa, displeased with you. *Vastly* displeased!"

The Viscountess Rackham regarded her husband with no great surprise, for, all the way home from Almack's last evening, he had been silent and uncommunicative, not to say surly. Having reached the house on Berkeley Square, he had retired to his chamber with only the most abbreviated courtesy.

"I hardly know why, sir."

She suspected, of course, that when the Prince Regent had sent her off to dance with his aide in such a summary fashion, he had something of particular import to impart to her husband, but, even now, she hardly could say why *she* should be considered the source of her husband's irritation. She used old tactics which had served her well among the beaux of her country upbringing, a widening of the eyes and an expression of exaggerated wonderment, which she fancied underscored both her innocence in the matter and a very slight amusement at his lack of the understanding of it.

But Rackham's tightened jaw could not have expressed more exasperation. "I believed you had more sense than to make a spectacle of yourself."

Her eyes widened in truth at that, and her teacup rattled against its saucer. "Whatever can you mean? I did nothing but dance, and that with only three persons: one of whom you surrendered me to, one who is your old schoolfriend, and one who is the titular monarch of this land!" Her pretty lips began to tremble, but she steadied them resolutely. "If you wish to delegate all my dancing partners, your lordship, I think you would do better not to go striding off to the tables at the first opportunity." She turned away and looked at the window so that he should not see the extent of her consternation. "I wish I had never agreed to accompany you last night. I am sure I could have found more amusing companions, not to say more thoughtful."

Then, as will sometimes happen on such occasions, they both began to speak at once.

"If you think that I . . ."

"If I had known . . ."

Each backed off, proudly leaving the field to the other. After a moment of confused silence, it was her ladyship who resumed the conversation, which spawned an unworthy triumph in the breast of her spouse.

"If you think, Rackham, that it was at all amusing to be carried off the floor by the Prince Regent, of all people, exactly as if I were a schoolgirl about to be sent to her room in disgrace, you may think again! All of those people staring and whispering behind their hands, I was never so mortified!"

"I must say that to that extent he had good reason."

"How perfectly wretched of . . ."

"The man I most distrust . . ."

There, they had done it again. This time, though, Clarissa stopped in midbreath. "Who?"

"What? You never listen, do you?"

"The man you most distrust is who?"

"Why, Francis Carlton, of course!" He spoke truculently. "You knew that."

"I did not. How in the world could I be expected to know it?"

His eyes blazed and rushed on, allowing his words to come out unchecked by any censor of politeness. "How could you not know it? The world knows it and, I expect, profits by it. Your gossips tell you everything else including the succulent details of my past private life, how could they have left Carlton out?"

Clarissa very deliberately buttered a bit of muffin. She knew that her lips had grown quite white, for she had felt the tingling as the blood left them. There was a little knot beginning to form in the center of her stomach, but whether it was a knot of anger or of anguish she could not yet tell. She very well knew that it restricted breathing and made her vastly uncomfortable, but sometimes, if she sat very still and tried to make her mind a blank, the feeling would go away. The effort took her husband quite by surprise in midsentence.

"To find oneself being censured by a man for whom you have little but contempt is . . . I say, Clair, are you all right? You've gone quite pale." When she did not answer, he quickly rose from his chair and came round the table. "Clarissa? Clair?"

She raised a face to him that was so full of suffering that his annoyance with her dissolved at once. He half-knelt beside her chair and tried to take her hands in his own, but she instinctively snatched them away.

"Clarissa, forgive me. I know that I am often an unfeeling brute, but it wasn't at all a salutary experience for me, you know."

The tears welled up out of her eyes at that. "Th-that is what I was trying to te-tell you. I didn't know *what* to do. I didn't like to be rude in front of everyone . . . and you had gone off . . . and then there was the Prince Regent, and everyone was staring . . . and heaven knows what they were thinking."

Her husband's face was much closer now.

"There, my girl, I do apologise for . . ." In a morning of half-sentences he hesitated once again, racking his brain to hit the exact thing that had set her off, but he wasn't quite sure what it really had been. ". . . For everything," he ended lamely. With one finger he reached up to intercept and brush away a tear, leant closer into the vision of her deep eyes swimming up at him and . . .

The door of the breakfast room fairly banged open, and Dolly flew into the room. "Clair, what have you done? You must tell me every bit. Why did you not ask me to attend so that I could have seen it myself? They say the Regent has gone quite mad for you and is going to dismiss Lady Conyngham, which pleases everyone, of course, and that Greville Landon and Sir Francis are to fight a duel!" It was said all in a breath and, for Rackham, difficult to disentangle, but Clarissa had been used to it all through her girlhood. She dashed away her tears with the back of her hand.

"A duel? Dolly, don't be foolish."

Rackham rose uncomfortably from his kneeling position. "I do assure you that if anything so stupid as a duel is to be fought over my wife, I shall be the one to do the calling out."

For the first time, Dolly realised that she had sprung into the midst of a domestic scene, though of what sort she was not sure. It was rather daunting, actually. Until now Clarissa had merely been her older sister, companion, friend, confidante, even though residing at a different address. She sensed that this morning, though, something had changed: Clair had, by some obscure alchemy, become less sister and more wife. She had moved in spirit from the house of St. Minver to that of Rackham.

For a few moments it was daunting, but Dolly had never been one to relish confusion, and she filed this interesting knowledge away in her head until it could be examined more closely. Now, instead, she said brightly, "From what I have seen of London, you could not have chosen a better way to make your mark." She was pleased, of course, because whatever glory accrued to her sister was also, in some degree, reflected upon herself. And to be in fashion in fashionable London was a wonderful thing.

Rather grumpily, Rackham excused himself and left the room.

"Oh, Clair, have I said something I oughtn't?"

Clarissa sniffed and used her napkin to dry her eyes under the guise of brushing away crumbs, a matter of turning the head and making a quick pass. The falsity of the manoeuver did not fool her sister, but Dolly allowed Clair her denial without confrontation.

"Of course you have not. What a thing to suggest. Rackham has a busy day ahead of him, you know. I shouldn't think he could be expected to dawdle with two women who have nothing very important to say."

Dolly could not let *this* pass. "Oh, but I have! That is why I hurried over here this morning."

"Whatever do you mean?"

"I have suddenly become terribly in the mode today. It is not yet twelve o'clock and people have left cards and sent their footmen bringing invitations with names I scarcely recognise. Why, even Mrs. Landon, Sr., has laid her card on me."

Clarissa could not help laughing incredulously. "Mrs. Landon?"

"Yes, and you know that means that *you* have truly arrived."

"She gave you her card, and you interpret that as meaning *I* have become fashionable?"

Her young sister gave her a look of disgust. "Oh, Clair, stop being so silly! I hope I have the sense to know that it is not I who have turned their heads. If that were so, I should have been dining out with Papa every night since we came up to town, or going to a ball, or a levee, or a rout. No, no, they cannot patronise the popular young Lady Rackham, of course, for you have already climbed too high, and so they do the next best thing in their eyes and ingratiate themselves with your younger sister. I have become a sort of thermometer of your success. Does it not please you?"

Clarissa shook her head. "No, it does not. I think it quite a silly and shallow way of conducting things. Besides, Rackham is quite furious. It has all come about for the wrong reasons, you see."

Dolly's face grew long. "No, I confess, I don't see. This is quite a wonderful advantage for Papa and me, Clair. His reputation is quite back if I am to climb to fashion on your petticoats. I hope you will not be so mincing as to deny me that advantage." Despite her words she was not so much annoyed at her sister as hurt and rather dismayed. It certainly was unlike Clarissa to be so petty-minded. Clarissa understood it at once.

"Oh, my dearest, what a thing to think of me. I believe the heady air of London has addled all of us." Then she disclosed to her sister the true state of affairs on the evening past.

"So you see it was all sham," she concluded. "The Prince Regent did not so much want to honour me, I believe, as to snub Sir Francis for some reason, and, despite his affability, he did not so much want to show favour to Rackham, I believe, as to censure him for not keeping me in check."

"As if he could," giggled Dolly, her temper quite restored. "But what do you suppose Sir Francis has done that sets everyone so agog?"

"They whisper that he is not particular the way he wins at cards, for one thing."

"Oh, Clair, I think you are the only one to believe that. Even Papa doesn't, and he has lost to him! No, I expect it is just because he is rich and handsome. I expect most people feel cheated by him in that way. It must seem unfair. He has great courtesy, that I'll grant him."

Clarissa looked at her sister shrewdly. "What experience do you have of *that*, pray?" Dolly was not at all flustered.

"Why, you know as well as I. We met him at home that once, coming out of Miss Plumb's and then again in the Green Park."

But Clair knew her too well. "And?"

"I declare, sister, you talk as if I were being held to account for my every moment and action."

It was Clarissa's turn to giggle a little. "Well, if you are to climb up on my petticoats, I think I should know that your shoes are not dirty?"

Her mood of melancholy had passed as it often did when the two were together. "We sound as if we were scarcely out of pinafores rather than envied ladies of the mode. Now, what is this about Carlton?"

Dolly's eyes took on a merry twinkle. "I happened to see him just now at Georgiana Landon's where he was taking chocolate. Even you must admit that he is devilish handsome."

Then her eyes rounded and she asked, "Clair, you don't suppose the Prince Regent is down on him because of you know. . . ."

"I don't know. What do you mean?"

"I mean because of Her Royal Highness the Crown Princess."

It was a thought which had never occurred to Clarissa, and it went far to explain Prinney's behaviour, but what about Rackham, why was he so against Sir Francis? It must be quite serious, she supposed. She did not pretend to know her husband well, but she judged that no mere schoolboy rivalry would set him so much in enmity.

═ 17 ═

GEORGIANA LANDON HAD been quite pleased to entertain
Sir Francis Carlton for a variety of reasons, one being that
it said to her that she had, perhaps, begun to arrive.
Despite all the favour and alliances called in by Greville's
mother, the trio had not exactly been inundated by invitations to the many private balls and parties with which the
evenings were whiled away in town. There were, of
course, the many public subscriptions to be had, for which
her father's money paid many times over, and there were
the larger private affairs for which the guest list was neither
limited nor select, but all one needed to do for these was
make oneself available. Things in town were quite different
than she had imagined they would be. The older Mrs.
Landon had intimated (nay, all but promised) that she had
entree everywhere, could even sponsor Georgiana at court,
but so far it appeared that, even with the Austruck fortune
behind her, her resources were limited.

"Perhaps we should give a ball, my dear," her mother-in-
law suggested more than once and each time as if it had
never been presented for consideration before. "You remember what a success your engagement ball in the country was. Everyone came who had been invited."

And added with something like a titter, "Even some who
were not, though I am sure no one begrudged them their
importunity so long as they behaved themselves."

But, thought Georgiana, *how humiliating it would be to send out invitations, only to have them declined, or worse, that all the wrong people accepted.* She already understood enough of life here to know that her social death knell would be sounded if too many of the wrong people were seen in her drawing room with no leavening of the ton. She might as well pack up and return to Manchester, where she was already known and loved.

But now Sir Francis had paid his respects.

Not that she had received him alone, of course; the other Mrs. Landon had been there as well, though behaving in quite a surprising fashion, posturing and striking attitudes and all but simpering across the table at their guest. It really was astonishing how she had, in such a short time, won Georgiana's—well, not contempt, exactly, but certainly a sort of wary forbearance. Greville had been of no help in the matter, since he catered to his "dear Mama's" every whim, sometimes exhibiting no idea that it was at his bride's expense. (In a nonmonetary way, of course. Georgiana never thought of pounds and shillings. She had been raised to think them vulgar.) And "Mama Landon," as she insisted that her daughter-in-law address her, just as if she could replace Georgiana's own departed mother, would insist on repaying the compliment by using Greville as a prod to convert her son's wife to her own way of viewing things.

"Greville likes it done this way, you know, my dear." "I hope you will not think me interfering, but Greville believes . . ." For all the world as if Greville had not been taught to believe in that mode by Mama Landon herself.

This morning had been almost amusing. The servant had brought a *carte de visite* bearing Sir Francis's name as the two women were sharing morning chocolate, and, though Georgiana was almost certain that no such thing was intended, Mrs. Landon insisted that the servant be told to invite Carlton to join them.

"It will be a great thing to say he has done so, you know, Georgie," she explained, "and if he does not, no harm is done. Nothing in this world is gained by reticence, my pet."

But when, surprisingly, the gentleman had accepted the invitation, the woman's manner had changed quite out of hand. From a firm and rather formidable example of the previous generation, she had transformed into a fluttering belle before her daughter-in-law's startled gaze. Georgiana could not at once say whether the rolled eyes and flirtatious manner were merely what had been fashionable twenty years past or if Greville's mother had conceived a sudden passion for their handsome visitor.

To his credit, Carlton had not denigrated the woman's fancies by so much as a look or a gesture, although he did treat her with a grave and elaborate courtesy which was quite apart from the light, almost bantering tone with which he addressed the younger woman. Nothing he said was out of the ordinary or of much consequence, yet he infused it with a spirit which made it seem both witty and faintly provocative. Georgiana could quite well see why her mother-in-law found the man compelling. The age of forty is not so great, after all, and it might be that the spirit of romance dies hard.

By the time Dolly St. Minver arrived, Georgiana was beginning to wonder, in fact, if romance had not been born for the first time in her own breast this very morning. Sir Francis's eyes seemed to be constantly seeking her own across the rims of the chocolate cups as he parried the none-too-subtle approaches of Mama Landon. Quite, quite unlike Greville was these days.

When Dolly came, though, the atmosphere changed completely, as, of course, it only could. Dolly was that sort of person who carried freshness and charm wherever she went; a measure of real goodness emanated from her. Even Mama Landon appeared genuinely happy to see someone from her part of the country and put herself out to seem genial, surprising Dolly no end.

"My dear, dear gel, what a refreshing sight you are after

so many town misses with their airs and Athanasian ways. Do you know Sir Francis? But, la, I recollect I saw you together in Burriton, did I not? So pleasant, I always think, when old friends come together in a strange land."

Georgiana saw with a tiny pang how Miss St. Minver blushed and slightly tripped over her words as she acknowledged the reintroduction. "And thank you, madam, for the card you left on me this morning. Papa has asked me to bear you his good thoughts and asks if you and Georgiana—Greville, too, of course—will come to supper one afternoon. Perhaps, he thinks, we might make up a party for the theatre."

"Oh, what a lovely idea," answered the elder Mrs. Landon. "Georgie tells me that your sister has had a great success and has even been taken up by the Prince Regent. Had you heard that, Sir Francis? I understand he made quite a stir at Almack's."

Carlton nodded gravely, some of his geniality seeming to have faded at the mention of Almack's. "I happened to be quite nearby at the time, you see, and, yes, the Prince did show her singular favour.

"I had the honour of dancing myself with your lovely sister last night," he said to Dolly. Perfectly ordinary words, but Dolly blushed, and Georgiana felt her own cheeks grow flushed, for he had danced with herself as well and now seemed to have thought nothing of it.

"Will you have chocolate, Miss St. Minver?" she asked evenly.

"Oh, I will!" came the answer gaily. "Chocolate must be one of the great delights of the world, don't you think?"

"Quite," said Georgiana, then chided herself for silliness. Here she was, a rich young woman with a handsome husband, languishing because an eligible young man of the ton was paying attention to someone other than herself. Her father, she reflected, would quite properly call her a prig for such mangerish behaviour, but, oh, if Greville only looked at her in the way that Sir Francis was looking at Miss St. Minver as she sipped her chocolate.

But when she glanced across at her mother-in-law, she saw she was not alone in her envy. Lettice had a pinched look about her nostrils, a sign to Georgiana that she was practicing great self-control.

"And then I must be on my way," Dolly was now saying. "I wish to hear from Clarissa's own lips of her great triumph. The Prince Regent, just think! I am sure she is set up all out of herself. I know I should be! It is so very odd, you know, the way they do things here in London; Clair has a success, and invitations have been arriving all morning for my Papa and me, which I am sure they never did before. I suppose I shall grow accustomed to it."

Sir Francis had arisen not merely from politeness. "Perhaps you will allow me to accompany you to Berkeley Square, Miss St. Minver, so that I may pay my respects to your sister?"

But both Mrs. Landons were astonished to hear Dolly set the gentleman firmly in his place. "Oh, I do beg your pardon, sir, but my sister does not follow the fashion of receiving in the mornings. Except family, of course. I shall be glad to carry in your card, if you like. She cannot object to that."

A lesser man might have been chagrined, but Francis Carlton merely smiled in an amused way. "How very right she is," he agreed without a look at his hostesses. "I daresay it is a barbarous custom, but what would you? The world does what it does."

When their visitors had gone, the two women sat morosely over the remains of the repast. Somehow the edge had been quite taken off the morning, though neither was confidante enough to the other to mention it. When their son and husband returned from his morning canter in Hyde Park, he found them still sitting there in their pretty morning costumes.

"Here you are," he said with annoying jollity, "my two nonpareils."

"Greville," said his mother, "you are going to give a ball."

He looked quite thunderstruck. "A ball, old dear? Quite impossible. This is our first season. Besides which it would be too damnably expensive to give another so soon, eh, Georgie?"

But his wife seemed hardly to have heard him.

The sign along the front of the meeting hall had been abbreviated, and the undertrodden discreetly banished from its consideration, *for*, thought Phyliss, *if I were undertrodden, I shouldn't like to be told of it over and over*. It was possible that she was being too nice in the matter, for neither Jeddy nor Mr. Peacenark seemed quite to take her point in the matter. Nevertheless, it now merely mentioned the Pargate Society and left the specifics to others. Left them to others in many ways, actually, for though Phyliss sensed that the neighbourhood needed and deserved a focal point, she was not sure what the thrust of the made-over society should be. On that score she need not have worried. Barely had she moved her possessions into the two rooms vacated by Mr. Wearthy, than she was honoured by a distinguished visitor.

Jeddy informed her of it, half-tumbling up the stairs in his haste to bring the news. "Issa lady, miss—a lady!" as if he had never beheld an example of one before. And perhaps he had not. Phyliss, of course, guessed at once who it might be and hurried downstairs to meet her aunt.

Lady Dedham had dressed with uncommon restraint, yet she had such an air about her that Phyliss understood at once why Jeddy had been so impressed. She realised with a faint shock that to have been apart from her ladyship for even this little time had given her, after her long period of service, an entirely new vision of the old woman. From one step away, as it were, a bit removed, the woman she saw now was nothing at all like the benevolent despot who had designed her every move.

"So," said Lady Dedham matter-of-factly, "this is the business you were going to sink your money into. What do you intend to do now that the man in question is gone?"

"Perhaps you will think I am foolish when I tell you."

"You have already so astonished me that nothing more can truly give me pause. Say on."

"I expect, then, that I shall still 'sink my money' into it, as you said," answered Phyliss without the faintest hint of defiance. "You were very kind, Aunt, to set up the conditions of my portion as you did."

This elicited a wintery smile. "I believe I imagined that since you had fairly earned it by attending me so well, it should be yours in fact, not only in name. I have managed my own life for a very long time, as you well know, and I think I have not made a bad job of it. If you had proved to be a ninny, of course, I should have done quite otherwise, but *if* you had been a ninny, I shouldn't have had you around me for long in the first place. You are an independent thinker, Phyliss, and I admire that. The fact that you have not just faded away since that *person* deserted you goes far to confirm my opinion.

"Now suppose you tell me all about this place and what you intend to do, since I gather from your sign that the 'undertrodden' have been banished."

Phyliss had spent many sleepless nights untangling just this knotty problem, and she had still not decided quite how to go about it, but she found herself explaining to Lady Dedham what she had learned about the people here and their needs. She told her of Mrs. Peacenark, for example, who cooked marvelously, but had no idea how to manage money in such a way that would ensure her larder being filled from one fortnight to the next. She mentioned sharp-tongued old Mrs. Appleton who had managed her husband into his grave and now had no outlet for a tremendous natural energy, which had become so bottled up that she had the reputation of being the most unpleasant woman on the street. There were the Baldwin children, offspring of a Gypsy mother who slaved for pennies at a greengrocer's so that she could fill their bellies on fruit and vegetables with the spoiled bits cut away. And Phyliss talked about Jeddy, typical in exampling the quarter, bright but unlearnt. Capable, but unskilled.

"So you mean to run an almshouse, do you?"

"Not at all, Aunt! Quite the contrary. I want to give them a place where they can learn to manage their own lives. Mrs. Peacenark cannot keep a sixpence from one se'nnight to the next, but I expect Mrs. Appleton has the first ha'penny she ever earned."

"A fine woman, I daresay," interjected Lady Dedham. "A woman of my own sort."

"But do you follow me? They are a natural couple. And Jeddy . . . Jeddy can teach the Baldwin boys as I teach Jeddy."

Lady Dedham shook her head. "You have no protection whatsoever. You will lose your respectability overnight. A woman alone in this part of the town? You know what they will say of you."

"Yes, I have thought of that," said Phyliss, "but I can see no way around it."

"And you are undeterred?"

"Oh, quite," Phyliss answered in surprise. "I thought you knew me better than that."

"No man will want to marry you, you know. I have never understood that trait in you. It wasn't natural for you to turn Rackham away."

"I daresay it was not, Aunt, but Alexander and I would never have suited. I believe you know that."

"Perhaps I do. He has met his match now," the old lady all but cackled. "Lady Clarissa will lead him a merry dance once she gets the bit in her teeth. I quite look forward to the spectacle of it."

She looked around her, poking here and there with her umbrella. An arm fell off one of the old church pews they used for partial seating. It was very odd, Phyliss found, but they had a greater attendance now than when Mr. Wearthy had been there to inspire them.

"Rackety old place," said her ladyship. "It will take a bit of repair."

"I believe they might be intimidated by anything grander just at first," Phyliss observed. "Changes can be made a little at a time."

Lady Dedham looked at her approvingly. "You are a bright girl, I never doubted that, but you've bitten off a good deal, you know."

"Yes, I know. But I must put my hand to the work that is nearest, I think."

"I daresay. What is the name of this again?"

Phyliss said it patiently. "The Pargate Society, Aunt."

"Yes, I remember. No more undertrodden."

"No, Aunt, no more."

— 18 —

"WILL YOU HAVE another slice of saffron cake, Alexander?"

"No, Mama, I have already had two slices," protested Rackham. "You will turn me into a tug-mutton. But I will take another spot of tea."

His mother poured and handed it back to him carefully, then gave him an enquiring look. "This is an early call for you, surely?"

He answered rather pensively. "Yes, I know that it is, Mother. Am I too early? Am I being an inconvenience?"

"Not at all," she assured him. "I am glad of the chance to see you. It has been a trial reclaiming this house after so many years away from it, though I must say that the Mercers treated it well."

"You have happy associations here then?"

"Oh, very. This was my home all during my childhood, you know. It was only after my father moved on to the higher realms that it was let. I expect I shall be quite comfortable again very soon."

For, of course, the dowager Lady Rackham had not returned to Rackham House when she came up to town this year, though Clarissa would have welcomed her. She had chosen, instead, to live in this smaller Queen Anne dwelling in Friarsgate Street. Her own papa had been a respectable enough solicitor, but hardly of the upper class, and the house reflected this. It was for her, however, a welcome retreat to the scenes of her childhood in an establishment modest enough in size to be manageable with a small staff of devoted servants.

She became aware that her son's attention had wandered. "Something is wrong, is it, my boy? Not with Clarissa, I hope?"

"With Clair? Oh, no, not at all." He paused, though, as if to reconsider that. "Well, perhaps to do with her slightly, but not in the way that I believe you to mean."

"Wrong, nonetheless?"

Rackham shrugged. "Not *wrong*, exactly, but beginning to be a touch difficult."

She waited patiently, guessing that he would complete his thought when it had sorted itself out in his mind. "It is Carlton, you see," he said at last.

"Oh, dear," she sighed and made a face. "I was afraid it might be."

His attention was quite regained. "Why, have you heard something?"

"No, no. It was only a surmise. It seems to me that you have become increasingly concerned with him over the last few months. I hope you do not intend anything rash?"

Her son withdrew from her stiffly. "I shall not if he does not, but I shall not allow much from him."

"I have never understood your bitterness."

He moved to the window and looked out, then turned back to her to say, "If you will forgive me, Mother, I have never understood *your* calm acceptance of the matter."

She spread her hands. "What would you have had me do? It was out of my hands from the very beginning. My marriage to your father was, like yours, based less on love than on convenience. For a lawyer's daughter to marry up into the peerage was considered a great coup. I must say I have never regretted it."

"But you loved him at last?"

"At last, yes, but not at first. And not at the time to which you have reference." She lifted her own teacup to her lips and said, not unkindly, "Life is at once more simple and much more complicated than you allow, my dear."

Rackham did not answer that, for it would have led to an argument which he did not wish to pursue. "Can you never forgive him?" He knew she did not mean Francis Carlton. "He has been dead for so many years. Will you carry this anger to the grave?"

He shrugged meaninglessly. "I would honestly be glad to be done with it, but this is not possible so long as Carlton continues to provoke me. One day he will go too far, and I will, as you say, do something rash which I will regret forever. But I fear it cannot be helped."

His mother's face became closed. "It could be helped if you chose to help it. You simply enjoy your little feud too much to let it go."

He collected his hat and stick, his face sad but determined. "You have never understood, Mama. I do not do you the dishonour of intimating that it is because you do not choose to understand.

"You may be right. Perhaps every man has one mote in his eye, and Carlton is mine, but he once tried to steal my inheritance away, and for that I expect I shall never forgive him."

"In his way he has succeeded," said Lady Rackham," for he has stolen away your regard for your father, and that is an inheritance far greater than mere money."

They regarded each other gravely for a long moment. Then, "You really loved him, didn't you?" he asked.

"Yes," she answered, "at last I did."

"I wish, Mother, that I *could* feel the way you do about it, but I am sure that Carlton will be a bone in my throat forever. It is unfortunate that we have both come up to town at the same time."

"That is not the way life has to be lived, Rackham."

He knew, of course, that she was right, and, when he left her, he strolled aimlessly through the streets of Westminster wondering just what fate would permit him to do.

"But Papa, you can't mean it? Go back to Burriton now when everything is just beginning for me?" In the last month she had felt her star's ascent.

Sir Wilton did not look at Dolly but at the autumn garden outside the window, seeing but not registering the brilliant splashes of colouration there. "It cannot be helped. The fact is, dear, I have been a deuced fool. I thought I could win back everything I had lost, but I made the same mistake most gamblers do, I did not know when to stop. I was ahead when the cards began to turn against me, and I thought I could outwait them."

"You have lost everything?"

"As near enough as matters."

Dolly considered. "What about Rackham, will he not back you?"

Her father was horrified. "Rackham back me? At the table, do you mean?" When she nodded, he said, "I hope I shall never hear you make such a suggestion again. What sort of man do you suppose your father is?"

"He would be glad to do it. I know he would." But the look her father gave her stilled the words in her throat.

"You have never shamed me, Dolly. I pray you will not do it now."

"I don't mean to, Papa. It is only that . . ." But she could see from the look in his eyes that his suffering went deep, and it was more than she could do to mention her own dwindling hopes in the face of his despair.

"I know that I have failed you, daughter. Clarissa, at least, had the sense to make a clever marriage despite me. What we shall do about you remains to be seen." He sighed. "They say that God will provide, but I expect it was not meant for old fools who squander their children's future."

He was sitting, now, disconsolately slumped in a chair, the flickering emotions across his face melting any residual drop of resentment in Dolly's heart. Quickly she crossed the room and knelt beside him. Putting her head on his knee, she whispered what words of encouragement she could summon. "It will all come right, Papa. You'll see," she murmured. But all the time she was telling herself that Clarissa was the one who must find a way to sort this out. Much as she hated to leave her father alone, she persuaded him that he would see it all quite differently when he had taken a nap.

"You have not slept since you left the tables, have you? For shame. How can you expect to think clearly when you have had no rest?" And when his eyes had closed, she threw convention to the winds and fled around the square alone to lay the problem at her sister's feet.

"It is obvious that you must come to Rackham House," said Clarissa when she was informed of the turn of events. "Rackham likes Papa enormously. It is a better address for you as well. It seems obvious that we must launch you at once and properly. It could never be done from those small chambers you and Papa have been inhabiting."

"But Papa will be dead set against it, Clair. He has become very proud. When I mentioned Rackham to him before, he grew quite agitated."

"That is because he feels his honour is impugned, but if you are to be dragged back to the country, Doll, all will have gone for naught. The vogue you are enjoying will fade and the ton will have forgotten you by the time you can return. I know there is a way out of this pickle. It only requires some thought."

When Clair saw her father later in the week, though, she had still found no tactful way to broach the subject. Finally, knowing that he would abandon town without it, she made up her mind to say what was in her heart, come sun or snow.

"Really, Papa, we owe it to Dolly to have an equal chance with the other belles of the season. Her opportunity will be lost if we wait another year." She pressed his arm. "I know it is difficult to swallow pride, but Rackham does not see it in that light, and, heaven knows, I certainly don't. If my husband were backing you at the tables it would be one thing, but there is nothing odd or demeaning about sharing his house, surely?"

"No," said her father, "I suppose there isn't, and, as you say, there is Doll's future to think of." He seemed quietly resigned.

Quite frankly, Clarissa was astonished she had won him over so easily. Perhaps, if she had thought, she might not so easily have trusted his capitulation. But, believing she had achieved a victory, she soon began her preparations for Dolly's launching on a grand scale.

The dowager Lady Rackham was the first advisor she enlisted. The conversation proved to be a most interesting one.

=== 19 ===

Brunswick Terrace embodied in its original plan a portion of the Prince Regent's dream of recreating London to rival Napoleon's Paris, but, as often happens, the reality fell short of the vision. It had been designed as a part of a great double circus with a great national monument in its centre; it ended as merely a truncated crescent of rather stodgy proportions, with chambers of those single but affluent gentlemen of the town who chose convenience over aesthetics. Visitors were often surprised that Sir Francis Carlton, notoriously a man of fashionable taste, had chosen to live there, but the building had certain advantages to one of Carlton's temperament, not the least being a certain freedom of behaviour not possible in apartments subject to closer scrutiny.

Oriana Pennant had been, over the years, a visitor of such frequence and longevity that she might almost have been considered a resident, were not the chambers let to gentlemen only. Her relationship with Francis Carlton dated back to the earliest days of his sojourn in town when he had been unknown and she had only just begun her career as a Cyprian. There were no defined bonds between them, but consistent use of each other had thrown up certain ties which each found it convenient to maintain. Therefore, though she was mildly surprised when the freshest and youngest darling of society came calling in the middle of an afternoon, it was not the visit but the chaperonage of a maid which was astonishing. Ardent young women rarely desire a witness. The manservant who admitted them seemed unperturbed, but it seemed to Oriana, hiding in the next room, that Carlton, too, was somewhat surprised, though he covered it well, striding across the drawing room with his hands spread forward in welcome.

"My dear Miss St. Minver!" It did not escape him that she was accompanied. "To what stroke of heavenly fortune do I owe this most welcome visit?"

Dolly smiled at him timidly. It had seemed such a good idea when it first occurred to her, and even in the carriage she had been sure that once she was in the Brunswick and facing Sir Francis, her nervousness would go away, but she found that such was not the case. It was proclaimed, she was sure, by the very way she sat at the edge of her chair, her eyes flitting anxiously about the room. It was the first time she had ever been in a man's rooms. She hardly knew what she had expected. It was a relief to know that Prosser waited upon a chair in the anteroom, easily within call.

"Can I offer you refreshment, Miss St. Minver?" he suggested. "Tea, perhaps, or a cordial?"

"Nothing, thank you." Now that she was here, Dolly hardly knew what to say to him or how to broach the purpose of her visit. "I imagine that my call will seem unusual to you, Sir Francis, even unprecedented, but, you must understand, I have no one else to whom I can turn."

Not even your beloved brother-in-law? her host thought to himself, but he did not ask it aloud. "Anything which brings such a delightful surprise is worthy of attention." He moved a chair a little nearer his guest and Oriana, watching, smothered a little laugh. Carlton was running true to form. It would be against his nature not to attempt the seduction of any young woman who came to him in this way. Dolly, on the settee, seemed unaware of his advance. "How can I help you?" he asked.

She turned wide innocent eyes toward him, her fingers nervously twisting a handkerchief in her lap. "It is about my father, you see."

"Your father?" he asked almost stupidly. "Oh, yes?" He raised a half-mocking eyebrow, then quickly suppressed it. Archness was uncalled for in this situation. An expression of sympathy, on the other hand, provided the excuse to join her on the settee, and to take her hands in his own.

"Please, Miss St. Minver, feel that I am your friend, your devoted admirer, to whom you can say anything at all. Is your father in trouble of shade? I will certainly do anything I can to be of assistance."

"Yes . . . no . . ." Dolly extracted a hand from his and lifted a finger to her lips. "I hardly know how to say this, but my father seems to have lost a great deal of money since we came up to London, you see, and I thought that . . ."

Kindly, he caught her hand again, clasping the two between his own and patting them sympathetically. "I know, I believe. The thought came to you that perhaps I could advise you. Perhaps I am, in your mind, even the author of his misfortune?"

She looked away.

Gently, he touched her jaw with one finger, turning her face back toward him. He looked earnestly into her eyes, his handsome head perilously near her own. "What a villain you must think me," he murmered.

Dolly drew back. "Oh, no! Did you think I meant that?" She blushed. "It is only that Papa has never been such a gamester before."

"He is not accustomed to losing?"

The girl dropped her eyes. "He has always seemed to play well enough except when it is with you. There seems to be some . . . I don't know . . . some spell you cast over him."

Carlton knew very well how to use his voice artfully, and he dropped it an octave, now, as he said reproachfully, "I hope you do not suggest that I am guilty of jinking him?"

With a man this would have been taken as provocation enough for drastic measures, Dolly realised, and she was truly taken aback. "Oh, but you are a gentleman! I expect that it is that every man has his master at something, doesn't he? It is just that . . ."

"It is just that I am your father's master at cards?"

"I expect so, amn't I right?"

Carlton pretended to consider this, though he well knew the answer. "It cannot be denied that your father never seems to win when he plays against me, but what is it that you suggest I do? I cannot give insult by refusing to play him." He now allowed his eyebrows to ascend quizzically. "Or is it in your mind that I allow him to win?"

It was obvious from the look on her face that this was just what she had hoped he might suggest as a solution. "Since you have taken away his pride as well as his income," she said, "I had hoped that you could be so persuaded. Not to return his money, you understand, but that you would know some way it could be done."

Sir Francis looked straightforwardly into her face and lifted her fingertips to his lips. "I will think what can be done," he promised. "Will you trust me?" He turned her hand palm upward and she felt his lips on the soft skin of her wrist. "You are a very lovely creature, Miss Dolly. I believe that we could make each other very happy, don't you?"

It was as if all the breath had left her body. "Oh, yes," she whispered. From the door of the anteroom sounded a discreet clearing of the throat.

"Excuse me, miss. Will we be going now?"

Oriana, behind the door, bent double to contain her laughter. It was quite like a play, and the duenna fully prepared to do her job, wasn't she? Such an elusion might even be a novelty in Carlton's experience; the handsome devil was more accustomed to women throwing themselves at his head than anything else. This must seem both a prohibition and a grave temptation at the same time. She had never seen the rake at such a disadvantage before. It was deliciously amusing. Sir Francis was such a notorious wrecker of hearts that it was only fair that his intentions be foiled from time to time. She felt she had been privileged to have watched it happen.

Prosser's well-timed intrusion had at once jerked Dolly back to an appreciation of her delicate situation. But though aware of the maid's sharp eyes on her, she allowed Francis Carlton to contain her own small hands in his. "You see, sir," she said frankly, "I must put my trust in you. I am sure I do not know what I am asking, but I believe I shall find my faith is justified."

Even Oriana was open mouthed at this, but Carlton seemed to take it in easy stride, exactly as if young maidens threw themselves blindly upon his mercy on every day of the week. The lovely Cyprian bit her lip enviously, for she thought she could discern something quite new in her lover's eyes. Something she had never seen there for herself.

"That was shocking bad behaviour, miss," declared Prosser as they reached the street. "I am sure I don't know what you would have allowed if I had not taken my stand."

"I daresay I am lucky to have had you nearby," Dolly admitted, "but, oh, Prossy, he has such deep eyes."

"We are lucky, then," snapped the maid, "for you might have fallen in!"

When she emerged from hiding, Oriana was still convulsed with laughter. "Oh, Francis, you are as good as a play! I had no idea, sir, that you were in training for knight errantry! Am I to suppose you will return to that poor child's father all the money you presumably swindled?"

Carlton was not amused, but he covered it nearly well enough to fool her. "Was there never a charitable impulse in your whole life, Orry?" he asked ruefully.

"No, not one!" she hooted," and I never saw one in you!"

"I had not thought I treated you too badly over the years?"

She came forward and kissed him on the cheek. "Oh, my dear, generous to be sure, charitable, no. I suppose it was that façade of innocence which prompted it? Believe me, within a week she would be as venal as the rest of us. In any case, I had thought it was her sister whom you had your eye upon? Has that changed?"

Carlton gave her a curiously guarded look. "That is true, of course, but only because the man to whom she is married is a particular antidote of mine."

Oriana poured herself a glass of wine. "Oh, of course, the famous Carlton/Rackham feud. You must explain to me sometime what is the basis for all that."

She and Carlton, though they had often quarrelled, had always been jolly companions, lively and amusing; but now there issued from him no warmth at all. It was as if, in fact, she had presumed upon an area of his life which was in no way a concern of hers. It more than surprised her, but she took it well. Their association was long-standing and mutually advantageous. Oriana knew well enough that it would return to an even keel. When she and Carlton had first met, she had been a relatively uncorrupted maidservant, and he a penniless wastrel. Now he had become an immensely rich and enormously elegant rake, but, in spirit, she knew he was much the same. Men like Francis Carlton do not alter. It was a quality for which she respected him. It was a quality she respected in herself.

"Do you remember," she asked, "how we pulled that swindle on my lady and you took me out of service and set me up? That was a pretty set of rooms I had then. My word, I thought you was the bravest and the best."

"Do you not now?" he asked, his good humour returning.

"Well, you've become a fine gentleman to look at you, haven't you? I daresay it does me no good to remember the old days."

"So you think I have changed."

She gave him a saucy wink, but it carried an element of seriousness as well. "You're rich now, m'lad, ain't you? And I expect you intend to be richer. *And* you ain't got much conscience the way you get it.

139

"I'll say this, money is real to you. You know how to use it and make it grow."

"It comes of too many lean years," he answered, "and too uncertain a future for too long a time."

"But what is it you have against Lord Rackham? You seem determined to do him all the harm you can."

His face had become quite still, his eyes curiously flat. Dolly, who had so rhapsodised about their depth, would not have recognised them. "They say that blood is thicker than water, do they not? I wonder if it is true even when the blood is spilled?"

Oriana could not help but shiver. "Why are you talking of bloodshed? What is Rackham's blood to you?"

"Only this," he said, his voice devoid of expression, "Lord Alexander Rackham is my brother."

Oriana Pennant turned quite pale. "Oh, my dear, surely you are joking?"

Francis Carlton looked at her curiously. "My word, old gel, you don't tell me that it would have made a difference?"

— 20 —

LADY DEDHAM WAS the sort of woman who examines corners and looks into closets, and not metaphorically alone. Since she had begun to take an interest in the Pargate Society, she had spent a substantial amount of time in such poking about. "What d'you mean you keep no books?" she demanded of Phyliss one morning. "How have you any notion where your money goes?"

"I find I have little need to know," was the reply. "The bills come in and the money goes out."

"And what shall you do when the demand exceeds the supply, eh? When the money is all gone, what will you do then?" She gave a scornful shake of the head. "Do you have more money coming in?"

"Only from you, madam."

"No, no, not from me! It comes from your own portion, not from mine, and, though you depend upon it, you seem to have taken no steps toward increasing it. Haven't even thought of it, I'll wager. Head in the clouds." She sat in one of the uncompromising pews they now used for seating, but shifted uncomfortably. "I don't approve of extravagance, but if you will allow me to make a donation . . ."

"That is not necessary, Aunt," Phyliss hastened to assure her, but her ladyship held up a silencing hand.

"Allow me to finish, *if* you please?" Chastened, Phyliss subsided.

"I was only going to say that though I disapprove of

extravagance, I will provide you with cushions for these seats. Old bones poke sharply through the flesh."

But she considered as she sat so that her niece could almost see the wheels turning and the clockwork ticking. "What of this Appleton woman?" she asked presently. "You remember, the one you said still cherished her first ha-'penny."

"I hope you do not think of bringing her into the Society?"

"It would not be my decision but yours, but why not?"

Phyliss struggled to speak fairly. "Oh, dear. She *is* a gem, I am sure, but a sharp-cut one."

The old woman gave her a sour smile. "And having served your time out with me, you are not certain you wish another of the same, eh?"

"I admire her immensely, you know," Phyliss protested, "but she is not easy."

The ferrule of Lady Dedham's parasol struck the floor in a sharp rap. "Easy? You don't want someone who is easy! You want someone who is clever at numbers. If you lack the ability yourself, you must find someone who has it. Fetch her to me, if you please. Let us see what she has to say."

Jeddy was duly dispatched, but returned alone. He was sent a second time with a written message couched in Phyliss's most tactful language. When he came back this second time a small, sharp-eyed woman accompanied him, though somewhat resentfully.

"Here now, what is it I am wanted for? D'you think I have nothing better to do with my life than to run about like a dog to a whistle?"

Her ladyship did not allow this. "Pray, what else *do* you have to do with your life rather than oblige a civil invitation by a neighbour?" she asked severely. "I should think, indeed, that you would be glad of an opportunity for a bit of change from staring at the wall."

The other woman's eyes snapped back at her through

old-fashioned octagonal spectacles. "And who, pray, may you be when you are at home?" It was said with a brusqueness to match but not surpass Lady Dedham's own. It seemed to Phyliss that they were an odd but beautifully matched pair. Her ladyship did not so much as blink when Mrs. Appleton announced matter-of-factly, "I may as well tell you, I am not fond of strangers telling me my business."

Phyliss's aunt seemed almost to relish this defiance. Thrusting her boney hand forward she replied, "Dedham, the name is. You appear to be quite a sensible creature, and my niece, here, says you may know the numbers. Is that true?"

The woman, surprisingly, did not resent this method of interrogation. "Yes, Mrs. Dedham, if you mean the adding and the subtracting and so on? My husband was a clerk in a counting house before he passed over. You should have seen him gobble up a column. Like lightning he was at finding a sum.

"But what makes you think it is proper to ask such a thing of a complete stranger?"

"Expediency," answered her ladyship. "Expediency, my dear woman, and you may find yourself glad of it."

"Sir Francis Carlton is my husband's brother?" asked Clarissa incredulously.

She had received Rackham's permission to give a ball, and it was quite naturally to his mother that the young Lady Rackham turned for advice. Rackham House had, after all, been the elder Lady Rackham's fiefdom for a great many years. Clarissa had, perhaps, been just the tiniest bit afraid of a polite but definite rebuff, but she need not have worried, for her mother-in-law seemed genuinely delighted to provide any assistance needed. In the course of an hour's conversation, she dredged up memories of Rackham House balls past, spring cotillions, summer dances, and the great affairs at Christmastide when the house was overflowing with merriment and holly. She had remembered where the accoutrements for each were packed away, and even suggested which servants might be relied on for what responsibilities.

"I would be a little careful with Mason, my dear," she suggested, and Clarissa related her first meeting with the footman of that name.

"I cannot think why Rackham still keeps him," said the dowager. "I expect it is as an inheritance from his father, though, I must say, he was more than once close to discharge without a character in my time for sheer impertinence. I believe in my husband's other establishment Mason was spoiled by being allowed to do what he would. Perhaps you will find a place for him in which he may not insult your guests."

"Your husband's *other* establishment, madam?" Perhaps it was less than polite to ask, but the question had sprung involuntarily to Clarissa's lips. Her companion did not sigh, nor did she seem discomfited or even shy to speak of what must once been a difficulty.

"It has been a very long time, you see," she explained. "Our marriage had been planned for us by our families, not ourselves. My heart had already been given to a man who could not accept it."

"He was already married?" asked Clair sympathetically.

"Not only that, but had children. It was a question of honourable behaviour and, of course, there was no help for it."

"And Lord Dedham, was he in love with someone else as well?"

"Irrevocably," the dowager said with perfect calmness. "I never minded it, because I knew all too well what it was like." Then she shook her head. "Or I did not mind at first."

"The lady my husband loved was the young wife of an old baronet, much revered in the countryside, who had run through two wives before her, neither with issue. If the line and the title, of which he was immensely proud, were to continue, there must be a son." She paused delicately. "But the baronet was old. Can you imagine the solution which was found?"

Yes, Clarissa could imagine it, for it was not an unheard of solution. Her imagination went even further. "You are saying that the heir of the baronet was . . . ?"

"Yes," said her mother-in-law. "The whole thing might have been managed easily enough except for two quite unlooked-for happenings." She fell silent and for the first time seemed affected by her story. "The old man died just before the child was born, believing in his continuance implicitly, but the luckless widow found to her shock that, despite the scale on which they had lived, he had left her almost penniless."

"How distressing," said Clarissa, "but the other thing?"

"The other was that I, too, was carrying Lord Rackham's child."

Young Lady Rackham's eyes popped wide, her pretty lips parting in surprise. "Madam," she suggested, "are you sure you wish to tell me this?"

The dowager nodded. "Do not disappoint me, Clarissa, by feigning an overniceness. We are alone here and it is essential that you know these things." Thus corrected, the young matron subsided into a nervous silence.

"My poor husband," the other woman went on, "was caught between two opposing loyalties . . . two households, as well. A beloved woman and a newborn son whom he could not acknowledge in one of them, and the offspring of an unloved wife about to be born in the other. The one thing the old man had not been able to do was to raise money by selling land, for the Carlton estate was entailed. There was no money to run it nor to bring it to the condition of profitability, but it could not, by law, be broken up or passed on to someone other than the infant heir himself.

"Poor man," she mused, "it must have been a dreadful time for Lord Rackham, though I felt little enough sympathy for him at the time. Our estate all but ran itself, and would have continued to do so had the revenue not been plundered to be put into the Carlton boy's land. The Holy Book says that where your treasure is, there will your heart be also, but, in this case, the reverse seemed true as well. Rackham House was closed (I had scarcely lived there six months), and I was sent to live in the country—'for your health's sake,' he said it was, but I knew that it was so he might be as near as possible his mistress and her son."

She rang for a servant, and the tea things were taken away. She did not go on exactly at once, and Clarissa did not press her, but, at length, the older lady said, "I was quite alone, you know, when the child—when Alexander—was born."

"And you resented it?" asked Clarissa. "Even though you did not love your husband?"

"I am afraid I did. You will understand it better when your time for it comes. It is rather frightening, you know, to be left merely in the hands of those who are hired to care for you. I fear I taught Alexander my own resentment over the years as well. Eventually I came to terms with the situation, bad as it was, but my neglected boy never did."

"He knew?"

"At length he knew. At length it could hardly be hidden. The whole county seemed to know of it. You could scarcely see Lord Rackham and the Carlton boy together without at once guessing their relationship."

"And that is why Alexander has such an antidote for Francis Carlton?" Clarissa observed. "What a burden it must be to carry."

For the first time she felt she had begun to understand something of the man to whom she was married.

= 21 =

CLARISSA HAD COME to look forward to the midmorning
repast she shared with her husband, not the least of the
reasons being that it was the only time of day she might be
fairly sure of seeing him. Following their early-established
pattern, the two continued to have their own particular
friends and move in their own circles, his being that of the
sporting world and hers the society of the ton which so
fascinated her. There were times when their paths unex-
pectedly crossed and they found themselves at the same
function, a ball or a theatre performance. At such moments
they always greeted each other with great good will and an
enthusiasm which led spectators to agree that theirs was the
perfect sort of marriage for the present age.

Otherwise Clarissa found she still knew very little of his
activities except in the broadest terms. When she thought
of the tale his mother had confided to her those several days
since, it seemed quite incredible in many ways. She supposed she could understand to a certain extent, if not
entirely sympathise with a father's desire to care for both
his sons, even that he might rather favour the elder, less
advantaged offspring. She wondered, though, if such childhood partiality truly accounted for the intensity of her
husband's dislike and distrust of his brother. Those days
had been, after all, a good many years ago.

The footman brought in the morning post, carefully
divided between them and presented on silver salvers.
Rackham idly looked through his as he finished his tea.

"When is it, exactly, that your father and sister are coming to us?"

Clarissa was surprised at the question. "In a day or two, I think. My father agrees that it would be best for Dolly, you see, but drags his heels about it." She raised her eyebrows at her husband. "I say, Alexander, you don't mind that they are coming here? I believe my father may not be altogether sure of his welcome."

Startled, he looked up from his letters. "Good Lord, are you serious? I shall be most happy to have your family living here. It is not only as a gesture to you, but because, quite honestly, I like them and wish them well."

He gestured with the missive in his hand. "I find I must go down to the country for a few days, but when I come back I shall take the matter firmly in hand. Neither Dolly nor Sir Wilton must ever believe that they can be anything less than welcome in Rackham House. I hope you will take it upon yourself to assure them of that until I can communicate it to them myself."

It pleased Clarissa that he was making such a point of it. It was a sign to her that the opinion of society was correct in its assessment of her marriage and that Rackham's attitude was no mere gesture but true generosity.

"How long will you be away?" she asked. "I am thinking of the opera party on Thursday."

"Ah, I had forgotten. Well, I shall do my best to return by then. Was it something you particularly wanted to hear?"

"Yes, it is a new production of *Amletto di Denmark*, but I expect I shall not lack for company if you do not return."

Rackham's eyes seemed to hold a faint twinkle as he said, "No, you rarely seem to do so." But when she again looked at him, he was innocently perusing his papers again.

She returned to her own letters and found that the next one lying on the top of the pile bore a badly formed handwriting which was more than familiar. She also discovered that her hands were trembling slightly when she broke the seal. The message inside was terse and scribbled in great haste.

"Imperative that I talk with you. Shall call midafternoon." The signature was merely an initial, but she recognised it well enough. She remembered the long winter afternoon when she, Estrella, and Greville had taken their lessons together in the library of Landon House. Estrella had developed a beautiful hand, but Greville, she recalled, had preferred to spend his time upon perfecting an elaborate rendition of his initials alone. Though it was simpler, now, she knew that the outsize G at the bottom of the page stood for the name of her former beau, and when she saw it she made an involuntary little sound.

Rackham looked up. "Something, my dear?"

His wife's face was carefully composed as she answered, "No, nothing really, nothing at all."

When Lord Rackham had finished his breakfast and left the room, Lady Rackham rang for the butler. "You may have them cleared, Hobbs."

He nodded sedately. "Yes, milady."

"And Hobbs . . ." she paused, then continued choosing her words with precision. "If Mr. Landon should, by any chance, pay a call alone this afternoon, please say that I am not at home. Is that clear?"

"Yes, madam."

"But if he is accompanied by either his wife or the elder Mrs. Landon, however, I shall, of course, be happy to see them. You understand that."

Hobbs, who had seen and understood a great many things in his day, merely answered, "Certainly, milady, I understand perfectly."

The opera had been particularly enervating, and Sir Wilton St. Minver had made his escape in the second interval. *Amletto di Denmark* was well enough in Shakespeare and chock full of devilish good quotations which a chap could use in company, but, somehow, the notion of the melancholy prince being impersonated by a stout female, however deep and rich her voice, was one which offended the St. Minver sensibilities. Much better to place oneself in the surroundings where one was most relaxed, even if there was precious little coin in one's pocket with which to play.

He looked about him happily. The click of the dice boxes and the soft shuffle of cards were as soothing as anything he could ever remember. How he had waited so long to come to it was more than he could imagine as he watched in delighted fascination as the cards fell out across the table in a jumble of black and red. Sir Wilton had only the merest trifle riding upon the play, but there were fortunes fluctuating all around him. Over there a hard-faced woman, liberally decked out with flashing gems, played a card with almost fanatic concentration; beyond her he could see the familiar visage of the Hanovers upon one of the several younger brothers of the Prince Regent; at the table to his left a famous courtesan lost in a few moments the small fortune it had taken an admirer years to amass.

Ashley's Club had not the cachet of Almack's nor the exclusivity of White's but the staff was unobtrusive, and the dealers were not the arrogant tyrants sometimes found in such places. St. Minver had put himself on a tight leash so far as money was concerned and had little enough to wager these days, but he found it difficult to resist the intoxication of the atmosphere. Were he not a gentleman, he sometimes fancied, it would be amusing to be the proprietor of such a club for the rejuvenating powers of the magnetic energy alone.

"Ah, the temerarious trio," a voice behind him murmured mockingly. He had no need to turn to identify the overcultured tones of Lord Tendril, for he had come across him often enough in society. That the foppish slug was slandering his betters, St. Minver had no doubt; only curiosity made him look to see who was being singled out for Tendril's brand of honeyed venom.

"I would give a dozen guineas to know what transpires between those three," said another voice, but a more cautious companion voiced a warning.

"Take care what you say. It might be perfectly innocent." But the gossip was having none of it.

"There is no such thing, my friend, as perfection. Neither in innocence nor in any other quality known to man. No, no, mark me, when a dull man has a pretty wife and makes a close acquaintance of a rake, there is such recklessness there that it quite takes my breath away. You will see the scandal break in a month or two, but remember that you saw it here in its incipient form." He giggled. "Don't you just love being in on the beginnings of things?"

When Sir Wilton looked about, the only trio his eyes fell upon were young Greville Landon, his pretty wife, and, just a step or two away, his *bête noir* of the tables, Sir Francis Carlton. Georgiana seemed to have acquired a distinctive bloom, though whether it was marriage or London, he could not tell. Greville, on the other hand, looked wan and paid little attention to either his wife or his surroundings, though his eyes kept flitting nervously from place to place as if he were searching for a particular something or someone. Hoping to find that they were not the objects of Sir Tendril's darts, Sir Wilton turned his head covertly from side to side, searching for another trio, but none was to be seen. Pairs, even, were in short supply, for most of the players stood alone in order to preserve their concentration.

Truth to tell, he remembered snippets of malice told him about the Landons, but he had paid little heed. Society, so easily bored with the usual, must needs always have something to whisper about, and if one marriage was not under attack, it must be another. But now Landon, looking up, caught his former neighbour's eye and came forward with extended hand, setting into turmoil the nest of vipers at Sir Wilton's back.

"My very dear sir, I trust you were not going to avoid an

old friend? I trow it must have been an age since we met, for only yesterday Mama was complaining that she never sees you or your family since Clarissa has been taken up. She is very fond of your girls, you know."

"Is she, by Jove?" asked Sir Wilton in mild surprise, surmising to himself that it must have been a recent affection.

"Are the girls here with you tonight?" Greville pursued. "I have been hoping to see Clarissa for some time."

"Lady Rackman and I attended the opera this evening, but I do not know if she intends to join me here," Sir Wilton replied, hoping by the use of his daughter's title to dampen the lad's familarity. Clair was a married woman now, after all, and it was hardly proper that she should so be spoken of in public even by an old friend.

"What do you hear from Burriton?" Greville went on, then asked still another question without attending to the answer of the first. "And how is dear Dolly finding the whirl of London?"

But it was all mere chatter, for Greville's greedy eyes seemed to be in a constant flit from table to table and game to game; looking everywhere save to his wife and her admirer, the very place where his gaze ought to rest. Really, the man must have no sense of the gossip which was endowing him with such a fine set of horns. Sir Wilton had always been a little surprised at Clarissa for languishing after such a stick, but there you have it, he had never pretended to understand women. Lucky thing that Rackham had come along when he did. Sir Wilton quite liked his son-in-law, and it had nothing to do with his liberality, either.

"Greville, my dear . . ." began a matronly woman, bustling up, then seeing St. Minver. "Sir Wilton, what a pleasant surprise!" He might not have recognised his old neighbour if he had seen her alone, for she was quite transformed from the dowd he had known in the country. Her evening dress of apricot crape was in the latest style, ornamented with a multitude of little Vandykes depending from the corsage, each velvet triangle being finished off with an ornament of black chenille. Upon her head was a toque of matching crape tipped rakishly forward. What he could see of her Titus-cut hair was equally surprising, for it seemed since he had last seen it to have acquired a distinctly saffron hue. The fact was that she looked almost smart, but failing, for the town fashion used in less excess might have suited her admirably.

"Greville," she returned to her address of her son, "do you not think you should be with your wife?"

Greville looked merely uninterested. "The purpose of a gambling club, Mama, is to gamble. I daresay Georgiana can amuse herself."

"She may find someone else to amuse her," said his mother caustically. She took Sir Wilton chummily by the arm and drew him away. "Such a long time since we have talked, sir. Shall we not join my daughter-in law?"

Ah, you need an extra pair of eyes upon her, do you? thought Sir Wilton, but when they turned about the room, the young Mrs. Landon and her escort were nowhere to be seen.

"I daresay we shall find them in the supper room," said Lettice Landon. "She is such a lovely creature that all the men want to take her in upon their arm."

But the supper room was nearly empty. It held only two couples and neither was the one Mrs. Landon sought. "The terrace?" suggested Sir Wilton.

"Oh," said the country woman in nervous displeasure, "I can hardly think that they would . . . by all means, let us take the air." There was something vastly determined in her look, far outweighing the mere discovery of a straying daughter-in-law.

But the terrace was empty as well. Amused though he was by the set of her jaw beneath the hussar's toque, Sir Wilton thought he might reasonably return to his game. "If you will allow me, madam?"

Reluctantly, she allowed him to lead her back inside the gaming club where, at a table in the corner Greville Landon sat at cards, pleasant and relaxed, with a delighted smile upon his face. Across the table sat Sir Francis, eyes narrowed and lips pressed into a thin line of annoyance, tapping his fingers on the table in frustration. His appearance, thought Sir Wilton, was quite unlike that of the urbane opponent of the past who won or lost with equal aplomb. Young Mrs. Landon, sipping a glass of wine, smiled at them over the crystal rim and delicately licked a stray drop from the corner of her mouth. Her mother-in-law approached her at once.

"Where have you been, you naughty girl?" she asked with a false laugh. "I have been searching all over for you."

Georgiana's expression did not change in the slightest, but something flickered in her eyes. "Why, Mama Landon, what do you mean? I have been nowhere at all. Greville and Francis have been playing at cards and I have been watching them."

What a cool piece she is, thought Sir Wilton. *Who would have imagined it?*

"And, do you know, Mama, Greville has been winning!" Georgiana leant forward and said in a conspiratorial whisper which was, nevertheless, meant to carry to the card-players, "I think Carlton is the tiniest bit put out, don't you?"

"Four sevens!" Greville cried triumphantly. "I have you again, Carlton."

"So you have, old fellow," said Sir Francis. "You are getting too good for me." Since St. Minver believed Greville Landon to be an indifferent player at best, and since he knew to his own cost how sharp a player Carlton was, he found this exchange more than surprising. But then, looking over at Georgiana Landon, her cheeks flush slightly with wine, he was less astonished than he had been.

22

HER LADYSHIP HAD come up to town for two reasons, perhaps three. The first was to lend her inestimable experience and advice on the preparations for the Rackham ball and another was to view a marvel whose fame had been reported even in the depths of the countryside. So it was that one afternoon Lady Dedham, Lady Rackham, Dolly St. Minver, and Lady Dedham's new companion made an excursion to the ware rooms of Messrs. Flight and Robson to seé and hear the fabulous Apollonicon, the grand musical instrument, which, by the careful application of scientific principles, performed the overtures to *Le Nozze di Figaro* and *Der Freischutz* every day between one and four. The price being only one shilling, Lady Dedham, who paid for her companion as well as herself, felt it was quite worth the expenditure. They had no such inventions in her part of the world and certainly not in Pargate.

Dolly and Clarissa found themselves quite delighted with the new companion, a bright, birdlike woman named Mrs. Appleton who displayed great respect for her employer, but was unlikely to accept ill-treatment from her. She took no liberties and held her tongue, but it was obvious to all that she was a woman of great conviction and well-formulated opinions who would be bluntly frank when the occasion required it. The two sisters agreed that Lady Dedham could not have found a more perfect foil.

"I have come up as well, you know, to find sponsors for dear Phyliss's society, which is doing such fine work amongst the lower classes." A small warning sniff from Mrs. Appleton punctuated her ladyship's statement. "I try to help a bit, you see, but what is needed is broader recognition. Dear Rackham has been our real inspiration, of course. I imagine you are immensely proud of him."

"Rackham has been your inspiration? In what way?" asked Dolly, giving her sister a look of surprise.

"Oh, the Pargate Society would have been nothing without his support. He has contributed both time and money in large amounts.

"Has he mentioned nothing of his visits to Pargate?" Lady Dedham asked Clarissa.

Lady Rackham, when she thought of it, realised that her husband seemed to be travelling down to the country with greater frequency these days, but her attention had not really been engaged by the matter. So he had been in Pargate? And interesting himself in a charitable society of all things?

"And how does Miss Powley (I forget her married name) do with her new husband?" she asked her relative. "I had rather thought you prophesied nothing good in the marriage, but now you seem very enthusiastic. Has he changed so much with matrimony?"

"La, my dear, did you not know? I was quite right about him. The man ran off and left her!"

"What, with her dowry? You must have found that a blow. I am sure I am very sorry to hear of it."

By the time Lady Dedham had rehearsed the entire story—in complete detail and with many asides—the Apollonicon had twice run through its repertoire. "And not a word has been heard of him until this day!" she concluded.

"That isn't true," said Mrs. Appleton. "I knew Mr. Wearthy very well—by sight, at any rate—and I have seen him more than once since he ran off. Pargate is not so large a place as all that."

"Do you mean to say you have seen that man and never told me?"

Mrs. Appleton seemed genuinely surprised. "Your lady-ship never asked. And, besides, it was before I came into your employ."

"Surely you knew my interest?"

"I know my place, madam. You explained it very care-fully when I began to work for you." Lady Dedham favoured her companion with a hard stare "I am sure I don't know why your ladyship is taking on so. If you were to turn your eyes to the street, madam, you might, I believe, see him this moment. I noticed him hanging about when we came in."

"See him? Where should I see him?"

"Outside the shop, madam, talking to the gentleman in the blue coat." The other three women followed the indica-tion of her slight nod, then, almost in unison, gasped.

"Do you recognise the gentleman in the blue coat, Ap-pleton?" Lady Dedham demanded. "Have you never seen him before?"

The companion moved closer to the glass for a better view, then nodded. "Oh, yes, madam, I believe I do know him. Is it not Lord Rackham?"

"And you are certain that it is *he?*"

"Oh, I have seen Lord Rackham many a time with Miss Powley in Pargate. I know him well." *With Phyliss?* thought Clarissa.

Lady Dedham cast her eyes to heaven. "*I* know Lord Dedham, you dullard! He is my nevvy. The other man, you are sure it is John Wearthy?"

Mrs. Appleton bridled at her employer's tone, pulling her head back quickly, chin drawn in and with an expres-sion of hurt pride. "I don't know that you have any call to speak to me like that, your ladyship. The other man . . ." But, even as she was speaking, they saw Rackham place something in the palm of the other and the two parted company. The man Mrs. Appleton had called John Wearthy went off down the street with a look of only marginal satisfaction, and Lord Rackham entered the ware rooms where he paused for a moment on the threshold, accustoming himself to the dimness.

"Rackham! Rackham!" cried his aunt, waving her handkerchief above her head. Rackham crossed the floor.

"Here you are, my dear," he said, bending to kiss his wife civilly on the cheek. He hardly had time to greet the others before his aunt assailed him.

"How can you have anything to do with that dreadful man, Alexander? You astonish me!"

It was Rackham who appeared to be astonished. "Perhaps you will be so good as to identify the gentleman we are discussing in such virulent fashion. What man, dear aunt?"

"Why, the wretch to whom you were just speaking, John Wearthy."

"I think you are mistaken, madam," he answered her. "Or, rather, you are mistaken in believing I am acquainted with the man who accosted me. I don't remember ever having seen him before. I believe he is one of those professional imposters who masquerade as out-of-work curates or chaplains of some ship which has gone down in the Indian Sea with all hands lost but himself. I did not really listen to his story, though I am sure he told it well. They all do. At any rate, I gave him no time to trot it out, but bought his silence with a few shillings to spare my conscience in case it should be true."

"But what did he say to you as he went away?"

Rackham smiled at her imperative interrogation. "I believe it was a hope that God should bless me, to be sure, I hope He will, for I do not understand the import of this close examination."

She reconciled herself quickly. "You must forgive me, it was only my agitation. Mrs. Appleton, you see—you do remember Mrs. Appleton from Pargate?—was certain that the man was that scoundrel who once aspired to Phyliss's hand and dowry."

"Ah, so that is the crux of it? Well, I cannot say for I

never saw Miss Powley's intended save that once at the Landon ball, and I am not sure I should know him if I came across him at the foot of my bed."

The Apollonicon trembled and wheezed, then again struck up its rendition of the *Figaro* overture, which made Rackham put his fingers to his temples. "May I invite you all to some teashop where we can escape this infernal din?"

"Why, dear boy, I made sure you would enjoy it. I believed that you prided yourself on your musicality?"

Lord Rackham made a face, then raised his voice against the volume of the music, but, as luck would have it, just at the moment he was answering, the mechanical musician wheezed again and ground to a stop, leaving his lordship in the position of shouting, "It is precisely because I *am* musical that I wish to go away!" which might be construed as a direct insult to Messrs. Flight and Robson concerning the worth of their attraction. Heads turned, and one or two rude people guffawed rather loudly until they saw that the gaffe had been committed by a person of quality. Then they turned their heads away, pretending the remark had not been heard.

"Come, let us escape before I am arrested," Rackham laughed, but as they moved toward the exit, the door opened again, and Crown Princess Caroline entered on the arm of a dashingly befrogged and moustachioed hussar.

"Ach, Lord Rackham! Vot a choy!" She extended a plump, none-too-clean hand to be kissed. "Und who are dese preddy t'ings? I t'ink dey must be respectable, eh, wid de old duennas to attend dem?"

Lady Dedham grew quite rigid with annoyance, recognising the princess, and constrained from reply, but Mrs. Appleton laboured under no such restraint. She had no idea who this fat stranger was, and she said exactly what she would have said in Pargate, "Mind your manners, you old trout!" Her eyes travelled scornfully over the youthfully beflounced frock, heavily feathered hat, and plunging décolletage. Encouraged by the silence which fell over the ware room, she went further. "Anyone got up like a guy at a circus has no place speaking so of their betters!"

The mouth of the Crown Princess formed an almost perfect 0, and the blood drained from her face even as the hussar beside her flamed with indecision. Dolly's eyes went wide, and Clarissa found it imperative to bite her lips and cast her eyes to the ground. When she had brought herself under control, she stepped forward and curtsied gracefully.

"May I remind Your Royal Highness that we have met before? It was in the Green Park some weeks ago."

"My wife, Lady Rackham, Your Royal Highness," said Alexander, lending her support. The complexion of the princess returned somewhat to normal, and she blinked at Clarissa as if emerging from a spell.

"Ah, yes. Wid Carlton, *nein?*" She inclined her head graciously, turned to Dolly, "And your sister, eh?"

"Yes, madam." Dolly sank into a curtsey as well. The princess passed straight over Lady Dedham, her eyes coming back to rest on Mrs. Appleton, now fully aware of her *faux pas*.

"If I vere queen," Caroline said grimly, "you vas in big trouble, ain't?"

Mrs. Appleton stood stiffly, battered but unbowed, ready to accept her punishment, but unwilling to compromise her principles.

Suddenly, astonishingly, the Crown Princess began to laugh, her plump body fairly jiggling with the vigour of her amusement. "Old trout! Dot is a good vun!" Reaching out, she slapped Appleton none-too-lightly upon one cheek. "Old trout is a good vife for de Prince of Vales, eh?"

Her audience responded uneasily to her sally, but as it passed about, repeated to those who had not heard, the laughter grew and became genuine until the shop rocked with it. Caroline turned to Lady Dedham. "I haf de big mouth. I don't mean nodding. You vill excuse me?"

Her ladyship was quite taken aback, for once bereft of a

sharp retort. "Why . . . ah . . ." She sank into as deep a bob as her age would allow. "Of course, Your Royal Highness. I am your humble servant."

Nein, nein, up!" and she extended her hand to help the old woman rise. "Hoopla! You are perhaps lucky to haf such a defender as dot one, I t'ink."

Mrs. Appleton blushed a deep crimson and, wonder of wonders, made her own leg to Her Royal Highness.

"Rackham," said the princess. "I onderstand you are giffing a ball, is dot right?"

He assented. "It is to introduce Miss St. Minver to society, madam. May I hope that Your Royal Highness will attend?"

Caroline broke into a wide-mouthed smile. "May I be sure of not meeting my husband dere?"

"With all respect, madam, no, I cannot say that."

She seemed understanding of the delicate problem. "Vell, ve shall see." She said to Clarissa, "I do not vish to make trouble, eh?"

"Your Royal Highness is very thoughtful."

"Now, den!" the princess cried out. "Let us hear dis moosick! I luff *Der Freischutz.*" The mechanical musician pumped a moment, puffed, and enthusiastically began the overture.

Beaming, Princess Caroline began a triumphal progress through the crowd, bowing and nodding and smiling. In a way it was quite a pleasant thing to see; in another way, considering the bed she had made for herself, it was more than a little pathetic. Hers was not an easy life, that of a wife who was no wife at all, a Crown Princess who would, if her husband had his say, never ascend the throne.

= 23 =

IN THE NEXT few days Clarissa turned over in her mind what she might ask Rackham concerning his involvement with Miss Powley's venture in Pargate. Remembering his matrimonial linking with Phyliss in the past, she suspected that his participation was in some degree connected to it. She wondered how far she might go in questioning him, if at all.

There was, as well, the question of John Wearthy, for Clair very well remembered him from the evening of the Landons' ball and had no doubt that this was the same man to whom her husband had been speaking outside the ware rooms. What was the connection between them? It seemed to her quite certain that it must be something to do with the Pargate Society and, consequently, with Phyliss Powley. She could not say anything to her husband about it for a few days, in any case, since he was attending a racing meet at Epsom, but she made up her mind that when he returned she would advance the subject. She must not be too concerned, though, if he declined to discuss it under the terms of their marriage bargain.

She looked about her with pleasure. The boudoir was the earliest room in Rackham House upon which she had put her stamp, and she was considerably pleased with the result. It had been panelled in blue silk, the window hangings of a lighter blue and painted in the Spitalfields fashion. The furnishing she had chosen with an eye to lightness and comfort. There was a tall cheval glass and a smaller looking glass, books by the bed and, on the wall, a painting of her mother which had lately hung in the parlour at Burriton. Little by little, the remainder of the house would surrender to her personal taste, one room at a time. It was a renovation much encouraged by her mother-in-law, who prescribed it as a way of making the old mansion her own.

"You will find, my dear," she had advised, "that not only will it please you to set things in your own key, but that the servants will better respond to you as a mistress and not cling so much to what they consider the tradition of the house. That sort of thing is always plaguey. Good service is one thing, but finicking is something else."

Certainly it gave Clarissa an occupation beyond her social round. All parties, routs, and soirees seemed so much the same to her by now that she varied her entertainment as much as possible. Tonight, for example, Papa was accompanying her to a lecture by a disciple of Mesmer, which might prove to be diverting, though she suspected that Papa would like it more than she would. Dolly was attending a small dance for young people and had begged Clarissa to break a rule and join her, but Clarissa had already learnt too well that Lady Rackham might dampen the frolic in a way that Clarissa St. Minver had never done. Her young sibling had not altogether understood the scruples involved.

"It is only innocent fun. Oh, Clair, I cannot believe that you are becoming an old dragon at twenty-two. I expect you believe you *should* think a lecture greater fun than dancing!"

"Not at all," Clarissa had protested, but the truth was that she sometimes felt, even this early on, that she might have made an error in exchanging a carefree life—even in the country—for one of doubtful interest. When one had put aside the questions of security and position, what did one have as Lady Rackham? Acquaintances, but few real friends; money, but little real pleasure; responsibility, but little real satisfaction. She dined out as often as she chose, went to the theatre and the opera with whom she chose (though always in mixed company), attended all the new exhibitions, the gambling clubs, and generally idled away her time. This was not to suggest that such leisure was unattractive, but what did one have to show for it? Perhaps that was why Rackham was interesting himself in the Pargate Society.

There was a discreet rap at the door of the chamber, and, when she answered, "Come," the door was opened and Mason announced, "Mr. Greville Landon, madam."

It was a standing principle of the household, and Mason knew it, that Lady Rackham discouraged morning calls, that she *never* received a visitor in deshabille, no matter how fashionable the practice was, and that no gentleman save her father was admitted without the accompaniment of a lady if one of her own family was not present. Mason was quite well acquainted with these rules, and certainly Greville himself had been turned away from the door because of them often enough to have absorbed the information, if he did not know it already. She had no intention of being coerced into acceptance.

"Mr. Landon," she said coldly, "if you will be good enough to wait in the drawing room, I shall be with you presently.

"Mason," she added, "I will speak to you later."

"Very good, madam," he said imperturbably.

"Oh, come along, Clair," Greville protested. "If there is blame, let it fall on me. I practically pushed by the chap."

"You may push by him again on the way out," she informed him sharply. "Mason will show you to the drawing room unless you would prefer to wait in the library where you may amuse yourself until I come down."

He retreated, though with little grace. Clarissa rang for her maid, dressed leisurely, and made her way downstairs in her own time. Mason was standing in the hall and, when he saw her, made to open the door of the library until she stopped him.

"You may go belowstairs, Mason," she told him. "Please say to Hobbs that I will see him as soon as Mr. Landon has gone."

"But my duties, madam . . ."

"Your duties are suspended, sir, until I have spoken to Lord Rackham. I do not wish to see you until that time. Please be kind enough to give my message to Hobbs and despatch Biggs here to the hall in the meanwhile."

For the first time a look of worry crossed his face, only to be replaced by a self-confident smirk. He expected, she assumed, that he would be on safe enough ground once Lord Rackham was consulted, since he was a retainer of long standing. Well, that remained to be seen.

Her annoyance was not lessened by Greville's plaint.

"It was an error, Clair, I guessed that from the beginning, and I never should have let Mama persuade me not to marry you."

"Well," she said in a real effort to be fair, "the estate is very important to your mother. It represents a great deal, and Georgiana's fortune, I am sure, made all the difference."

"I should have known that money was not the only thing," he said despondently. "You see, Clair, all those years I had you to depend upon. You and Estrella rather kept me in line. I know it is no good telling you that my marriage is dreadfully unhappy and all that; none of that matters now."

"What is it you are saying?"

He knelt beside her chair and took one of her hands in his. "I am saying that I love you, Clair, and that I want you to forgive me for what is and love me again."

She snatched her hand away. "Do get up and stop being silly. I am a married woman."

He retreated and flung himself into a chair nearby. "But,

dash it, you don't love Rackham. You only married him to spite my mother."

"Even supposing that were true, how does it alter this situation?" she asked coolly.

"London is a hotbed of emotional intrigue, Clarissa. No one minds in the least. At house parties lovers are placed near their mistresses and distant from their wives, don't you know that?"

Yes, she had heard of it. Nothing seemed to matter if convention was preserved.

"Everyone has affairs, Clair."

"Not everyone."

"Do you mean your husband? Do you mean to say you don't know about his little friend down in Pargate?"

Lady Rackham stood up. "That is enough, Mr. Landon. You have no call to slander my husband in his own house."

"Dash it, you don't love Rackham," he repeated, "You love me!"

And Clarissa realised that she did not!

She was not prepared for the rushing sweep of disillusion that came over her. That Greville had repudiated their long understanding and thrown her over for an heiress was, knowing his mother, almost bearable; that he even broke into her house to declare his love was ungentlemanly but forgivable; that the argument he used was her husband's infidelity was not. It was close to being caddish, certainly not the reasoning of a man. In her mind Greville was merely a silly boy.

Disgustedly, she pulled the bell cord. Instead of Briggs, whom she expected, it was Hobbs who answered. He stood in the doorway, impressive as only an authoritative upper servant can be. "Yes, my lady?"

"Mr. Landon will be leaving now, Hobbs. My previous instructions remain. If Mr. Landon, or any gentleman, calls in the company of his wife, or another lady, I shall be happy to receive him, but not alone."

"Very good, madam."

Greville, chagrined, rose from his sprawl in the chair. He gave her a curiously boyish grin. "See here, Clair, don't make too much of what I have said."

For a moment she did not understand what he meant, but when she did the last illusion fled. "You needn't worry, Mr. Landon, Lord Rackham shall hear nothing of it."

Orianna Pennant dipped the last strawberry in cream and then into sugar, popping it into her adorable mouth with the sublime expression of a greedy child. Leaning her head back against Carlton's naked shoulder, she giggled and continued the recitation of her itinerary.

"And then, he tells me, we shall go to Firenze for the spring, and perhaps to Como for the summer."

"What happens if he becomes sated with you before autumn?" asked Sir Francis lazily. "Does he guarantee your *partie* so that you can come back to London?"

Oriana sat up and sneered at him in mock indignation. " 'Ere, then, d'you think I don't know me trade? I never 'eard *you* complain, me buck, and that's a fact!"

Carlton, chuckling, swiftly flipped her over his knee and swatted while she flailed her arms about delightedly, pretending, but never quite convincing him, that her protests were valid. When he swung her back, she threw her arms about his neck and pressed her lips to his. "And as for you, me lord, what will you be doing whilst I am burning it blue? I wager you'll have more than one broken feather in your wing by the time you see me again. Is it the Landon woman you're after, or are you still set against poor Rackham?"

He pushed her away. "Poor Rackham? You, of all people, should know what sort of unaccountable muskin he is!"

"Don't speak of him that way. He never did *me* any harm. God knows, with what he had he was more generous than you."

"Oh, generous? He demmed near did me in on your account."

Oriana nestled into the hollow of his shoulder and blew softly into his ear, then gently nipped the lobe. "He thought he loved me. I always thought him rather sweet."

Carlton grunted and dug deeper into the bed. "I expect you were excited by his murderous rage when he came after me with that iron club."

"It was only the fireplace poker, my love, and though he threatened, he never would have struck you with it. He is too gentle a man for that, and you must remember he thought he was defending my honour. Why, he even wanted to marry me, you know."

Her bedmate murmured drowsily with quiet satisfaction, "Yes, I know he did. His father would never have permitted him to go through with it."

"Then I should probably have had a handsome piece of change if you had not mixed into it." She sat up. "Tell me again."

Indulgently he laughed. "Tell you what?"

"About your father and all that you told me before. It is an incredible story, isn't it?"

"Is it?" he asked with some bitterness. "Not if you were forced to play it out, my little minikin. Rackham got the gravy whilst I was left with the bone."

"Why do you hate him so, or do I guess?"

He turned his back, but she pulled at him. "No, Francis, tell me. I want to know."

"It is none of your affair," he said irritably. "Don't plague me!"

"It *is* my affair! *Both* of you were my affairs, if you'll remember. Why did you never tell me then that you were brothers?"

"Half brothers. I did tell you."

She laughed derisively. "Not above a month ago. Why did you never tell me before?"

"Perhaps because I thought it would set you up too much."

Yanking the pillow from beneath him, Oriana began to

beat him about the head and shoulders until there were feathers floating about the room. "Will you tell me about it? Will you?"

At first he protected himself with crossed arms above his face, but as she would not leave off, he reached up and savagely caught her wrists. "Stop it!" he snarled. The harshness of it startled her into momentary obedience. "Never mind! Never mind about me and Rackham unless you want me to throw you out the door in your shift!"

But the Cyprian would not let it be. "I have a right!" she continued to protest. Carlton looked at her with what she recognised as the beginning of one of the cold rages that sometimes came upon him. She should not have pushed him so far.

"Yes," he said, "you have a right. You have a right to know that I would never have taken up with you in the beginning if *he* hadn't wanted you. You midden-slut, d'you think you were anything in those days to tempt the likes of me?

"You were a weapon to me," he spat. "You were a weapon to cut his heart out!"

— 24 —

THE HOUSE SMELLED enticingly of beeswax and flowers and, thanks to the advice of the dowager Lady Rackham and the indefatigable Hobbs's memory, presented something of the elegance of the previous reign while basking in the rejuvenation of the new. The servants had already been lined up for inspection, one sent back for fresher gloves, another chided for an unusually luxuriant growth of facial hair. Mason, given still another "one last chance" by Rackham, was smirkily obsequious to Lady Rackham and coarsely arrogant to his fellow servants.

Clarissa, self-contained but excited by this, her first major entertainment as a peeress, made one last tour through the drawing room and library, the retiring rooms, and, at last, the great blue and silver ballroom, with its tented ceiling making it so like a giant azure pavilion. The musicians were already in the gallery, trying out bits of the popular tunes of the day: *O, Dear, What Can The Matter Be?*, *The Curly Headed Boy*, *High Randy Dandy O*, and, especially poignant for Clarissa, the haunting *Pretty Blue-Eyed Stranger*. She recalled that when she had last danced to that tune it had been in Greville's arms, and she had thought herself safe in a friendly and limitless world. Now Greville was no longer even her friend, and her world had become constricted by the demands of her position in a way that she had never suspected was possible. She enjoyed London and her new life, but it was a little sad to have found the great world, the bon ton, so empty and, though certainly spirited, essentially spiritless.

Rackham, splendid in evening costume, came from his apartment to join her at the top of the stairs. She had not seen him for several days, since he had been off again on "affairs," as he spoke of them, and she thought, not for the first time, how handsome he was in his coat of *bleu céleste* from Weston, his dazzling white waistcoat, and his pantaloons of blue stockinet, strapped over his varnished black shoes. In his hand he carried a tiny bouquet of roses.

"Good evening, my dear," he greeted her. "You are particularly beautiful this evening, but, allow me," and he reached out to carefully replace an escaping tendril of hair at her temple. "There. Now you are perfection."

The roses were faintly flushed with pink to match her own costume. "Shall I fasten them at the shoulder, or will you carry them?"

"Fasten them, I think, or they will wilt too soon." And, even as he finished pinning them to the edge of her corsage, the first arrivals were announced by Hobbs in a rich, stentorian voice.

"Lord and Lady Frinton—Lord Dilling—the Duke and Duchess of Bristol."

And there were, presently, as well, Lord and Lady Ravenspur just back from a long sojourn in Rome with her ladyship's sister, the Countess of Eriskay; the formidable Lady Battledore; Mr. Brummel in the perfect cravat for which he was renowned; the famous musical conductor Mr. LaValle and his still beautiful wife, who had been the singer Muriel Findlay; and, of course, the eccentric and fascinating Lady Holland, doyenne of all the wit of London, who gathered in her famous salon. All these, the great of society, made their way up the marble stair of Rackham House. It was amusing to their hostess, and she greeted them with added pleasure, for when she had suggested to her mother-in-law that many were sure to send regrets, the dowager had snorted amicably.

"Never think it, my dear. Rackham House has been virtually shut up for years, and many will come to see what you've done to it; others will come to inspect you and pass their judgement; some will come to gaze upon their betters and so on. No, you need not fear an empty ballroom. I expect you had better plan for the uninvited interlopers as well, the footmen cannot keep out all who do not belong."

"Do you think the Prince will attend?" Clair had ventured.

"Why not? There are so many houses these days where he is unwelcome that he must certainly cultivate new acquaintances."

Clarissa had seen nothing more of the Prince Regent since their encounter at Almack's, and, so far as she knew, neither had Rackham, though a morning or two after the event a basket of flowers had arrived accompanied with the prince's card, though unsigned. If he came, of course, her career as a hostess was virtually secure. If he did not, there was always another time, though, as the enchanting Duchess of Towans had reminded her, "It is difficult, my dear, to be friend to both the Prince Regent *and* the Crown Princess. You must, at the least, invite them on different nights." And, even as she was turning this over in her head, she heard Hobbs roaring "His Royal Highness, the Prince Regent." She saw the pressing crowd fall back and Prinney begin his majestic progress up the stairs, on his arm Lady Conyngham, her complaisant husband three steps behind.

Clarissa swept into a low curtsey, but His Royal Highness took her hands in his and, lifting her up, said sincerely, "I scarcely dared hope that you would be as lovely as I remembered you, my dear Lady Rackham, but I see that my memory failed me, for you are even lovelier." He sought the agreement of his stout mistress. "Isn't she lovely, Lady Conyngham?"

The other woman favoured her hostess with a cool nod. "Lovely," she agreed unenthusiastically, but her unpreposessing husband echoed the words with a tone of real enthusiasm.

"What a handsome house you have, Lady Rackham. I have not been in it for years. I hope you will not mind if I rove about somewhat?"

So that was how he kept out of the prince's way? "Not at all, Lord Conyngham. Perhaps a little later I can persuade my sister to act as your guide."

"Capitally done, my dear," murmured Alexander out of the corner of his mouth as the royal progress continued on its way. "You have pleased the gods and your reputation is made."

He favoured her with a roguish wink just as Lady Dedham presented herself. The old woman raised a warning finger. "Try to control yourself, Rackham," she advised tartly. "Don't bring your wife down with your Corinthian ways." But to Clarissa her withered face presented a smile. "You've come off in grand style, my dear," she said. "Just don't let him get out of hand." And, to Clarissa's delighted surprise she, too, winked broadly.

The music began in earnest, and Lord Rackham led his lady into the azure ballroom. Everything was moving in perfect time. They stepped off into an aristocratic mazurka, in this instance the wildness being sublimated to pride of bearing. The Prince Regent danced it well, but Lady Conyngham seemed unaccustomed to the beat.

The waltz, the contradanse, the quadrille (at which Rackham partnered Lady Conyngham, and the Regent, Clarissa) all went well. The prince called for an *Écossaise*, "Because of my other kindgom," he explained, which rather amused his hostess since the one the musicians managed raggedly to play had nothing in the least Scottish about it.

But if the Prince Regent was the center of attention, Dolly was the attraction about which all the dancing moved, for other young women were engaged for a turn about the floor dependent upon the dance card of Miss St.

Minver. If they were at all aware of this, they showed no sign of it, but not a young man in the room (or even some older ones in whom the blood still ran warm) was less than acutely conscious of Dolly, where she was, and with whom (lucky devil) she was dancing. In her ravishing ensemble of white lace over rosepink, she could have engaged every dance, but she diplomatically took an occasional aside to enjoy a cup of punch or seek a breath of air. It happened that she was not in the ballroom when Hobbs's voice rang out for the final announcement of the evening.

"Her Royal Highness The Crown Princess Caroline and Sir Francis Carlton!"

"Caroline!" rumbled the Regent turning alternately fiery and pale. He faltered in midmeasure and looked toward the door. There she was, indeed, unmistakable in yellow silk, looking like nothing so much as an absurdly oversized lemon. Lady Conyngham's low warning was needed to recall him to himself.

"Remember who you are, sir."

By which he knew she meant that he could not give way in public to the sort of tantrum he sometimes enjoyed in private, and she was right. The game would not be worth the candle. Still, he could not absolutely control his rage, and it roiled and boiled inside him.

"You must dance, sir," commanded his mistress, and it was not until he caught her sibilant whisper that he realised he had, in fact, stopped, and that the music had stopped with him. Briskly, he nodded to the leader of the orchestra and the tune struck up again. His mood was hardly set for a *galop*, but he willed himself into it and was amazed at the therapeutic value of the dance.

The sum of those present was about evenly divided between those who revelled in the discomfiture of their sovereign and those who did not. Even among the former, Caroline had few genuine supporters; she was of too piquant a flavour for the upper crust. It was among the common people, whom she so much resembled, the honest and earthy ale-quaffing mob, that she had her champions for the most part. The response to Francis Carlton was similar: some were deluded by his easy charm and some prided themselves on their perspicacity in seeing through him. There were even a few of a third kind, those who recognised his casual duplicity and did not care about the results of it so long as they themselves were safe.

A few eyes turned curiously to Lord Rackham, but, like the Prince, his lady was exercising a certain amount of control. "You cannot put him out without a scandal," she reminded her husband whose inner promptings urged him to do that very thing. "He is under the protection of the Princess." Purposefully, she crossed the large room to welcome the late arrivals, though others, for their own reasons, were already crowding about them. Carlton saw her progress and the determined look upon her face.

"Dearest lady," he said in a carrying voice as he stepped forward to take her hands familiarly, "how generous of you to allow me to attend your brilliant affair."

Clarissa's eyes widened a little at the swaggering conceit of the man, but she answered as clearly as he had spoken, "How good of you to honour us."

"Ja, you see, Carlton?" said the Princess in a way which seemed to exonerate the adventurer from any blame, "I haf told you dot Lady Rackham vill nod turn you avay, eh?"

In that moment Clarissa felt a curious wave of warmth for the outrageous woman. Her perceptions of propriety might be faulty, her friends raffish, her convictions askew, but she would always be loyal to them. Pray God her friends would always be as loyal to her.

"Is your Royal Highness aware that . . ."

"Dot de vale is here? Ja, I know." She spread her nostrils and there was a light of battle in her eyes. "De question is who stays and who goes avay?" Peering into Clarissa's distressed face, she added, "But dis might destroy you, ain't? It is a pickle. Vot shall be done?"

Rackham joined his lady's welcome of Princess Caroline

with his own. "It is a privilege to have Your Royal Highness in my house no matter what the circumstance," he assured her. A look of decision came into the woman's face, and she pressed his hands gratefully.

To Her Highness's escort the host merely inclined his head coldly. "Carlton," he said.

"Rackham," replied Sir Francis in an almost perfect mimicry of intonation, though with a look of deviltry in his eye. "Handsome house you have here."

The irony was wasted on those who did not know that he had once tried to wrest it from his half brother's grasp. He smiled at Lady Rackham. "Dear lady, may I engage you for . . . ?"

Dolly, emerging from the conservatory on the arm of a pallid admirer, hurried over to them. "Sir Francis, what luck! You are just in time for the one dance I saved you on my card!"

Carlton's eyes mockingly sought Clarissa's permission, and then he swept her sister off in a sensuous *valse*. "What an amusing chap he is," said a voice at Lady Rackham's shoulder.

She saw that it was Lord Tendril, and she allowed him to lead her out after she had ascertained that Rackham was attending the Princess. For such a slight fellow, Tendril was astonishingly masterful upon the dance floor, firmly leading and directing her in the swirling rhythm with no effort at all, still retaining energy for conversation.

"A word to the wise, my lady. Your sister might be in safer hands."

And, indeed, Dolly seemed to have become quite transfigured since beginning to dance with Francis Carlton. Clarissa found she was quite inclined to agree with Lord Tendril, but she had no idea what could be done about it.

Georgiana Landon, too, was distressed as she saw the look on Dolly St. Minver's face. Her own heart had leapt up when Sir Francis had entered the room, and she had had to force herself to remain calm or she, too, would have run across to him as joyously as the girl had done. Only a few hours ago she had lain in Carlton's arms, realising, even then, what a fool she had allowed herself to become. Now she began to believe what she had already suspected, that she had been—perhaps even was now—merely a piece in a complex puzzle to which only Sir Francis Carlton held the solution. Sadly she surrendered her hand to her husband and was led by him onto the floor. It crossed her mind that of late she hardly knew Greville, and that his mother, with whom she almost always spent her morning hours, was their only connexion, save in a social way. She could not be unhappy, though, that he had chosen to occupy a chamber of his own.

= 25 =

It HAD BEEN quite shocking that Georgiana Landon had taken a bit too much refreshment and come up to Dolly and Carlton, saying such dreadfully vulgar things. When Dolly slipped out of the ballroom to escape the unexpected attack, she only went as far as the conservatory. It was odd, she reflected, that hardly anyone had come in here this evening except herself when she needed a respite from the crowd of admirers and well-wishers. One or two of her dancing partners had been bold enough to lead her in this direction, but once they had discovered she was not interested in a romantic interlude, each seemed ill at ease and soon led her out again.

Now she saw it as a refuge, and she paused here, listening to the conversation in the room outside to see if anyone was remarking her sudden exit. She also hoped that Carlton had been watching and would follow her out. The only solution had seemed to be flight, but she had not expected to be left so long alone. She did not feel that she could go out again just yet although she was already impatient and half-ready to cry because Carlton had not seen fit to follow her at once. Certainly the attention he had given her in the past few weeks had led her to expect otherwise.

At first, she had not been at all suspicious that he suddenly seemed to be present at every function she attended, be it grand or intimate, from parties for young people, which were hardly more than the innocent sort of entertainment given to those who have left childhood but not yet become adults, to any evening party, fête, or diversion she chose. She came to accept that any time she went out she might expect to meet him. He never actually pursued her, but within a fortnight it seemed inevitable that he would be nearby to delight her with his lazy charm, to fetch her an ice or a cool drink to quench her thirst. Gentleman that he was, he had never once alluded to her visit to his chambers, though *she* always seemed conscious of its memory hovering over her, subtly affecting the tone of their relationship.

But then on Tuesday last, at the little supper party given by Lady Ranleigh, he had laughingly stolen a kiss from her during a game of forfeit. She had been rather disturbed, but everyone present seemed to think it a capital sort of jest. Still, though it began lightly, it had ended by leaving her rather shaken. Sir Francis was quite old, after all, as old as Rackham.

Now she heard a man's discreet footsteps approaching with what seemed like stealth or at least caution. She moved quickly a little further back among the ferns and waited for him to find her there. If he had seen her come in he must know she was still there, since there was no other exit. She could easily see the door from her vantage point, and she expected he would soon discover her. He came in, looked about, straightened a sleeve of his jacket, and looked not toward her but to the door. It seemed, indeed, that he had not so much marked her escape as that he was awaiting someone else. She was about to make herself known when the other person, Georgiana Landon, came into the glass room.

"Francis, oh Francis, how can you be so cruel as to do this to me?" Dolly heard her ask, then saw her throw her arms about Carlton's neck, laying her cheek against his lapel. Since he was only slightly taller than she was, it was only a matter of a small movement before his head was turned toward her uplifted face and his lips were on hers. It caused Dolly a great wrench in her heart, but she found she could neither announce her presence nor tear her eyes away from them.

How happy she was to hear Carlton now attempting to ease himself out of the situation. "Georgiana, you must think of your husband and your reputation."

"Do you no longer care for me?"

"I care for you far too much to wish you unhappiness. No flirtation is worth demeaning yourself in the eyes of society."

"And is that all this has meant to you? Only a flirtation?" Georgiana had stepped away from him and was staring in astonishment up into his face. "I had not thought you so heartless." Tears sprang into her eyes.

Sir Francis pretended to be very surprised at such a reaction. "But, Georgie, my dear, what else could it be? You are a married woman."

Georgiana began to cry in earnest, and for the first time Carlton seemed rather alarmed. "My poor girl, could it be anything but a brief attraction? How can you take all this so seriously?" Taking her hand, he asked, "Why torture yourself and me, as well, over a mere fancy? You must have known it would come to nothing in the end."

"I know what it is," she said accusingly. "I know perfectly well what has changed you!" And Dolly was astonished to hear herself being referred to with a word that had never even passed her own lips, though, being from the country, she knew full well what it meant. She had had no idea that Greville's wife held her in such disrespect.

"And if it were true that she had come between us?" Sir Francis was now asking in a reasonable tone of voice. "Miss St. Minver is a charming young woman of a good family."

"And marriageable, I suppose?" asked Georgiana in a voice that was half-derisive and half self-pitying. "I wonder if she knows you would never consider marrying her once you . . ."

Dolly could see Carlton laying his fingers across Mrs.

Landon's mouth. "That is enough," he said tersely. "Did you come to me so unwillingly? Do I remember any promises or vows between us? I swear, Georgie, I never thought you took it for anything more than the lark I did."

This might have set off another flood, but the woman's eyes seemed to have gone dry. "I thought there were promises, if not vows. I thought I heard you saying all manner of things to me."

Although there had been a bit of an edge to his voice for a brief time, now all his old charm returned. Putting a finger under her chin, he lifted her face so that he could look into her eyes. "No, no promises, my dear child. I never make 'em. Certainly not to a married woman. I am very careful about that. I am sorry, truly I am, if you believed you heard something I never had any intention of saying."

Georgiana pulled away from him, and Dolly could see that she had completely left off crying, though her eyes were necessarily a little red. *What will happen now?* she asked herself and realised how, in her own mind, the answer would affect her future.

"What a wretch you are, Francis Carlton," Mrs. Landon said, and Dolly saw her stand up very straight. "Thank God, I was never *completely* taken in by your honeyed tongue." But she looked almost longingly into the man's face as if she hoped he would repudiate her words.

Carlton laughed out loud, a pleasing sound that held no mockery at all. "A wretch? Why, of course I am, Georgie dear, a complete bowyer, the choicest spirit in society, and that is the whole of whatever fascination I have for ladies the like of yourself, unhappy in their marriages and eager for diversion. You never hunger for the good men, do you? Of course not. Only the wretches like myself who make you feel for a little while quite alive and sparky." He drew her to him and kissed her. "But I swear upon my honour, my girl, that I thought you knew the game. Now go running back to safety before you are terribly burnt."

The slap Mrs. Landon gave him quite reverberated

throughout the conservatory. White-faced, she all but ran from the room. Sir Francis waited for a moment until he was sure that she had gone, then crossed and firmly shut the door. He waited a brief moment only, then said softly, "There now, Dolly, do you see what a terrible person I am? Do you still want me to love you?"

Lady Dedham to Miss Phyliss Powley of Pargate (fragment):

> ". . . and, certainly, to have seen them circling about each other on the ballroom floor like two great galleons, all sails out, but being very careful not to be thought at all in the vicinity of the other was better than a play! Stout Lady C_ N_ _ _ H_ M stood off to the side and set him up with partners, for he is, truly, a gifted dancer and she is *not!* I expect she is clever enough to guess that it is better to have the choosing of them, rather than allowing the P. Rgn't to do it for himself. Twice with pretty Dolly, once with Mrs. Landon the yngr and *three times* (!) with his hostess, our beloved Clarissa. I thought it such a shame that her father was not there to witness her triumph. I have no notion where he had got to, but he was missed by many (not least by myself to whom he is the only link to his wife, my departed cousin.)
>
> Speaking as I was of Mrs. L——, there was a moment when I had quite a turn, for she came flying out of the conservatory with the look of Medea upon her face! Though my curiosity was great as to whom she might have abandoned inside, my courage was not great enough to open the door & see! Lord Tendril was standing quite near me and, I am sure, will add his own speculation, for you know I have said to you what a talebearer he is.

Without doubt, the most handsome and ingratiating gentleman at the ball (always excepting dear R——, of course) was one of whom I had often heard, but never met. I speak of the cavalier who escorted the Mad Princess (as many are calling her), but who did me the honour of a *very* spirited *valse*, the memory of which I shall carry with me until my dying . . .”

Long after everyone had gone, the candles extinguished, the servants sent to bed, Lord Rackham tapped softly at the door of his wife's boudoir and, being admitted, entered with a bottle of French wine in his one hand and a pair of crystal glasses in the other.

“I believe, dear wife, that congratulations to you are in order. It is my considered opinion that you did old Rackham House very well tonight in the face of some very dicey situations.”

Clarissa blushed with pleasure. “It is very good of you, Rackham, but I was so terrified all evening long that I enjoyed very little of it myself.”

Alexander uncorked the wine and poured. “I am sorry to hear that,” he said as he handed her the glass. “And surprised, too. You certainly did not leave that impression.”

She held the glass up, admiring the clear amber of the wine against the light. “Do you think the Prince Regent will ever forgive us?”

“I think he should, instead, praise us. He may have set a record.”

“What do you mean?”

“Do you think he ever before spent an entire evening on the dancing floor with his wife without a word of vilification?”

“They did not dance *together*, and, so far as I know, they did not speak.”

Rackham gave her his curious, lop-sided grin. "That is what I mean. So much the better if it were always that way."

"Would you rather *we* did not speak, sir?" asked Clair with a slight air of provocative archness.

He looked deeply into her eyes as if searching for something there. "I hope, my dear wife, that you do not propose to take the royal marriage as a model for our own? If that were so, no man in England would marry, and no woman bear a child."

She found herself returning look for look. His eyes promised things she had not suspected. They confused her, addled her thinking. "It comes to my mind that . . ." But he could not know what she was about to say, for she veered away to another subject.

"I think you did well with Carlton."

"By avoiding him, do you mean? It was not easy," Rackham said with a grimace. "I was persuaded that it would be unseemly to provoke him in my own house. I am glad to report that he appeared to conduct himself with admirable restraint." He gave a short chuckle. "You can be sure I watched him carefully."

"Do you think you may have misjudged him over the years?"

"Hah! Hardly that. What I meant to say was that I know he is up to some deviltry which I have not yet discerned. His bland behaviour tonight had something behind it, I do assure you. Francis has never performed one action lightly in his life. Everything is calculated."

"And yet he is well liked and respected?"

"No, no, Carlton has left behind him in his career a broad trail of broken faith and broken troth that would doubtless circle the world. Did you not see poor Georgiana attack him? And in public, too. Luckily, all eyes but mine were trained on the royals to see what they would do next."

"Georgiana? Georgiana Landon? Do you mean you believe that she . . ."

He lifted his glass and sipped meditatively. "I hardly know, but from what I saw this evening I might suspect that Carlton has made inroads there if nothing else."

There was a light tap at the door, then more insistent. "Madam? Madam!"

Rackham opened it. "Yes, Prosser, what is it?" He saw the footman lingering a little way along the passage. "That will be all, Mason. Good night."

"Good night, sir. Sleep well." Rackham noticed, not for the first time, how sharp and attentive were Mason's eyes, peering out from his ferretlike face. He turned his attention back to the maidservant. "Come in, woman. What has agitated you so?"

"What has happened, Prosser?" asked Clair when she saw the woman's worried eyes. "Is Miss Dolly ill?"

"She's not yet come home. I don't know what to think, and with Sir Wilton gone, I thought I had best waken you."

Clair was bewildered. "I had no idea she was not in the house."

"Did you not say good night to her?" asked her husband. "I thought you made a small ritual of that."

"No, I was so long delayed downstairs that I assumed she would already be asleep.

"What time did she go out?" she asked Prosser.

Rackham exchanged a look with Clarissa. "And with whom did she leave?"

Prosser wrung her hands as if she knew she shared some responsibility in this. "It was toward the end of the ball, madam, but she did not go alone. There was a whole party of young people."

"Sir Francis?" asked Clair and Alexander almost in one breath.

"Oh, Rackham," she added, "if anything has happened to her, Papa will never forgive me."

He put his arm about her shoulders, a gesture not unnoticed by Prosser even in her state of nerves. "Here, here, none of that until it is called for."

There was the slight rattle of a carriage in the silent street, and all of them hurried to the windows. Below, at the front of the house, Dolly St. Minver was alighting from a brougham, assisted by a man whose face was hidden until they approached the door of the house and the moonlight fell across his face. Dolly lifted her head, and the man kissed her.

"Carlton! By gad, if . . ." He headed out of the chamber and towards the stairs. "I knew that devil was up to something!"

"Rackham, wait!"

"Wait? For what, madam?" He hardly paused.

"Wait for me to speak to my sister before you do something which you may well regret!"

When he looked back at her his eyes were blazing. "Ruin for your sister is not a matter for anger?"

"We don't know that. Dolly may have been vasty indiscreet, but . . ."

As they hurried down the stairs, Mason looked up at them, then straightfaced, opened the door and admitted Dolly. He paused there fractionally as the girl came in.

"The gentleman will not be staying, Mason," said Rackham from the stair.

Clair ran the remainder of the way down the steps. "Dolly, where have you been? We have been dreadfully worried."

Her sister stood in the light of the candelabrum held in Mason's hand, her colour high. She had never looked more vibrant, more full of life and barely contained excitement. "Oh, Clair, wait until I tell you! Rackham, why on earth are you scowling? Prosser? Why are you all hovering about on the stair?"

Clarissa spoke before Rackham could. "Where have you been, Doll?"

"Nowhere very wicked, only at Ashley's with Papa."

"It was not your father who brought you home, my

186

dear," said Rackham as evenly as he could manage. "I think some explanation is in order."

"Oh, Rackham," Dolly laughed. "I hope you are not going to go all head-of-the-clan and declare that 'while I am under your roof' and so forth?"

"Sister, you know that Rackham has no love for Sir Francis."

The girl blinked. "But *I* have no quarrel with him, and Papa even gambles with Carlton." She seemed genuinely bewildered.

"I hope," said her brother-in-law quietly, "that you will give consideration to my wishes while you are my guest to the extent of accepting my view whether or not you understand it. There are circumstances here beyond your ken, Dolly."

Her look turned petulant. "I do not see why I should not be allowed to choose my own friends. You do, and Clair does; she quite often goes out without you, Rackham, and with other gentlemen, too."

"Your sister, Miss St. Minver, is a married woman, not a chit, and may do as she chooses within the limits of propriety. You on the other hand . . ." He stopped, took a deep breath. "We will not discuss it further tonight, if you please. I am sure we are all overtired."

"Oh, Alexander, dear," Dolly went on, not wishing to relinquish the point, "please don't be stuffy." She said it so winsomely and with such a smile of complicity that it was all made to seem a huge joke. "I have heard of the scrapes *you* have been in! Wasn't there a run-in with the watch?"

He could not help smiling ruefully back at her. "I am a man. You are an inexperienced young girl. The difference is immeasurable."

She shook her head at this. "My word, all he did was bring me home. Or is it the kiss which bothers you? All this for a kiss?"

"Is Papa still at Ashley's?" asked Clarissa.

"Lord, yes! And having the run of his life. I don't expect elephants could drag him away from the table, let alone a daughter. He was winning a fortune when we left. The counters were piled so high in front of him that he could scarcely see past them."

"God bless him," said Prosser fervently. "Perhaps I'll have my wages for these three years past!"

"And, as for Carlton, Papa said he might bring me home. "Though he said nothing about the kiss," she giggled. Then to Rackham in a conciliatory fashion, "I know you have some sort of grievance with him, but I do not. He has been a gentleman with me."

"As long as you keep both feet on the floor," muttered her brother-in-law darkly.

All of the women stared at him in surprise. "I know what that means!" said Dolly in a further burst of giggles. "I think you are very wicked!"

"As I do, Rackham," said his wife. "Most unsuitable. You are certainly a poor example to an impressionable girl.

"Nevertheless, Dolly, I hope you will not be alone with Sir Francis again. His reputation is far from savoury."

They had been moving up the stair all this time, and Dolly stood at the corner of the passage to her own apartments. "I expect you have been listening to Mrs. Landon," she said, a little worried by their persistence. "It was not Carlton's fault, really it wasn't."

"What wasn't?" Rackham asked.

"Well, Georgiana practically threw herself at him, you know."

The husband and wife exchanged uneasy glances. "On what authority do you say this, dear?" asked Clair.

"Why, I . . . on my own authority. I was in the conservatory, you see, when it happened."

"When what happened."

The girl became round-eyed. "Oh, Clair, it was quite dreadful! She actually made advances to the poor man. He could scarcely keep her off."

"When was all this?"

"Tonight . . . during the ball."

"You'd best come along to bed, miss," said Prosser. "What remains can be told in the morning, surely, can it not, sir?"

"I daresay you are right," said the master of the house. "I think we can mull it all over at breakfast."

The women went to their chambers, but Rackham lingered behind, then went a part of the way down the stairs where he could see the footman locking up again.

"Mason."

"Yes, sir?" It was asked uneasily.

"I believe that the wages I pay you are quite generous, all things being considered."

"Why, they are, sir. You have always been very open-handed with me."

The master nodded. "Then, old fellow, I expect you will in future find that you need not accept tips from our guests."

"Guests, sir?" The innocent look was almost convincing.

"Yes, such as Sir Francis."

"Oh, sir, I . . . I would never . . ."

"Quite. I hope it is understood?"

He made his way back up the stairs to bed, while Mason extinguished the lights of the candelabrum, muttering to himself. He had been that careful. "Now how the devil did the sharp-eyed beggar know?"

=== 26 ===

By EIGHT OF the clock that morning, Sir Wilton was still not in occupancy of his bed, his eldest daughter discovered. Overtired and overwrought, Lady Rackham had awakened again and again during the night, fancying she had heard his return, only falling into a deep sleep just before dawn. But, now, when she awakened again, she was still filled with dread. Crawling from bed and throwing a wrapper around her shoulders, she crept along the passage to Papa's room and rapped on the door. As she had feared, there was no answer, and, when she cautiously opened the door, she saw that the bed was undisturbed, the chamber empty.

She hurried next door to her sister's sleeping chamber, not even bothering to knock in her agitation. The curtains of the bed were drawn despite the unusual warmth of this autumn, probably so that Dolly could sleep undisturbed. But her bed, too, was empty, although it showed evidence of recent occupation. Almost frantically, Clarissa threw open the door to the dressing room. Empty. The lovely ball dress had been carefully hung in its muslin covering, but Clair could not judge whether other garments were missing.

With a sense of panic constricting her throat, she ran along the hallway and beat frantically upon the door of Rackham's apartment. He opened it almost at once, his face half-obscured by lather, a razor in his hand.

"Good morning, my dear. You're up early."

"Rackham, Dolly is gone. Do you suppose . . . ?"

He seemed unperturbed. "First your father, then Dolly. Do you think it may be an epidemic?"

"Pray, do not joke, sir. It is not a time for humour."

"No, Clair, of course it is not. But, pray, just look out the window." Her husband's view was over the garden, and when Clarissa looked out, there was Dolly, in a morning robe, walking barefoot over the wet lawn.

"What on earth is she doing?"

"Watch," he counselled.

Bending, the girl wet her fingers in the dew and lifted them to her face, then repeated the gesture. It was an old wives' recipe for beauty, but a perennially popular one. Clair felt a rush of tenderness sweep over her as she watched her sister. Then leaning from the window, she softly called the girl's name. Dolly looked up, smiled angelically and waved her hand, moving on towards the garden walk. Just as she reached the edge of the lawn, she stooped again and washed her face in the dew, then, in a fit of exuberance, threw her arms above her head and spun around, the skirt of her robe flying out as she turned.

"Dear heaven," said Rackham with surprise, "one would think she was in love. I can think of no other reason for such behaviour." His eyes met those of his wife, each recalling Dolly's return from Ashley's.

"Do you suppose it could be true?" asked Clair. She hurried down the backstairs and into the garden. "Doll, come into the house at once, you will take a chill. What are you doing out here without even slippers on your feet?"

The girl laughingly threw her arms about Clair's neck. "Nothing, nothing, sister dear! My slippers are over there somewhere." She lifted on her toes and pirouetted like a rope dancer. "Oh, Clair, don't you ever miss the country as Papa and I do? I woke up and looked out into this absolutely glorious morning, and I simply had to come outside."

Clarissa breathed a sigh of relief. "I can't think what Prosser was about in allowing you to do such a thing," she said, but was glad the impulse was merely one of wishing for concourse with nature. Odd that she had not noticed that her father and sister were not content in London, but still longed for the countryside. Tugging gently, she drew Dolly towards the house.

"Poor Prosser knew nothing of my escapade," Dolly protested, instantly defending the servant. "She was still snoring when I peeped in on her." She retrieved her slippers and, leaning on Clair's arm, slipped them on her feet. "Did Papa come home the possessor of a fortune again?"

"Not yet," Clair said, "and I am worried about him. Was it at Ashley's he was playing, did you say?"

"Yes, but that was hours ago! He wouldn't still be there in play, would he? Papa is not one of those Marathonian players like Lord Howell who will sit at the table for days."

"I shall ask Rackham to enquire. Even if he is gone, they may know where he can be found.

"I daresay he is all right," she added with an attempt at consolation which she did not feel. "He is probably somewhere sleeping off the result of his sudden return to wealth."

The stale smell of a gambling club in the daytime hours is quite like the sated spirit of those who are sometimes still found there. At night with the winking candles, the high excitement of the bets and the merry clink of coin make an almost carnival atmosphere, but after the sun has risen the place is like a house of mourning. The servant who answered the door to Rackham's pounding spoke in appropriately hushed and lugubrious tones.

"No, sir, I ain't no idea. I have only been on duty for an hour, you see." But looking closer and recognising his lordship, he readily admitted him. Yes, sir, he believed the proprietor was on the premises, and if Lord Rackham, sir, would take himself a chair, he would enquire.

But Rackham was too edgy to sit. While he waited for the proprietor, he wandered about the establishment, reflecting upon the folly that brought mankind into such a mad pursuit of pleasure as was to be found here. He counted himself among them, for he had no illusions as to his own fallibility. The most astonishing stories were told of Ashley's, and of fortunes and futures and lives, even, which had been wagered on the turn of a card. He thought of the great gamesters of his father's day; Selwyn, Admiral Pigot, and the great parliamentarian Charles Fox, of whom it was said that he prepared the speeches with which he dazzled the house while sitting at the faro table. Rackham himself had once sat here with £ 10,000 in bullion lying on the center of the table and had seen it taken by a chap who only the day before had begged him for a guinea. Faro had replaced hazard as the favourite sport, but that was only the exterior look of the marvel. The game, he knew, might well alter over the years, but the urge would go on forever, so long as men had coin to wager and a taste for living on the edge of life.

The woman who crossed the deeply carpeted room towards him was one whom he had not laid eyes on, save from a distance, for five or six years, but she was still a prime article. Unlike many of her Corinthian sisters, she had kept herself up and was in many ways, he suspected, far superior to the wench he had thought himself in love with so many years ago.

She greeted him with a faint mockery of courtesey, as though their heads had never lain side by side upon a pillow. "Lord Rackham, I believe?"

His lordship replied with a graceful half-bow. "Mistress Pennant, I am your servant. I thank you for seeing me when I suspect you are deuced busy counting out the cut of the house. I hear that it was deep play last evening."

She agreed with a wry twist of her pretty mouth. "Steep, indeed. I heard old Marsten say when he ran low that he would have coined his heart and dripped his blood into drachmas to continue playing, the excitement ran so high."

"And you were too cold-hearted to lend him the where-withal to do so?"

She shook her head, or rather tossed it, for it was

transformed into a flirtatious movement by the look which accompanied it. "Not I! The old goat is anxious enough to borrow, but he always argues the interest. I am happy enough to take his money, but I do not wish to lend him mine."

Rackham had heard of the exorbitant rates she demanded of the poor devils who had contracted the fever, but he made no remark. Instead, he said, "I believe that one of your patrons last evening was my father-in-law."

There was a crinkle of affection about Oriana's eyes. "That dear old man; always a gentleman, win or lose. I wish all my clients were like him. Yes, he was here, but not for last night only. He arrived much earlier. I think he must have been gulling me, for he arrived at this time yesterday or a little later and asked me for a job, as he called it. I recollect that he said that since he had paid out so much to me over the years, it was time he began to see some return on his investment, the clever old jester. There was still a game running from the previous night, and I expect he inveigled himself into it with a small sum, then with a series of *parolis* made himself the master of the table. I only wish he might have had the good of it."

"I am sorry to hear that he did not. Did you see what happened?"

"Oh, certainly," she said, then continued, watching his face carefully. "Your brother returned, and Sir Wilton has never been able to resist playing against him. I expect he hoped that his run of luck was so strong that their history together would not matter."

He was staring back at her, and she could not see if it were enmity or only amazement in his eyes. "Pray, never use that word again in describing the relationship between Sir Francis Carlton and myself—neither to me nor to anyone else."

Until now Oriana had retained a certain barrier as befits that between merchant and customer, but now she softened. She laid her hand lightly upon his arm. "Forgive me,

Alex, I suppose I was testing the truth of it. If I had known . . ."

"What, all those years ago?" He shook his head. "I was a green lad with much to learn of the world." Slyly he continued, "And I found as careful a teacher as any man has ever done."

Oriana was silent for a moment, then said, "I, too, was very young. Too young to know the worth of what I was doing.

"Will you tell me something . . . now?"

"Perhaps I will, though you must not mind if I beg off when you cut too near the bone."

"Would you have kept your promise?"

His eyebrow quirked upward. "Promise, madam?"

Oriana's professional mask dropped back into place. "Ah, you have forgotten. It is no matter, is it? Not anymore."

Now Rackham seemed ashamed. "Of course it matters, Oriana. I buried the sting of it for years, but I have not forgotten it. You are asking if I really would have married you?"

She bit her lip. "I wonder if I really want to know the answer."

Rackham made a small, indecisive gesture. "It can come as no more of a shock to you than . . . ," but he did not continue. Instead she finished it for him.

"No more of a shock than my desertion to Carlton was to you?"

He nodded. "Something like that. The truth is this, that yes, I would have gladly married that girl, no matter what was said by anyone." His voice dropped a register, and he said quietly, "I loved her, you see."

"Even though she was an illusion?"

"Even so. Perhaps love is always an illusion?"

They stood rooted there, staring at each other. Oriana would have liked to reach out tender fingers and lightly touch his face, but she did not dare. "What a fool I was. But we could never have been happy, and you have married better now."

The servant arrived with coffee, and they sat at a table to sip it.

"Yes," Rackham agreed, "I have made a vastly convenient alliance." Then abruptly, he aroused himself. "Tell me, if you will, what have you seen of Sir Wilton."

Oriana wrinkled her brow in thought. "There is not much for me to tell. I recall that at one time Miss St. Minver was present with a group of youngsters her own age. I try to discourage them, you know; for the most part they are not serious, but think it is a madcap adventure to come to a gaming house. Once they are here, they play recklessly or not at all. They are a disturbance to the regulars and of very little profit to me."

"Was Sir Wilton aware that his daughter was here?"

Oriana was emphatic about that. "Oh yes, and he was even more aware that Francis was here. I remember thinking that he was very clever in disposing of two distractions at the same time."

"Do you mean that it was Sir Wilton himself who sent Dolly off with Carlton?" He shook his head. "I can scarcely believe it. Carlton is up to something, of that I am certain."

"Yes," Oriana agreed. "He holds you in as much dislike as you hold him. Am I the cause of all this enmity?"

"No," Rackham assured her, "you were only a small part of it. It reaches back before any of us were born." Oddly, the answer did not seem to please Mistress Pennant so much as pique her, for she sniffed disdainfully and smoothed her skirt.

"Did Carlton come back?" asked his lordship.

Her jaw tightened a little, and the stretching skin made her face seem hard. "Yes, came back and jeered that poor old man into playing against him and, I would swear though I could not prove it, jinked him royally. I know that Francis left this morning at about four, but Sir Wilton sat at the table for another hour, gazing into nothing. Everyone had been on his side in it, you know, for he is so gallant an old man, but no one remained when he lost everything he had won."

"What became of him, if you know?"

"I fear I do not. I went into the counting room, and when I came out again he was gone. The people who are on duty now are the day staff, so I doubt that they would know anything more. I am sorry I have been of so little help."

"On the contrary," said Rackham, rising from the table. "You have told me much more than I had expected." He took up his hat and stick. "I thank you, Oriana . . . for everything."

She thrust her cheek forward to be kissed. "No, I thank you for telling me something that makes me very proud. I am sorry that I did not deserve the honour you offered me.

"I hope . . . ," she paused, ". . . I hope that your marriage to Lady Rackham will be very contented, but take care, my dear friend, for Francis will strike at you where he can. He has no sense of fair play."

Rackham chuckled wryly. "Bad school, I expect. Improper values and all that."

When Lord Rackham had gone, it was Oriana who sat staring off into nothing for a few moments, wondering what her life might have been. Then, being an eminently sensible creature, she went back to counting her money.

= 27 =

CLARISSA WAS SUPERVISING the general return of the household to normal conditions when Hobbs sought her out in the morning room, asking, "Madam, is Miss Dolly about?"

"I believe she is dressing for an afternoon engagement. Is there something I can do for you?"

"There is a lady, madam, who has asked to speak to Miss Dolly, but I hesitate because . . . well, madam, she is rather overwrought."

A veiled and shrouded figure thrust past him and, coming into the room, threw back the covering over her face to reveal a countenance made haggard by extreme anxiety and lack of sleep.

"Georgiana!" said Clarissa in surprise. "That will be all, Hobbs, except, perhaps, for some refreshment. Chocolate, Georgie?" With an impatient wave, a hand dismissed chocolate and refreshment in general.

"I hope you will forgive me, my dear," said Clarissa when Hobbs had gone, "but you look perfectly *distrait.* What can be the matter?"

Young Mrs. Landon did not speak for a moment, but sat looking with peculiar intensity into the face of her hostess. At last she spoke, but in a hoarse, rasping voice quite unlike her usual one. Clair guessed that she had, for some reason, spent many hours in continuous weeping.

"Lady Rackham," she said, "I have not slept all night long. I daresay I must seem very odd to you, but I had asked to speak to Miss St. Minver, is she here?"

"I believe she is presently occupied," answered her hostess a little nervously. "Perhaps you would tell me what it is about?"

The huge eyes stared out of the drawn face. "You cannot protect her forever, you know. Someday she must face the real world and become accountable for her actions."

"What ever do you mean? Are you suggesting that my sister has committed some action which she should not have done?"

"Ah, don't you know?" asked the other passionately. "Could you not be aware of the things happening at your own ball—in your own house?"

Clarissa was tempted to laugh. "A great many things seem to have been happening all at once last evening," she said. "There were rather a lot of guests, you know, not to mention the Prince Regent and the Princess Caroline."

Georgiana cast a deep sigh and said, a little spitefully, "Yes, perhaps what I have to say will seem very small indeed, except that it concerns your own family."

An alarm seemed to ring in Clair's head. "A concern of my family? Please make yourself clear, Georgie." It struck her that she had been using her visitor's Christian name, and even its diminutive, since the woman had arrived, but Mrs. Landon had been punctiliously formal. She all but forced the swaying figure into a chair. "Georgiana, what is it? Perhaps I can help."

Young Mrs. Landon threw her hands across her face. "No," she moaned, "I know that nothing can help. It is all done and cannot be undone!"

Hobbs entered with a silver tray upon which reposed a pot and a pair of cups. He placed it on the table and raised a discreet eyebrow and looked enquiringly towards the ceiling. Clarissa interpreting this as a question concerning Dolly, shook her head emphatically, gratified by his look of comprehension.

"Come, Georgie, have a bit of chocolate. I always feel it does wonders when one is having an attack of the vapours."

But it was still refused. The young woman, beautiful even in her distress, sat in her chair, head bowed and shoulders sloped, a picture of complete abjection. When at last she raised her head, Clarissa could see that there were fresh tears upon her cheeks.

"Good heavens, tell me what it is? Is it Greville?" This was presumably a mistake to say, for Mrs. Landon's control broke completely, and she dissolved into racking sobs. Seating herself beside her, Clair put her arm about the woman's shoulders. "Whatever it is, I fancy a few days will make it all come right. Now then, drink some of the chocolate. No, don't push it away. Drink it. It will lift your spirits."

In between sobs and gulps of air, the Niobe did as she was bid. At last she seemed in moderate control of herself, for she said quite clearly, "He will never marry her, you know, if that is what you think. He will throw her aside just as he has done with me."

"Who, dear?" Clarissa asked, although she already had an inkling of the answer. "What is it you are talking about, and what do you mean?"

The voice was becoming a trifle incoherent again, but Mrs. Landon continued to babble on. "He doesn't care for her, you see. He doesn't care for anyone excepting himself. He uses us all, can't you see that? Uses us and then discards us when we have served our purpose." She looked up with a moment of lucidity. "I know I sound like a jealous fool, and perhaps I am, but you must not let Dolly fall into his hands!"

"Whose hands, Georgie? What are you talking about?"

"Did not your precious sister tell you? She is his latest jilt, I believe! Or is it common knowledge, and I am merely the last to know?"

"Carlton? Carlton and Dolly?" Clarissa found it hard to catch her breath.

"I believe he asked her last evening to marry him!" cried Georgiana in another spate of tears. She looked up at her hostess through drenched lashes. "You know it isn't Dolly that he cares about! How can you let her do it? It is all against Rackham. He only uses us all to reach at Rackham!"

Clarissa wanted to shake her. She could not believe this nonsense she was hearing. "Are you saying that Sir Francis Carlton had asked my sister to marry him?"

Georgiana Landon all but snarled in her impatience. "Carlton, Carlton, Carlton, yes! Who did you think we were talking about?"

Miss Powley was completely astonished when she realised the identity of the man snoring gently in the last pew of the meeting hall. For a respectable person to be sleeping as the sun stretched towards its zenith was peculiar in itself, by country standards, but to choose such a place for it was beyond belief. She had no idea how he had gained entrance, for she believed she had carefully locked up before she went to her own rooms, and, so far as she knew, she had the only key. She had, of course, been about her errands all morning. Quite nonplussed, she leaned forward and shook his shoulder.

"Sir Wilton! Wake up, sir, if you please. Sir Wilton!"

He merely snored contentedly on, and now she noticed what a state he was in: unshaven and unwashed, clothes torn and muddy, hat broken where it lay on the floor beside him. Her nose wrinkled. Quite unlike the gentleman she remembered. And what in the world was he doing in Pargate? Had she not heard from Aunt Dedham that he was living in town since the property at Burriton had been leased? What a puzzle.

Going to the door, she called for Jeddy. "I want you to find Mr. Peacenark at once and bring him to me." He pulled his forelock, but his eyes grew big as he peered over her shoulder at the sleeping man.

"Oi, have we taken in lodgers, then, miss?"

She could not help smiling at his impudence. "Never mind about that. Run along and find him!"

"Perhaps I can be of some assistance, Miss Powley?"

She was startled to hear the familiar voice, and as the man came towards them over the cobbles, she felt an unexpected blush rise to her cheeks. "Good day, Mr. Wearthy."

His austere face was as reserved as ever, but was she imagining a sense of a change in him? Something of his old manner seemed to have softened, grown, if not tender, at least more amenable. "I expect I can solve your mystery," he said to her and held up his hand. In his fingers she saw a key. "I have never relinquished this," he explained. "Perhaps it was wrong of me."

"Lor'," commented Jeddy, "you did give us a turn, sir. We thought you must be dead!"

Wearthy looked quite taken aback, as if such an idea had never crossed his mind. "I never meant such an interpretation to be put upon my actions, Miss Powley." He stopped, confused. "I don't know exactly what I did expect you to think, but it was not my death, I do assure you."

It was the first time that either Phyliss Powley or Jeddy had ever heard anything approaching an apology from the former president of the society, and both were silent, wondering what it might imply. Wearthy seemed to be aware of their curiosity. "As for Sir Wilton," he explained, "I found him wandering about in the streets and brought him here. I thought it was the safest place I could leave him until he recovered from his . . . indisposition."

Phyliss remembered that only a short time past, Sir Wilton's "indisposition" would have called forth a strong moral lecture on the evils of drink. Truly, Wearthy seemed to have undergone a sea change of a most drastic kind. *What is he up to?* she wondered, then felt ashamed of such doubt. Was she so far from charity that she could not forgive a man who seemed to be exhibiting remorse for his previous behaviour?

"A thousand guineas . . ." crooned Sir Wilton from within the hall, ". . . a thousand golden guineas . . ."

"We had best see to him," said Phyliss decisively. "Perhaps the two of you will move him to my . . . to the upstairs rooms, where he can reacquaint himself with the condition of a gentleman?"

The two males moved towards St. Minver as he rose joyfully from his couch, continuing to croon to himself in a sweet monotone. "Money money money money money." But he paused and looked about him in surprise. He seemed befuddled; he blinked, rubbed his eyes, and murmured, "The devil," in a completely bewildered way at the three who came towards him. He spread his hands apologetically. "The trouble with the drink is," he confided, "that you forget the sequence of things at times."

"If you had any money about you, sir," Phyliss said gently, "we have seen nothing of it." The others concurred.

"Nay, nay," mournfully said Sir Wilton, "you would not have done, for I had it, but lost it again. I had not the sense to stop, you see. And I could not resist the lad," he said half to himself. "I owed it to him, you see. I've lost my house, my property, lost my fortune twice over . . . but I owed it, didn't I? I owed it to him."

"A good wash up and brushing down will do you a world of good," promised Jeddy cheerfully. "If you'll come along with me, sir, I'll have you straight again in no time." He looked back at his companions. "Would you just be good enough to bring the gentleman's hat, Mr. Wearthy, sir? And would you unlock the door to the stair, miss?"

"Where are we going?" asked Sir Wilton. Jeddy led him first to the rear yard, where he carefully removed St. Minver's cherry-coloured coat and untied his stock.

"If you'll just put your head here, sir."

"What, under the pump?"

"It'll do you good, sir. Clear your head."

Reluctantly, Sir Wilton agreed. "Begad, I need it cleared."

An hour later the beggared but refurbished gentleman again sat in the pew where he had slept; this time with a steaming mug of tea in his hand, listening carefully to what Wearthy was saying to him.

"And according to the ostler at the Three Feathers, you know, you were expelled from the London coach for disorderliness, sir. He did not know your destination."

"As to that," admitted Sir Wilton, "I believe I was headed for Burriton. It had quite slipped my mind that the property no longer belonged to me, and when I thought of going home it was to the house in the country." He chuckled. "Can you imagine what the new owners would have thought if I had come banging at their door for admittance? I daresay I should have been put away in a madhouse."

"The question is what we can do to help you now?" mused Phyliss. "I wish I had the money to provide your fare back to London, but we manage here on a narrow margin, you see."

"Now as to that," said John Wearthy, taking a leather purse from his pocket, "I believe I can be of aid and repay a debt at the same time." He counted out the exact amount.

"I stand in your debt," vowed St. Minver, "and I fear I do not even know your name, though it comes to me that I have seen your face."

"There is no debt, Sir Wilton, for I stand in debt of that exact amount to your son-in-law, who advanced the sum to me when I importuned him that I might return to Pargate where I had business still unfinished."

Miss Powley's soft look revealed that she understood what he was saying, that it was as much to her as to Pargate that he had returned. "I have a position here," Wearthy explained, "in a counting house, and I expect to prosper enough to take myself a wife."

"We had best hurry, your honour, sir, if you are to catch the coach to London," warned Jeddy.

The three walked St. Minver to the Three Feathers and waited with him for the coach. He still looked a little the worse for his adventure, but at least more respectable than when he arrived, for all that the driver looked sharply at him when he climbed atop.

"All sober now, are you, sir?"

Sir Wilton tipped his battered hat. "Quite sober, my good man, and ready to be about my business at your pleasure." He waved cheerily at the three below.

"Off we go then, sir. Tally ho!"

=== 28 ===

SMIRKING, MASON TAPPED discreetly at the door of Clarissa's chamber. "He is here, my lady. I have shown him into the library."

"Thank you," she said coldly. "You will remember my instructions?"

"Oh, yes, madam: I am to inform you at once if either your husband or Miss Dolly should return." How she hated his tone of oily complicity. It was obvious that he thought himself party to a romantic intrigue.

"That will be all, Mason. I shall be down presently."

To stand at the door of hell is one thing, she reflected as she descended the stairs, but to face the devil in your own home is quite another. There had been no help for it, of course; she could never have gone to his rooms, the scandal would have ruined Rackham forever. So here she was, dressed in style, painted to perfection, going to beard the lion in her own den, so to speak. Mason hovered near the foot of the stairway. Eager to please, he ran ahead of her and opened the door. Francis Carlton, glancing at a book, put it down and moved toward her, all broad smile and élan.

"My dear Lady Rackham, what a surprise and what a joy that you should see fit to summon me. May I hope it will be to the gratification of both of us?"

She waved him to a chair. "I think you have misunderstood my motive, sir. This is not intended as a *liaison*, but a straightforward discussion of a certain difficulty which I hope that you may solve."

"I am chagrined, but, as always, at your service," he said gallantly. Why was there such a dancing light in his eyes? He moved his chair nearer to where she perched uneasily upon the edge of a sofa.

"I have it in my mind," he said confidentially, "that you have asked me here for one of three reasons." He ticked them off on his fingers. "One: to vilify me for your sister's sake. Two: to plead with me—for your sister's sake. Or three: to strike a bargain."

Clarissa relaxed against the back of the sofa and smiled faintly. "Perhaps for all three, Sir Francis." She let that sink in, then added silkily, "Or perhaps I have invited you here to give you a warning."

The handsomeness of his countenance was somewhat diminished by the faint sneer it wore as he replied, "Not from Lord Rackham, I hope? I have been issued ultimatums of one kind or another from that direction for many years now. The day of reckoning has yet to come."

Looking at his still smiling face which so belied the falsity of his behaviour, she thought how great a contrast was this man with his brother. "No, it is a warning from myself. My enmity may not count for much, but as you have already ruined my father, I will not allow you to ruin my sister as well."

"Ruin? Is an offer of marriage a ruination, then?"

"I cannot think of another man who would make her so unhappy."

"What a calumny. I challenge you to produce more than hearsay for such an accusation."

"Mrs. Landon was closeted with me for an hour this morning," said Clarissa quietly. If she had expected a pronounced reaction, she was disappointed; his smile grew only slightly more mocking.

"Dear Georgiana, so literal in her expectations."

"You do not deny her accusations, then?"

He took up a decanter and a glass. "Will you?" he asked, offering the wine. She shook her head, and he went on with his reply. "Deny? What is there to deny? A flirtation the like of which takes place thrice in a week, nay, more often, amongst every level of the ton. You have brought your country morals into town, I fear. In the great world, Lady Rackham, pleasure is never ruled by prudence; that is half the pleasure of it. When one has already lost one virtue, how can losing others really hurt you? It is a game, a folly in which all may indulge themselves. I had thought when you first came up to London that you were to be our brightest star."

His manner became even more studiedly casual, his warmth more palpable, his eyes widening in amusement as if at a jest which both he and his hostess shared. "You speak about preserving what you perceive as your sister's virtue, dear lady. There could be, you know, another way." He leant upon the arm of the sofa and took her hand in his, lifting her fingers to his lips, his eyes never leaving hers.

For a moment she did not know what he was suggesting, but when the enormity of it became clear, she felt almost physically repulsed by him. "You are grossly insulting, sir," she said and quickly rose from the seat, almost knocking the glass from his hand.

"I say, I believe you mistake me, your ladyship," he said smoothly. "I merely suggest that with persuasion I might alter the direction of my affections."

"I understood you perfectly, Sir Francis," she said coldly. "I wish I had not."

"I don't believe you really do. You must think me a very great villain to respond in such a way without hearing me out. I want nothing from you which you would not choose to give. Gad, I am not a ravisher! Only what you would choose to give . . . in your own time."

She surveyed him wonderingly, having no idea how to answer this last bit of impertinence, but before she could speak he went on persuasively. "Everyone knows that you do not cherish a *tendre* for your husband, that it was a French marriage, a marriage of convenience, and that you each feel free to go your own way."

"You say this as if it were common talk."

"It is common talk; the talk is just as common that your husband, of whose honor you seem so chary, visits a certain seaside town at frequent intervals."

"And what of that?"

"Only that they laugh because it seems so awkward. His last Cyprian lived only in Finsbury Pavement."

Clarissa bit her lip. So all the world knew what she suspected of Rackham and Miss Powley? "As you say, sir, a marriage of convenience."

"Inconvenience, I think you mean, if the husband does what he chooses, but the wife cannot play her own tune to dance by. If he cares so little for his own reputation, why should you be overcareful of such a trifle?"

Clarissa had been looking sightlessly out into the garden, now she turned back into the room. "I think I know, sir, why you wish to add me to your long catalogue of conquests."

"Do you?" he asked insinuatingly. "I wonder if you do not underestimate your value. A throwover by a fool like Landon and a marriage to a stick like Rackham must leave you with very little in the way of a yardstick, surely?"

"However unflattering it might be, I believe I could explain to my sister that you wish to possess her only to wound my husband further."

"And would you not like to wound him just a little, to repay him for his visits to Pargate?"

"You must not always judge the world by the standards of your own life, Sir Francis. The rest of us do not always jig to that same tune."

She began to move towards the door, but he followed her, quickly blocking her progress with an outstretched arm. "I suppose there is no brief in telling you of your own irresistibility?" He caught her by the shoulder and spun her towards him, drawing her towards him and pressing his mouth harshly down on hers. Struggling, she forced herself away from him.

"Oh, you are comtemptible!"

He laughed with an air of genuine amusement. "One stolen kiss, contemptible? Perhaps. I wonder if your sister believes it so?"

"Yes," said Dolly, "I do." She was standing in the doorway, white as paper, and behind her was Lord Rackham.

The rumour of an impending duel spread quickly through the ton. The piquancy of the relationship between the duellists, known to everyone, added the necessary spice which lifted the occasion beyond the banal. Though, perhaps, no one ever fought a duel for pleasure, the chance of seeing such an encounter was, for certain minds, always a distinct attraction. The mere whisper of such an encounter, as with the promise of a boxing match, would sometimes draw such crowds as would prevent the event taking place at all. The brothers were determined that such would not be the case this time. To avoid interference, the setting had been fixed for Hounslow Heath, but the seconds had yet to set the exact time.

Lady Dedham was irate, and she spoke her mind freely. "People are killed in duels, Clarissa. Men die! One of them might be your husband."

"No, it is a matter of honour only, not a duel to the death, but only to first blood. Rackham means only to pink him."

"And if it should go awry? Carlton, they say, is no blunderer with a blade."

It was a thing Clarissa did not care to contemplate. Her feeling of responsibility in the matter was exacerbated by the refusal of Rackham to discuss the matter with her—or any matter, for he had scarcely spoken a dozen sentences to her since he had found Carlton, his nemesis, in the appearance of molesting Lady Rackham. When Clair had pleaded with her husband he had merely turned a bland face to her and assured her that he was easily his brother's match. It seemed ironic, however, that a husband who professed not to love her should find death brushing against his coat over a meeting she had arranged with a man for whom she cared not a button.

She had tried to explain this to Dolly, but the girl willfully refused to listen. Somehow she had attached all the blame upon her sister, not Sir Francis. "Yes, I see that he was not worth loving and that everything I had so carefully poured into my ears about him is undoubtedly true, but I don't *know* how I feel about him, Clair. If he asked me, I might still fly with him for a Gretna marriage, with your approval or no."

"Doll, you wouldn't!"

The younger sister was defiant. "Yes, I would! If he would have me!" Her voice trembled. "But if he was only using me to get at Rackham, I suppose he would not?"

Her ladyship hardly knew what to say. "I believe you will find a man who truly loves you one day," she comforted her sister. "This will seem to you a mere fancy, exciting but unreal."

"Do you never regret Greville?" Dolly asked.

"Not any longer," said Clarissa, and, saying it, realised that it was true. She and Dolly were talking in the morning room, and at that moment Lord Rackham came through the door. With a sudden shock, as she saw him, her ladyship discovered that far from merely tolerating him, or even admiring him, she experienced a lift of spirits when he entered. Could it be, she wondered, that this experience was teaching her a needed lesson? Was she, indeed, unfashionably attracted to her own husband? And was she allowing him to go towards the danger of his own death at daybreak without ever telling him so?

She had prepared for bed with great particularity, but

now she lay there staring up at the tester, a thousand thoughts flitting helter-skelter through her head. Was Rackham, as Lady Dedham suggested, truly in danger? And, if he were not, if the meeting was amicably settled, what would be the situation between the men? Or *could* it be amicably dealt with? Would either man allow it? The more she let her mind dwell upon the morrow, the more agitated it became. She realised that, until now, her calm acceptance of the outcome had been merely a façade cast up by shock. She began to tremble and then to shiver so strongly that her body was quite shaken on the bed. She wanted to cry out, but the words would not come. She wanted tears, but her eyes remained dry throughout the spasms of shivering. She wanted—she wanted not to be alone. She wanted the comfort of Rackham's arms about her.

When the spasmodic muscles allowed her to do so, Clarissa crawled from the bed. Slipping a pelisse robe over her nightshift, she sat beside the window and stared out into the night. A light rain was falling, and she wondered if the duel might be delayed or postponed because of it. Almost without thinking about it, she rose from the chair again and quickly ran a comb through her hair. Not stopping for slippers, she pattered down the hallway towards Rackham's door.

She could see enough by the light from the window to cross the room, but once beside the bed, she hesitated. Was she merely being a fool? Was he still angry? She listened carefully for the sound of his breathing, almost inclined toward retreat. The answer to her dilemma came as Rackham threw the covers back.

"Get in," he said softly. "You will catch your death of cold."

= 29 =

THE LONDON COACH, on the basis of a wobbling off-wheel, was delayed at Grutch. The lord of the hostelry was gratified to find his taproom full at this hour of the morning, but the passengers who must perforce cool their heels and their ardour for the joys of London, were ill-suited by the occurrence.

"In the old days," one of them began petulantly, "this would not have happened."

"Aye, things were better in the old days," agreed his fellow, but Sir Wilton, untainted by ale, cider, or gin-and-treacle, disagreed most heartily.

"In the grand old days," he reminded them, "the coach was an unwieldly machine, overloaded with luggage and wayworn passengers groaning in concert with the horses. These were, to my mind, tricked out with the worst of harness, ill-constructed, and at once unsafe to passengers and more tormentingly punishing to the horses than all the whips or spurs in England! I was a fair whip in my day, and I can assure you that the Flyers, and the Times, and the Telegraphs, and all their modern kind, are worth their weight in gold."

"Hear, hear!" cried the driver." 'Ee be givin' it right t'them, sir, and for that I'll stand 'ee a drink, if 'ee be not to proud to drink it!"

"Well, my good fellow . . ."

But the driver would not be put aside. "It be like this, 'ee see, I have taken a great fancy to 'ee in just this stretch o' t'road. Better company than by my guard, begad! Here, drink up, and I'll not have nay for an answer!"

And thus it was that in the two hours time, Lord Wilton was reduced on his return journey to much the state he had endured on the journey out. That is to say much, though, for on this lap he was riding atop and not inside. To while away the morning hours, he and the driver sang the old songs; *Pretty Peggy of Darby O*, being the odds-on favourite, to which he contributed a clear, though wavering tenor. At last the rocking of the coach and the lateness of the hour combined to lull him into somnolence.

In the matter of the duel, the seconds had made the final arrangements as always. The hour was dawn, the spot that part of Hounslow Heath closest to the Bath Road, just before the Cranford turn. This was done as much for convenience as for any other reason. Not only would the curiosity seekers be loath to travel twelve miles out on a rainy morning and so remain abed, but one could stay close to the highway. A trek to a wilder part of the heath would have served little purpose, and the nearness of transportation might, in the event of emergency, prove a deciding factor. There would be a surgeon in attendance, of course, though it was hoped he would need to do no more than staunch a scratch, honour having been satisfied. The seconds, though, had warned him to be prepared for more. They had discussed the situation at length and agreed that it was as well to be prepared for untoward complications, reasoning arrived at by a view of the long standing enmity between the men.

When the procession of carriages, four in all, began the twelve-mile run, they did not all depart from the same spot, but by the time their destination neared they were so close in line that an uninitiated eye might have thought them a funeral cortège. All things considered, the assumption might not have been far wrong. Contrary to custom, Rackham elected to ride alone with his wife, his second being banished to the following carriage with Lady Dedham and Miss Dolly St. Minver. There had been much opposition from the Rackhams as well as from Lady Dedham, on the suitability of Dolly's presence, but stubbornness won out, for she could be most obstinate when she chose. The next carriage was the doctor's, and the last was that of Rackham's opponent and his man. Oddly enough, just as the four black hacks converged, scarcely past the eighth milestone, still another carriage joined them, so that there were five in all. No one knew whom the last might contain.

Clarissa was very brave. She had lain all night in her husband's arms as though in the embrace of a lover, their newly discovered passion for each other heightened by the knowledge of its aftermath. Inside the carriage they did not cling, scarcely held each other's hand, but it was enough. Everything had been already said. Rackham's only words were mundane last minute instructions.

"Oh, my darling, please . . ." Clarissa whispered, and even these practical matters were laid aside.

In the second carriage Lady Dedham continued to expound her contempt of duels and those who were actively involved in them. Since, by implication, this also included the gentleman who occupied the opposite seat, the conversation was decidedly in one voice alone, though Dolly, from time to time, shot the young man a sympathetic glance from her warm brown eyes. His name was Oliver Bateman, it transpired when her ladyship's monologue had turned to the subject of family, rank, and breeding, and he was the second son of the Earl of Chudleigh; not landed, of course, but with a promising career in the church. Quite respectable, since the living of Chudleigh would be in his brother's hands. It was no small thing to be a socially prominent vicar, surely? Lady Dedham quite warmed to him.

The doctor, it may be supposed, was not given to self-converse, and in the fourth carriage nothing was being said at all, but in the fifth, that mysterious, closed vehicle, Georgiana Landon was attended by a most surprising escort. It had, in fact, been he who had come to her door as soon as the news was passed to him, and it was he who had determined the probable time of the encounter.

"Tradition places duels at daybreak, my dear," he had explained to young Mrs. Landon. "Can you slip out of the house so early?"

Georgie laughed derisively. "It will hardly matter. Mama Landon will be fast asleep and my dear husband, if his pattern holds true, will not yet have come from the tables. There is no reason, Lord Tendril, to think I should even be missed."

"Do you think we shall see an end to the famous quarrel?" he asked in his mincing way, saying one thing but meaning another. "Or will it be only the amusement of a morning?"

"I hope," she said vindictively, "that it may be the end of Francis Carlton."

"Do you really, my dear? Hell hath no fury, is it? I confess it will be, if nothing else, a joy to be in the position of having the truth in one's keeping instead of making it fit one's passion for embroidery."

And so, near the eighth milestone, this fifth carriage had joined the cortège. Luckily, Tendril had thought to bring a good French wine which made the waiting easier while the ground was being prepared.

And then, at last, the moment came. Carlton alighted from his carriage, the doctor from his, instrument case in hand, and young Chudleigh rattled the handle of Rackham's coach. His lordship came down, helped his wife to the carriage in which her sister and cousin waited. It was best that she not be alone. One never knew in cases of this sort. Coats were removed, rapiers tested against the air, the distances paced off.

Around the Cranford turn came the delayed London coach, flying hell-for-leather to make up time. The swaying of this "ship of the land" had long lulled Sir Wilton to sleep, but the bump and the squealing brake applied at the turn awakened him. And the first thing his eyes rested upon was the line of five black hacks waiting in a row like ravens on a fence. Intrigued, he tapped the driver on the shoulder and the man nodded that he, too, had seen them.

"Duelers," he shouted against the wind of their passage. "Young bloods which have no better business nor to go about killing each other.

"Over some silly fancy, I dessay," he added scornfully. "More's the pity they mustn't work for a living, that'd change their natures!"

But, once his eyes were open, Sir Wilton's vision was extraordinarily clear. He saw who the participants of the promised skirmish were to be. He clapped the driver upon the shoulder a second time.

"Here, pull over please, and set me down."

"What, man, pull over at this speed? Are 'ee daft?"

But Sir Wilton convinced him this was not a whim. "Pull over, you devil! Those fighters are known to me! The one of them is my son-in-law and the other . . ."

The look of horror on his face was enough to convince the driver, who managed to draw the horses up in time to stop not far beyond the other carriages, feather-edging them as he passed, but doing no more than causing them to rock. Almost before he reined in, Sir Wilton had clambered down and was running across the heath, arms waving frantically, shouting something incomprehensible both to the driver and to the men he was approaching. The other passengers curious at the delay, were poking their heads out of the window of the coach and exclaiming at what they saw. A duel amongst the gentry was something not to be missed.

"Yes, ye may climb down," allowed the driver, "but ye are to stay here. They'll not be thankful to have 'ee underfoot!"

The duelists were *en garde* when St. Minver approached

them, weapons at the ready, but when he shouted he gratefully saw Lord Rackham drop his arm. The older man ran up, breathless, and cried out, "Stop! You must stop!"

Lord Rackham shook his head. "This has been a long time in coming. You must not interfere with it, sir. The quarrel lies between me and my brother."

Sir Wilton's face became a mask of anguished misery. "Believe me, Rackham, you do wrong! Sir Francis Carlton is not your brother—he is my son!"

Rackham swung about to face his father-in-law in shocked surprise. His arm was down, but no sense of ethic had ever deterred Carlton from his goals. His way was open. He hesitated not at all. The blade went in under the shoulder, aiming for Lord Rackham's heart. The seconds flung themselves at Carlton, but the thrust had been made. His lordship, being distracted, had turned and Sir Francis had, knowingly, stabbed him in the back!

"Is he dead?" cried one of the coach passengers greedily, for Rackham had gone to the ground.

"Wouldn't you be dead with three inches of cold iron in your beef?" asked another jeeringly. "It's an earth bath for that 'un."

The surgeon had run forward and was bending over the fallen man; the seconds knocked the blade from Carlton's grasp and caught at his arms, but, small of stature though he was, he flung them off like importunate curs. There was not the slightest remorse in his face as he looked down at his fallen enemy. Instead, he pursed his mouth and spat, then flung away and, catching up his coat, made straight for his carriage. In a moment he was being driven away.

The coach driver banged against the side of his vehicle with the butt-end of his whip. "Get aboard now! All you people get aboard, the show's over, and we have time to make up!"

Clarissa had scrambled over the broken ground, and now she flung herself down on her knees beside her husband, but the surgeon motioned to the other men. "Please to keep the lady away. I need room to work." He finished his cursory examination and began to bind up the wound. "It appears to have missed the vital organs," he said, "although he is losing much blood. We must get him into town at once. I can do nothing for him here."

— 30 —

Lady Dedham to Miss Phyliss Powley:

I must say, I find your news of Mr. Wearthy to be very surprising, but I hope that you are correct and that he is substantially changed.

The news of Carlton's dishonourable act is now all over town, of course, since Lord Tendril has made it his business to be the crier of it. For once, I allow that the silly fellow has rightness on his side, though he has no more natural sense than a shock-dog. Carlton did, indeed, draw first blood, but in the way of a traitor—in his opponent's back like an arrant coward. He is finished now in good society, though I doubt it will deter him. Rascals, alas, seem always to make their own way. Luckily, Rackham mends or there might be a more serious charge laid at that young man's door. I would name him a murdering dog, but that would be to denigrate a noble animal. As for the news of Carlton's paternity, I vow the news has shaken us all . . ."

"I protest I do not need all this coddling!" Rackham pouted at his wife. "You treat me like a babby, and I must be up and about or I shall lose my mind before the week is out."

"Before the week is out, I daresay the doctor will let you

220

leave your bed, but if you continually worry at me about it, I shall have him prolong your punishment." She leant forward and kissed him on the forehead, but when he caught at her arm and would have pulled her down beside him, she laughed and moved out of his reach.

"I declare, my lord, that you are the worst of patients! If I did not love you, I would wash you off my hands." Her father entered the sickroom, and she called upon him for vindication. "Did you ever see such a man, Papa? He pays no heed to anything I say!"

"A woman who cannot manage her husband even in the bed, must have a very difficult row to hoe," he commented with a perfectly straight face, "but I daresay you will note that I am in my dotage and have very little sense of what is fit."

Then he grew more serious. "I have just come from your sister, Clair, and I confess I don't know where I'm at. I think she has yet to grasp the significance of what she knows."

Lady Rackham agreed. "Let me just finish with this new dressing, and I will talk to her again. You must admit that it must be shocking to a girl of Dolly's character and age to find that the man she believed herself in love with is possibly her own brother."

"That is just it," Sir Wilton said. "She all but refuses to accept my explanation of the matter. She seems to think it a delusion of some sort."

His daughter took up the basin of bloodied water and the soiled bandages she had removed and started out of the bedroom. "Have patience with her, Papa. I will see what persuasion my voice will add, but time alone will sort it out for her. One day, I expect, she will fall in love again and we shall see that it has all come right."

Rackham, propped up against the pillows, motioned his father to a chair beside the bed. "The problem is not with Dolly alone, sir. I think I, too, must hear it again and again before it finally sinks into my brain. I have lived too long with my old beliefs and prejudices to so easily surrender them now."

"Well enough said, I suppose," Sir Wilton agreed. "The fact is that it is deuced difficult to sort out the truth after so many years. Carlton might be blessed with many fathers for all I know. Old Sir James, the baronet might, for all we know, have given his wife a son, but it is unlikely. Your father, too, might have been the progenitor. Certainly he had reason to believe he was. I, on the other hand, may have had an even greater claim, for the old man's land abutted that of my father and he was vastly fond of me. My parents saw nothing wrong in my being a great deal at Carlton Hall, so long as the baronet did not mind having me underfoot.

"I was a sort of family pet: young, cheerful, and still very, very innocent. Will you understand when I say that Lady Carlton was not? I expect she was merely ensuring the inheritance, but I flatter myself that our *liaison* was a little more than that, just as I can maintain without a blush that my claim may be far greater than your father's."

Hearing the echo of pride in the older man's voice, Rackham asked, "And you have never told anyone else of this?"

St. Minver shrugged. "Who was there to tell, and for what reason? I was raised in the old tradition of being a gentleman, not that of the present age. Nevertheless, if you had known my father, you would never doubt that Francis is his grandson. The resemblance is remarkable, though the difference is that my father was an honest man."

"Was all this why Carlton could always jink you at the tables, do you suppose?" asked Rackham thoughtfully.

Sir Wilton raised his eyebrows. "I daresay. Perhaps I felt that it was his own due inheritance, eh? I expect there are things in this that we shall never know. But the row between you and Carlton, at least, is over."

"Yes," said Rackham, "It is certainly over on my part, though I wonder if it can ever be finished with him." He sighed, lapsing into a brown study for a moment, then, musingly, he said, "I find that I do not hate him any longer. He tried, I know, to cheat me, but in the long run, I see that he has cheated himself of even more.

"Besides, I am too happy to wish to be drawn back into that old enmity. It is over for me."

And Sir Wilton, seeing his daughter come back into her husband's room, and the look that passed between them, understood why.

If you have enjoyed this book and would like to receive details of other Walker Regency romances, please write to:

Regency Editor
Walker and Company
720 Fifth Avenue
New York, N.Y., 10019